International Standard Book Number 13: 978-1-60452-143-6
International Standard Book Number 10: 1-60452-143-0
Library of Congress Control Number: 2018951454

BluewaterPress LLC
52 Tuscan Way Ste 202-309
Saint Augustine FL 32092

www.bluewaterpress.com

This book may be purchased online at through our online catalog at www.bluewaterpress.com.

Please note that address information is subject to change. At the time of printing, the address was correct, but may have changed. Please check our website for the latest address information for BluewaterPress LLC.

A TAP-TAP AT SUNDOWN

Short Stories By

William Hallstead

Also by the author:

Raging Skies

Hard Days in Paradise

River of Madness

Pursuit of the Weapon from Hell

The Secret of Keystone City

Position of Ultimate Trust

Image of Evil

The Rebuilt Man

Chain of Vengeance

Secret Kills

Pursuit of Fear

Table of Contents

A TAP-TAP AT SUNDOWN

The scent of mingled spices drifted upslope from the city of Port-au-Prince. With it came an underlying pungency of open sewer and garbage too long in the sun. Then I smelled sweat not my own. That set me up, and I swung around in the creaky wicker chair.

Chretien, said the plastic badge on his rumpled tan waiter's coat. Christian. At breakfast, I had bribed this man amply – by local standards. He had enfolded my American ten-spot in supple sepia fingers, stared through my request, then padded back to the kitchen leaving me frustrated beneath the dining room's squeaky overhead fan.

"M'sieur," he said now, "the drink you ordered."

"I didn't order –"

He bent low over the table at my elbow, the planes of his face carved in oiled ironwood. "At sundown, M'sieur. The west end of the hotel. A tap-tap. Mostly blue."

He handed me the check for the rum concoction in its rippled glass. I fished out the required number of gourde plus an oversized tip. Blank-faced, he left the veranda without a sign he had spoken.

I'll be damned, I thought. Cast enough bread on the murky waters, and you get a taker. Tap-taps, I'd been told by the driver of the mufflerless taxi I had taken from the airport, were freelance station wagons, gaudily decorated by their owners, cheap to rent – "only one gourde, M'sieur" – which was cheap, all right. About fifteen cents. "But you may find yourself riding with chickens or pigs."

From the hotel's broad veranda, I squinted into the white sunlight that pressed down on Port-au-Prince. The softening pavement, the scruffy public monuments, the buildings from the rococo dazzle of the presidential palace to the dun-colored tumble of waterfront shanties – all seemed to cringe in the heat. Down there, though, I'd seen faces shining with pride, inexplicable unless it was pride in survival in spite of a government in perpetual unrest.

The Gulf of Gonave stretched from the two-mile distant waterfront to the sea of the Windward Passage, an expanse of molten iron that held the narrow Ile De La Gonave in its grip out there through ten miles of shimmer. Only the mountains that soared behind the hotel offered a respite from the scorching breath of mid-afternoon. The air conditioning unit in my room had clattered itself to death an hour ago. I slumped out here on the second-floor veranda – at least in the open air – and pondered what had brought me to Haiti.

What had done it, of course, was money. Specifically, the money for a proposed book. I had already been paid the standard 50% in advance. The balance would be mine on delivery of an "acceptable manuscript." That was why I was here on the scabrous porch of the Hotel Bien Venue, wondering how in the world I was going to gain access into certain arcane practices of this tiny, turbulent nation.

The working title of my forthcoming work was "The Dark Side of Justice." I had planned on strong doses of voodoo and obeah, leavened by kangaroo court tactics in certain

South American locales, seasoned with a dash of Klan, and possibly bolstered with a stiff shot of Third Reich Sturm und Drang. It would be the kind of text that appeals to progressive professors and just might make a public ripple, as well as… All right, so it was to be an exploitation book. No worse than certain cable TV offerings any night of the week.

Haiti was steeped in just the kinds of primitive goings-on I needed. And the airfare from my home base in Savannah was helpfully low. I had spent my first day here dropping hints to taxi drivers, hotel staff and a couple of likely-looking not-quite-gentlemen at the Bien Venue's gritty bar. I made clear I was not looking for tourist voodoo but the real thing.

For all that, I'd gotten blank looks, distant gazes, and a couple of hard stares that made me wonder whether the terror of Ton Ton Macoute might still be more than a memory. I had returned to my room, suffered the collapse of the A/C unit and taken refuge on the veranda. There I began to realize a writer of suspense fiction is not necessarily also a writer of esoteric fact. I had come face-to-face with the debilitating suspicion that I might not know what the hell I was doing here. And at the moment Chretien had appeared at my elbow with his whispered indication that my sowing of seed money had sprouted something.

I tried an early supper in the hotel's stifling dining room, opting for the tassot: tough, sun-dried turkey marinated in lime juice. The boiled potato with it looked innocent enough, but I found I could manage only coffee and the bread, spread with mamba, a kind of supercharged peanut butter. I finished too early and killed some tense time in the lobby.

As the sun hissed itself out in the gulf, I descended the hotel's broad wooden steps and walked, a little hesitantly now, toward the building's west end. Sounds of the city reached here, a distant gabble of uninhibited people threaded through with snatches of pounding meringue beat.

A stranger in the tap-tap at sundown... That would have been comfortably catchy in one of my novels, but living it had begun to tighten an ice cable across my chest.

I rounded the Bien Venue's hedge of dusty crimson bougainvillea and walked into the narrow side street, the unhappily named Rue Du Repentir. Repentance Street, if my high school French was holding up. I hardly had time to mull that over before a rattling blue Chevy station wagon at least 15 years old pulled to the curb. Apparently, its driver had been parked down the street watching my uncertain approach to the west end of the hotel. The multi-colored graffiti along its near side seemed to depict a ragged marching band.

The driver, a hulk of a man black as licorice, leaned across the passenger seat. The engine snorted and coughed so loudly that I had to stick my head in the window to hear him. Then I realized how chancy that little action was in a nation as unsettled as this one.

In a Creole accent that sounded flowery for such a huge man, he said, "You are the American to write the book?"

I was the American desperately trying to write the book. I nodded. With a huge hand, he shoved open the creaking door, and I climbed into his gaudy wagon. If he had indeed transported pigs or chickens on these threadbare seats, their lingering savor was drowned in the reek of blue exhaust.

As we bounced beyond the city's outskirts, the air freshened outside and in. I smelled something close to the delicate scent of frangipani. Then the harsh odor of decaying vegetation crept through the open window.

Through our climb into the foothills, my giant driver hulked wordless, a great opaque block in dark trousers and a white short-sleeved shirt. By now, the shirt was all I could make out in the thickening darkness. The tap-tap's sickly headlights barely illuminated the tunnel of jungle growth through which we labored upward.

The driver's silence was no help to my research. To break it, I thanked him for bringing me, but I wondered where I was going.

"It is not voodoo," he said over the engine's clatter, though I hadn't mentioned that buzzword to Chretien, our intermediary. "The tourists, they all ask for voodoo."

A tour guide. Had I simply fallen victim to the scam of Third World freelance tour guiding?

For another mile, I said nothing. A succession of poinciana fronds overhanging the road flew out of the darkness to slap the windshield like angry wraiths.

"We are Efik," he said as we abruptly slowed to swing off the pot-holed macadam into a dirt lane that climbed even more steeply. He clashed the manual shift into second. The old station wagon growled upward into yet deeper darkness.

"Efik, long ago from the River Niger. You know l'Afrique?"

I did not; not that well.

"We have some of the old customs, those worth saving. Customs that are taboo here. Comprendez?"

I wasn't sure what he was talking about, but I certainly understood taboo. Now we were almost an hour outside of civilization, high in the mountains that rose nearly 9,000 feet, southeast of Port-au-Prince. I began to wonder about my sanity in jumping into this battered circus wagon of a car with this immense stranger, all on the say-so of a bony waiter I'd bribed to gain entrée into God-knew-what.

The driver stopped the tap-tap. My panicky conclusion was that I had let myself in for a Haitian-style mugging. Cold sweat prickled my chest.

"Before I take you further, mon ami, we must make an agreement. You may write what you will see, but you cannot say here in Haiti that you saw it. And you cannot print the writing in Haiti."

Those were easy enough terms. I didn't know anyone here I would want to tell this folktale to, and Haitian book sales were surely beyond the consideration of my U.S. publisher-to-be.

"And you must be a watcher, comprendez? No matter what you see, you will remember that you are only here to see."

That sounded ominous – but at the same time, reassuring. Robbery of a tourist on this wild mountainside did not appear to be his aim after all.

"There is the small matter of cost, M'sieur. Let us say, for the gasoline."

Appropriately, the engine stalled. In the deep silence, I was willing to pay for gasoline, oil, depreciation – anything this ancient crock might need. "Would forty dollars America – "

"Bon. That will be sufficient." Twin Andrew Jacksons evaporated into his immense hand.

"It is not far distant," he said as the starter ground over and over. A rank smell oozed out of the roadside tangle, the stench of sweet rot. I heard rustlings in that black hedgerow. Then I realized fat raindrops had begun to fall.

The engine caught. My driver flipped on spastic windshield wipers, and we grumbled higher. Through an unexpected break in the roadside trees, I caught a glimpse of the city's light, far below and tiny. Then we were swallowed up again. Minutes later, the wagon bumped over some rocks in the narrow lane. We pulled into a small clearing and stopped.

A scatter of dilapidated vehicles flanked the bulk of a windowless hut with a corrugated metal roof. My driver hurried me inside where a dozen black men, all dressed identically in black slacks and white shirt, milled about in the light of several kerosene lanterns hung from the low roof.

As we entered, they fell silent. The place seemed airless. It smelled of nervous bodies and the sour earth of the hard-packed floor.

The only furniture was a battered wooden table and three stools behind it. At the base of the rough board wall opposite the single door was a row of straw mats.

My driver, whom these men seemed to have been waiting for, nodded toward the mats. All but one of the men sat. He walked to the table as my guide settled on the center stool behind it, looked at me and pointed at the row of men squatting on the mats. In the center of that row, a place had been left. I took it, feeling I had completely lost control of my situation – then realizing I had lost control of it the moment I stepped into the tap-tap.

"Bring in the accused," ordered the huge man who had brought me here. I had no doubt now that he was in charge, and he was using English for my benefit, which was considerate, as Creole was a mile beyond me.

The man who had remained standing left the hut to return silent moments later with a compact, scar-faced man dressed in ragged khakis. He was as close to pasty gray with fear as any black man I had ever seen. Behind him and his escort trailed a white-haired elder with a quart bottle of some pale yellow fluid and a small wooden bowl. Following him was a third escort, this one spidery small and carrying a larger wooden bowl.

They stood the terrified man in front of the table, facing the giant. I realized he was serving as judge in some kind of secret—and no doubt wildly illegal—trial.

As rain rattled on the metal roof, my giant driver-judge said in a voice as ominous as muted thunder, "Philippe Prise, you are accused of the rape of Angelique, the wife of our kinsman Emil Thibaud."

"Non! Non! Innocent! Je suis innocent!"

"That is to be decided." The judge paused. "By Efik custom." He nodded at the two men who had remained behind the terrified accused. The old man set the quart bottle on the table. He handed Philippe Prise the small bowl. The other "court attendant" walked off five paces from the table then carefully placed the larger bowl on the dirt floor. Now I could see that bowl was half-filled with some milky fluid.

"Philippe Prise," the judge said, glaring at the cringing man who faced him. "You know the custom. Eight calabar beans have been ground to powder and placed in this bottle. You will drink. You will wait ten heartbeats. Then you will turn and take five steps toward the bowl behind you. In that bowl is the antidote to calabar. If God lets you live long enough to drink the antidote, you are innocent in his eyes. If not, the Efik justice has spoken."

Calabar beans! I had already come across that devastating poison in my preliminary research. The beans are rich in the active component physostigmine, which almost instantly sedates the spinal cord. The resulting paralysis climbs rapidly from legs to chest. Death comes from asphyxiation.

My God! I had paid to be brought here to witness a poisoning. I came close to leaping to my feet in protest, but the huge judge threw me a glance surely meant to remind me of my promise to be "only a watcher." Lord knew what these people would do to me if I tried to interfere.

The white-haired man carefully poured a stiff dose from the bottle into the bowl held in the doomed man's trembling hands. Then he stood back.

Philippe Prise's face twisted in anguish. I wished they hadn't used his name, that he had remained to me only an anonymous man brought in from the night. He shot a look of despair at the judge. The two men who had brought in poison and antidote walked around the ends of the table and took the stools flanking his. They settled comfortably, anticipating what promised to be an appalling spectacle. The man who had brought in the accused stepped back against the wall. He folded brawny arms but looked ready to leap out, were the accused to make a break for the door.

I thought there should arise from somewhere the guttural throb of drums. But all I heard was the rain's tinny patter and the breathing of the men on either side of me. Theirs was a kind of gape-mouthed expectation I would have expected from witnesses at a sanctioned execution. But this was a dirt-floored hut in the Haitian mountains with surely illegal barbarism about to take place.

The accused man, quaking in terror, slowly lifted the shallow bowl. And drank.

My stomach revolted. I forced back the bile that bubbled into my throat.

Philippe Prise clunked the poison bowl on the table and stood immobile for what I presumed was his required count of ten heartbeats. My own heart thundered loudly enough in my ears for such a precise count.

Then he turned away from the table and fixed his eyes on the bowl of salvation that lay on the floor a dozen feet distant. He took one step. Two. He seemed unaffected, except by the fear that had stiffened his limbs since he had entered the hut.

Maybe he could–

His left leg gave way. He tried to lurch erect. His mouth fell open. The eyes bulged. He clutched his chest. His legs collapsed. He fell to his knees. Then he pitched forward, both arms outstretched, clawing futilely for the antidote only a yard from his grasp.

I was horrified. I had sat there in silence and watched…a murder.

The judge shoved back his stool and stood. He stared down at the fallen man. Then he looked at me. With the rest of the witnesses, I scrambled to my feet.

As I strode angrily to the table, the big man read my expression. He held up a broad palm to cut off my words before they tumbled out in violation of our agreement.

As I reached the table, I noticed he appeared perplexed.

He said softly and to me alone, "I truly believed the man was innocent, M'sieur."

The others filed out, the last two carrying Philippe Prise's limp corpse. And my driver-judge did something that stunned me anew. He picked up the nearly full quart bottle from the table and offered it to me!

"No need to waste good grapefruit juice, M'sieur. Because that is all that this is."

PHOBIA

"**O**h, Gawd, Mitch! You shoulda seen your face up there!" Henry Stanhope dissolved into giggles.

I cringed as a couple of late night strollers stared our way. "You son of a bitch, you told me the restaurant was only a few floors up."

But it had been at the very top of the John Hancock Center, 100 petrifying floors above Chicago. I hadn't been able to eat anything more than tea and toast – and that with my back to the windows. Couldn't wait to get down to street level again, hands shaking, knees rubbery, legs close to giving way altogether.

My problem – one of two – is acrophobia, fear of heights. Not just uneasiness. Sweat-popping, near-paralyzing, panic-threshold terror when I'm higher than three or four floors.

My other problem stemmed from that one: Henry Stanhope enjoyed cruelty. He got a bang out of my altitude hang-up. Maybe because I'm tall and lean while Stanhope is short and dumpy. I have hair. Stanhope was getting bald. Whatever the cause of his sadistic behavior, he never let up.

So why were we in Chicago together when we both lived and worked in Baltimore? The National Conference on Advanced Advertising Techniques. We had been sent here by Moody and Rusch Advertising, Inc. Stanhope was vice president, and I was chief copywriter. In the corporate pecking order, he was my boss. Which put me in a bind. Sue my boss for harassment because I was scared of heights?

So I put up with his jokes. "It's not the long fall that kills you, Mitch. It's the sudden stop!" Heard that one maybe ten times.

"As the jumper said when he dropped past the second floor, 'All right so far!'" Heard that maybe twenty times.

Stanhope's twisted fun had been verbal until tonight. Oh, there had been that presentation luncheon back in Baltimore last June in the revolving restaurant thirteen floors above Lombard Street. He seated me right next to the windows, and he sat at the other end of the table wearing a huge grin while I struggled through my part of the agenda. I don't remember a word I said. My brain was paralyzed by the realization that only a foot or two behind me, separated by only a thin pane of glass, was 130 feet of empty air.

Oddly, it's not the empty air itself that terrorizes me. ("It's not the – hee hee – long fall…") In fact, I have no fear at all in a jetliner 30,000 feet above God's green earth. That's so detached it's like looking down at a map. No, what throws me into a stomach-churning heartquake is a mere glimpse of a building's downward taper to its seemingly tiny, unsubstantial base that a mere breeze could topple. Don't laugh. The tall ones sway in the wind. I can feel them sway in the wind.

"Yeah," Stanhope chortled as we neared the hotel, "you shoulda seen your face."

The son of a bitch took lip-smacking pleasure in the weakness of others. Got Joe Pincus fired because Joe couldn't resist taking home company pens and pencils – especially when Stanhope constantly laid them on the table next to Joe's desk. And it was Stanhope, I'm certain, who happened to mention to copywriter Abner Coale that he'd seen our company president entering the Hyatt with a woman whom Stanhope described as a dead-ringer for Abner's wife. She wasn't, but Stanhope had a chuckle over what must have transpired at Abner's house that evening.

All of us who had to work with Stanhope hated the bastard, but when the bastard is your boss, what can you do?

"It's the sudden stop, Mitch. Hee hee." He pushed through the hotel's revolving door. We entered the nearly deserted lobby, a comfortable if slightly seedy lobby with places to sit and read. "It's one of the few grand old hotels still in operation," he'd told me when he'd had his assistant make the reservations. "Real tile in the bathrooms, windows that actually open."

"Oh, meant to tell you," he blurted. "I want to go over the Kitty Carsoner proposal with you before we turn in. It's in my room. I'll be right back."

Stanhope's room was down the hall then around the corner. I wasn't going to wait out here like a good dog at "stay." I opened the door, walked in and shut it behind me. Let him knock.

I took off my coat and tie, sat on the bed and began to untie my shoes. Knock he did. Review the Carsoner thing at this hour? It couldn't keep until morning? We weren't meeting with Kitty until next Friday.

I pulled the door open and turned toward the table between the two windows. "We can spread it out on-"

That was when I felt something jab me in the back, just above my belt.

"Don't turn around." A harsh whisper in my left ear. "Just tell me where it is."

"Where what is?" The seriousness of this hadn't yet sunk in.

"If you've found it, you know. If you haven't, you don't need to know."

"I don't know what the hell you're talking about." I started to turn around to get a look at this menacing whisperer. What had to be a pistol muzzle jabbed me hard.

"Don't turn around. Lock your fingers behind your head." Same hoarse whisper as if his vocal cords had been seriously damaged. "Where is it?" he demanded.

"Where is what?" What else was there to say? I hadn't the remotest idea what was going on here.

"Make it easy on yourself," he urged. "Hand it over, or I'll have to search the room."

"Go ahead. Search." I was surprised at my boldness, but the unreality of this clod's intrusion seemed to take the edge off its menace.

"Not with you here waiting to jump me. Over to the window."

Oh, my God.

The gun rammed into my kidney. "Don't make me use this. Over to the window."

Now fear rippled through me. This couldn't be happening. I caught his reflection in the window's ripply glass. Man in a black ski mask, just behind my left shoulder.

"I told you-" Now my voice was an embarrassing squeak. "There's nothing here that-"

"Open the window."

"Why?"

"Just open it." The viperish hiss was right in my ear.

Trying to control trembling fingers, I thumbed open the double-hung sashes' old-fashioned pivot lock. The lower sash had two metal finger slots. As I reached for them, I couldn't avoid looking beyond the narrow ledge out there, looking almost straight down.

Fifteen floors. One hundred fifty dizzying feet. My stomach constricted into a hard ball. I stumbled back. The gun muzzle dug in painfully.

"Open the goddamn window!"

My hands shook. My palms were slick. "Look, I've got a real problem with heights. Why don't I just stay in the bathroom while you do whatever you-"

"I don't give a damn about your problem. I've got my own. Now open that window!"

I prayed that it was stuck shut, glued tight with the revarnishing of decades.

It wasn't. The sash slid smoothly upward. I shrank back from the incoming gust of humid August air, from the canyon-bottom street sounds that rode in with it.

"Now," he grated in my ear, "step out there."

The floor tilted. I lost my balance. Grabbed the sill to catch myself. Swallowed bile that erupted in my throat. My legs were cold rubber. My gut congealed into ice.

His free hand slammed down between my shoulder blades. He shoved. I almost toppled through the open window.

"Out on the ledge."

Impossible. The concrete strip just below the window level looked to be no wider than a foot and a half.

I recoiled into the gun muzzle's hard jab. "I can't do that."

"Hell you can't. Get out there, or I'll drop you right here. One way or another, I'm searching this room without you in the way."

Would he actually shoot me? Wouldn't the sound bring people running? Maybe not, if the gun was small caliber and held close to muffle the blast. Would he take that risk? Depended on what he was looking for. A previous guest must have left it for him, and I'd gotten here before this guy did. A parcel of hot jewelry? Maybe a kilo or two of cocaine? Whatever it was, this bastard was ready to kill for it.

Against every instinct, fighting every reflex that impelled me back from the gaping window, I managed to get my right leg across the low sill and out on the ledge.

"That's a start," said the growl in my ear. "Now, the rest of you."

I bent the outside leg, kneeled on the gritty concrete. Then, fighting a near-paralyzing wave of panic, I slid across the sill and lay flat on the hard ledge.

He shut the window.

The horrendous impact of where I was hit me like a fist. Awash in hot sweat, I pushed up against the building's face below the sill. I didn't dare look to my right, to look into space – then down fifteen floors to toy cars and antlike people down in the street that waited for my screeching plummet off this impossibly narrow perch.

But I did look down, the way you have to look at a loathsome spectacle though you don't want to. I peered out, then down – and the building lurched. I felt myself slide inch by inch toward the abyss.

My fingernails clawed the unyielding surface. Found no grip. Skated across the concrete. My right leg slipped free, dangled in open air over 150 feet of nothing, threatened to pull the rest of me off the ledge to whistle downward, to smash against the distant pavement.

I was struck by that crazy impulse that hits acrophobes when, despite all precautions, we find ourselves high enough above ground to feel panic's hot grab:

Go ahead. Jump. Get it over with.

That insane urge struck me now as I groveled on the ledge, one leg dangling in space, with gravity's persistent pull telling me to let go, to let it rush me down, down…

The building wasn't moving. I was suffering an attack of vertigo. I managed to drag my leg back up on the ledge. Then I dared raise my head to look through the window.

No one in the room. I could see through the bathroom's open door that he wasn't in there, either.

I was locked outside an empty room. Could I break the big pane of glass in the bottom sash? The thought of untying a shoe then slamming it into the window brought hot sweat anew. The reaction to hitting the window surely would topple me backward into yawning space.

Was I truly locked out here? I didn't dare stand up to check the pivot lock on top of the sash. There were no finger slots on this side, of course, but there was room between sill and sash to wedge in the tips of my fingers. I managed that from a prone position, petrified to raise my body higher.

I stiffened my fingers, pried upward - and slipped. My fingertips flew free. I lunged backward toward the edge of my narrow perch. I barely managed to slam my left hand down on the concrete lip in time to check my rolling off.

But that moment of terror had been worth it. I found that I'd managed to raise the window a quarter-inch, enough to give me real purchase. I raised the sash cautiously, peered in on hands and knees. Then I crawled back into my room.

I collapsed on the rug, exhausted, leg and arm muscles twitching uncontrollably, mouth dry.

And I heard a rapping at the door.

I stumbled to my feet.

"Wh—who is it?"

"It's Henry, Mitch. With the Carsoner proposal. Like I told you."

I let him in.

"What in the hell," he said with eyes bulging, "happened to you?"

I told him, and he insisted on calling hotel security. A few minutes later, a sepia version of Raymond Burr arrived to take a lot of notes and urge me to be more careful of whom I let in my room. I was way ahead of him on that.

He left, I begged off on the proposal review, and I hardly slept at all.

Stanhope and I had agreed to meet at the elevator at eight a. m. sharp. I got there early, which gave me a few minutes to listen to the clankings and bangings in the shaft. Ancient machinery having a moment of revolt. I wasn't so sure I wanted to—

"Morning!" Stanhope, all slicked down and natty in boardroom blue. He gave me a smirky nod. I nodded back then jerked my head toward the elevator.

"Sounds like they're having some trouble."

Stanhope shrugged. Then he grinned—and said the most chilling words I'd ever heard.

"Don't turn around. Just tell me where it is." All that in a hoarse whisper. In the hoarse whisper that had terrified me last night.

"Jesus H. Christ!" I burst out. "That was you!"

He dissolved into thigh-slapping guffaws. "My God, Mitch, you should've seen yourself! What a kick! You were-you were-" he burst out laughing again.

"The gun," I croaked. "You didn't actually-"

He flipped out his Mont Blanc pen and hunched into a mock shooting stance. "Mightier than the sword." He fell into another giggle fit.

The ski mask. The room with easy-opening windows and a ledge. The son of a bitch had certainly planned it all.

I was infuriated. I didn't know whether to spit in his face, scream at him or slug him. I was ready to do all three.

Then, behind him, the elevator door slid open. Still laughing himself to tears, he eased backward toward the car.

But there was no car. Just the open door then gaping black nothing.

"Henry!" I grabbed for him. He ducked away, reared back— and found only air. He seemed to hang there, arms flung out, mouth frozen in a horrified O. Then he was gone, his screech of terror trailing him down the shaft.

It was then that I gave in to the strongest and surely most unworthy impulse I'd ever had. I stepped right up to the edge of the elevator opening and looked straight down into the diminishing howl. And I shouted:

"All right so far, Henry?"

HONEY MUSTARD

After the rush to O'Hare, the nearly missed connection in Atlanta, the baggage crush at Southwest Florida International, Jamie Saint was all nerve ends through the drive from the airport to Sanibel Island.

Stu was a classic Husband Hopeless. He had accepted this roller skate rental car without a murmur of complaint. Then there had been the argument over the route. "The girl at the counter said take Daniels to Summerlin," he insisted.

"The map the 'girl' gave you with the rental agreement shows Six Mile Cypress Parkway is much shorter."

"She told me Daniels to Summerlin," Stu repeated, and that was that. Typical.

Jamie's tautness diminished a notch after he paid the $3 toll, and they set out across the causeway to the resort island. She had thought this whole plan would be a breeze, but now she began to wonder whether it might be too complicated.

"Boy, look at that water!"

Boy, for God's sake. Stockbroker Stu talked like his father, two masters of passé expressions.

"It's beautiful," she said, forcing enthusiasm she didn't feel. "I've never seen such a lovely blue." Not Academy Award level, but she was a good enough actress to deceive Stuart Saint—who wasn't all that hard to deceive.

"Hey, look! A shark!"

"It's a porpoise, Stu. The fin is rounded, and it... I think it's a dolphin." She had almost told him the thing that had surfaced with the rolling motion, just like on the Flipper reruns. Then, instinctively, she had played "the game." Stu thought her childlike. Most of the people who knew her did, because that was how she wanted them to think of her: blonde fluff. Her dippy ringlets helped. So did the vapid smile. None of her friends nor even Stu really knew her. Except... She felt a delicious tingle when she thought of the Braydons.

The cramped compact dipped off the last causeway bridge. At the island's four-way stop, though there wasn't another vehicle in sight, Stu brought the car to a complete halt. Good old Stu. Not a rebellious capillary in his whole mushy body.

He accelerated slowly through the intersection, crossed Periwinkle Way and putted down Lindgren to East Gulf Drive. Minutes later, they registered at the Gulfpride.

Like a teenager, he couldn't wait to get on the beach. He plowed into his suitcase, whipped out his maroon swimming trunks with an exuberant "Tah-dah!" and stripped right in the little living room of their two-room suite. She slumped on the sofa, watching all of him emerge fish-belly white, big in the butt. The antithesis of Chuck Braydon, who had no sign of middle-age droop.

Sweet-voiced, she said, "You're putting on weight, honey."

"You're telling me!" The band of his swimming trunks bisected the early gestation of what would inevitably bloom into a formidable paunch. "It's jogging time, ah yes." Please, not W.C. Fields again. "Might you accompany me to the beach, m'dear?"

"In a while, maybe. I thought I'd wait 'til Chuck and Ella get here."

"They're not due until around five."

"I'll wait anyway. I'm kind of worn down by the trip."

She slid open the glass door to their second floor beachfront deck and waited until she saw him emerge from the foot of the balcony stairs. Only then did she pick up the phone and dial the desk.

"This is Mrs. Saint in 38. Our friends, the Braydons, are due in around five. I just wanted to make sure they have an adjoining unit."

"Yes, they do, Mrs. Saint. Number 36."

She set the phone back in its cradle with a satisfied little smile. Even with Chuck and Ella just beyond the connecting door, Stupid Stu wouldn't have a glimmer of what was going on.

A few minutes after five, the Braydons pulled their rented Buick into the Gulfpride's sand-and-shell parking area. Jamie waved gaily from the balcony, and an hour later, the four of them walked into the Jacaranda Restaurant a mile down Periwinkle. Charles R. Braydon, Jr., MD, had brought with him his health-club tan and his self-assurance. Tall, fine-boned, trim. A lot like Tyrone Power in the old gems she caught on the nights Stu went to bed early and left her sitting there in their big living room. Hooray for cable.

Ella, dear Ella, walked into the restaurant with Jamie, arm-in-arm, a vision in studied casualness: pleated white skirt, yellow cotton blouse not concealing those to-die-for boobs of hers, emerald silk scarf that set off her raven's wing hair.

"Did you arrange for the boat?" Chuck asked after they ordered.

Stu drew a blank. "Holy cow, was I supposed to do that?"

"You were indeed." Chuck's tone was doctor's office God-to-clod.

"Well, gosh, I'll get over to the marina first thing in the morning."

"Remember, Stu," Jamie said, "we want something around thirty feet, an inboard that sleeps four. And," she added petulantly, "I won't be stuck somewhere out in the gulf if the engine quits."

"And make it a gas engine, not a diesel," Chuck put in. "Should be easier to find refueling facilities."

Just the way she and Chuck had worked it out that snowy afternoon at the Highland Park Motor Lodge. It has to be an inboard, Chuck had told her. Inboard, she'd repeated, pulling the rumpled sheet back over them. She hadn't known what an inboard was, but at their next recreational get-together, Chuck brought a copy of Chapman's Piloting. He insisted she read the paragraphs he had marked in Chapter 12, "Safety Afloat," and the sections about small outboards, before they proceeded with that afternoon's diversion. "Now that you've read all that," he had said as he reached for her, "our challenge is putting it to practical use."

"Excuse me, ma'am."

"What? Oh." She leaned back as the waiter set down her garden salad. The house dressing was honey mustard, the mustard's sharp bite disguising the honey's sweetness.

In the balcony's early morning glare, Jamie watched Chuck "do laps" in the inn's swimming pool. He bounded to the bottom of the steps, danced first on one foot then the other to jiggle water from his ears. As she watched Chuck towel off down there, Stu appeared lumpishly beside her. In the rising heat, he was already sweating.

"Guess I'd better get over to the marina posthaste and make the arrangements. Want to tag along?"

Behind him, Ella had emerged from her unit, sleek as a mink in a pale blue sundress, coffee mug in hand. "Thank God for kitchenettes. Did I hear somebody mention the boat? Can't get out on the water too soon for me, friends."

Jamie turned to Stu. "I'd really rather just sit up here for a while." Had that been casual enough?

"I'll go with you, Stu," Ella offered. "A woman's touch might be useful."

"Fine with me," Stu agreed over his shoulder. He was already clumping down the steps.

Chuck draped his towel around his neck. "Think I'll head for the beach, soon as I've had a shot of coffee." He playfully patted Ella's rear as she passed him on the stairs. "You two take your time."

From the balcony, Jamie and Chuck watched Stu's rented compact disappear beyond the inn's entrance portico.

"The game's afoot," she whispered.

"Uh-huh."

Uh-huh? Last night, she thought she had detected just a tiny crumbling of Chuck's commitment. Now he was in spiritless uh-huh mode? She had work to do.

"At supper, I heard you say something to Stu about possible problems renting the boat. You're not thinking of backing out?"

He pulled the soggy towel off his shoulders and frowned. "He was pushing for a drive through the Everglades. I was only trying to keep him on track, Jamie."

That was fairly convincing, but she hadn't liked the frown. "They'll be gone at least an hour, love." She grinned naughtily. "Let's open the connecting door and get you out of those wet trunks."

A few minutes later when they were wrapped together in the big double bed, she murmured, "You're not getting cold feet, are you, Chuck honey?" He was, in fact, cold all over, but she hoped that was from his thrashing in the pool.

"It's one hell of a risk, Jamie."

"I don't think so. Not the way we've planned it."

"Maybe too intricately. Divorces would take longer, be messier, but-"

She pressed her forefinger to his lips. "You keep forgetting the premarital agreement. With you and Ella it would be a different story, but if Stu and I split, I get not one damned thing."

He raised up on an elbow. "How could you have signed such a thing, Jamie?"

"A trade-off. The good life against a life sentence behind one of Marshall Field's inventory computers. I never thought long term. Not like you and Ella. But you won't have to worry about her after all this is over, will you?"

She wriggled playfully. "Now make us happy, darling."

By the time Stu and Ella returned, Chuck seemed back on track. His and Jamie's final words as she rushed through the units' connecting door had not been ones of endearment.

"Chuck, you did remember to bring the—"

"Phenobarb capsules? Of course. Just use two each."

The boat, Stu told them, was a 35-foot hardtop sundeck trawler. "A real coup," he babbled. "It's up for sale, and the owner cut us a terrific deal for a big-bucks rental. It's got two sleeping quarters, two heads with showers-"

"Not a diesel."

"Not a diesel, Chuck. And just for you, Jamie, he'll hook a Zodiak on a tow line."

"What's a Zodiac?"

"An inflated dinghy. It'll have an outboard engine, just like you said. Now you've got nothing to worry about."

If you only knew, she thought.

When Stu told them it was a trawler, Jamie'd had visions of a bedraggled shrimp boat, but it turned out to be close to sumptuous. She would have called it a cabin cruiser with an oversized cabin.

They set out from the marina in the early afternoon on their third day on the island, swung southeast past Lighthouse Point to drum out of San Carlos Bay into the open gulf. A pleasure cruise. No need to race anywhere. They had the boat for four days.

Jamie wondered about Stu's ability to engineer a deal this good. "He let you have this boat just like that?"

"The guy's had it on the market for a year. He's getting desperate, so I made him an offer he couldn't refuse. And I told him I'd had experience handling a Grady White on Lake Michigan." Stretched out on the sundeck in his floppy maroon trunks, Stu folded his hands contentedly over his dough-white midriff.

"Some experience," Jamie scoffed. "Fifteen minutes behind the wheel of Doug Miller's boat."

"Hell, driving this tub is a breeze. Look how well Chuck's doing."

"It's insured?" she didn't want a prolonged, messy aftermath.

He twisted around to look at her. "Odd question. Since when do you worry about that kind of thing?"

"Oh, I don't know, honey. I guess it was something Chuck was worried about. He's so thorough about everything."

Stu's eyes still held hers.

"Look!" She pointed. "There's a porpoise!"

She and Ella had stocked the galley cupboard and small refrigerator. When the sun neared the horizon's slate edge, Chuck drove to just past Cape Romano, a half mile off the desolate Ten Thousand Islands. The gulf was shallow here. Their anchor found purchase with only three-quarters of the line out.

When Jamie slipped past Chuck in the narrow aft passageway, he wordlessly thrust something into her hand. The vial of Phenobarbital capsules. As the others finished up the canned spaghetti and toasted garlic bread, she made potent coffee. Then she laced each of the two mugs with the powder from the yellow capsules in the vial. She had thought she would be a wreck at this point, but her hand shook only a little.

In their cabin, the more difficult part was waiting for Stu to go under. He insisted on reading some damned investment magazine he'd brought along, fought his increasingly heavy eyelids with sudden jerks. Then at last, when she thought she would have to scream to blow off her suddenly galloping tension, he snapped off the light over his bunk. Seconds later, he began to snore.

She waited five minutes. Then she slipped off her bunk and began to dress. No, that was wrong. She pulled her pajama bottoms back on and dug in her suitcase for her housecoat. Then she opened the door a crack.

"Jamie?" Though she expected it, the hoarse whisper startled her. "Is he...?"

"Yes. How about with you?"

"Just as we planned. You know where the fuel line is?"

"Under that hatch in the back. I asked Stu."

"Nice irony there. I have pliers and a flashlight."

Together they lifted the engine access cover. Jamie took the flash and located the black tubing of the fuel line. She fitted the jaws of the pliers around the locking nut and loosened it until a thin stream of raw gasoline ran from the connection.

"You put on the coffee pot and lit the burner?" she asked. "Left the cabin door open?"

"I did all that. So we probably don't have much time, my love."

No, they certainly did not. The smell of gasoline fumes had begun to permeate the stern area.

They hauled in the Zodiac's line then piled over its rubber gunwale. Under Jamie's bare feet, it felt like the clammy skin of some sea creature.

"Untie us," she said. "I'll get this thing started." On her third yank of the starter rope, the small Johnson outboard kicked over. The Zodiac bounded free. They leaped toward the shore until she got the knack of steering and guided them parallel to the inky fringe of mangroves.

The rush of night air past the Zodiac was chilly and disagreeably damp. She shivered in her nightclothes. When they had glided across the dead calm water to what she judged would be a safe distance from the big boat, she turned the throttle on the tiller to idle. The trawler's anchor light was the gray night's only star.

"When the Coast Guard or whoever picks us up, remember: we couldn't sleep, we were in the galley making coffee, smelled gasoline, went out on deck, and the boat caught fire. There was no way we could get to them, no way at all. Right?"

"Right."

"So we went over the side. Then the Zodiac drifted free, and we got on board. We'll have to take a little swim to get salt water on our clothes."

The flash blinded her. The thud jarred the water around them. Then blood-red flame boiled at the base of the rising smoke pillar.

"I'm sure they never knew what hit them, did they, Jamie?"

"They never had an inkling, dearest," Jamie agreed. "Men like Stu and Chuck never do."

DEATH MAGIC

Six of us were aboard the Learjet that arrowed eastward toward the Palaus. Our lean, tall pilot. Our pudgy co-pilot. And we four passengers from Prime Global Import-Export, Ltd. By now, four hours out of Ho Chi Minh City, I was aware that the other three were in the mood to do me in.

Up front in the chartered jet's spacious cabin crouched Jack McClung, VP-Overseas Operations. The senior exec, he surely carried the most weight—250 pounds of it, his permanent flush showing the strain.

On the adjoining seat, nodding loyally at every McClung mutter, perched Tom Sennett, VP-Marketing. He'd no doubt been told more than once that he looked like Errol Flynn, and he constantly diddled his Flynn-like mustache.

The third company man up there, across the aisle from the other two, was Marty Belnap, Director of Public Relations.

An unctuous smoothie of middling height, he never spoke without a smile.

Technically, I wasn't a Prime Global employee. I'm Peter Palmer, hired marketing consultant. I was aboard this little excursion to evaluate the company's proposal to establish a Vietnamese branch operation.

And I had come to the conclusion that the time was not yet ripe for such a corporate investment. Which conclusion I had reluctantly hinted at under aggressive questioning earlier in this homeward flight. And which veiled revelation had sent all three of them forward for what now looked like a near-panicky heads-together confab.

I had kept my biggest concern to myself. A helpful Vietnamese police captain had come to my hotel room in the dead of night to tell me of an odd coincidence. These same three gents were under quiet investigation of a clandestine business they apparently already had underway there in what used to be Saigon. My informant was almost certain they were absentee entrepreneurs of lucrative but highly illegal import-export of tiger parts, exploiting a current health craze throughout eastern Asia. The demand for tiger bone, claws, gall, penis and other body parts already threatened extinction of the world's tiger population.

If my police captain was reliable, it was possible that my client was being set up as a patsy to subsidize a company office that would be subverted by these three ecological bandits.

No proof, but there seemed to be enough taint at least to advise Prime Global to hold off on its intended Vietnamese expansion. My intimation that I wasn't going to recommend the company's Asian plunge just yet was surely why all three of my fellow passengers now looked as if they'd like to kill me.

Figure of speech, of course.

Our sleek little jet's safe-side cruising range required a stop in the Palaus for refueling. We would overnight there,

500 miles east of the Philippines and eight degrees north of the equator. Then on to Majuro for another refueling overnight and finally back to Honolulu, Prime Global's home city.

At 3:15 p.m. the Lear's wheels kissed the runway at Palau International Airport—a single macadam strip carved out of the jungle on Babelthuap, the largest of the Palau Islands.

Our pilot had radioed ahead for ground transport to the Palau Pacific Resort. In a car with unyielding springs, we jounced out of Babelthuap, rattled across a seemingly endless causeway then traversed the ramshackle capital island of Koror. At Koror's east end, another lengthy causeway with no sign of guardrails took us to Arakebesang Island and the resort.

It had been built on a Japanese WWII seaplane base hacked out of the tropical forest. A five-star hotel, the resort had a big central building designed along the lines of a Polynesian meeting house. Numerous small "cottages" were scattered throughout the adjacent tropical growth.

"You'll join us for supper," McClung said - ordered - after we had checked in.

I smiled. "Glad to." Always the professional. "Though I'd like to take a walk first. See what there is to see."

We stood amid the main lobby's wicker, waiting for the porky Palauan bellman to trundle our luggage out to the cottages we had been assigned.

"What is there to see?" McClung gestured oceanward. "Sand and water."

"Some of the world's most interesting seashells. A plentiful supply of sea snakes that spend a lot of their time on shore. One of the world's-"

"You been here before?" McClung asked.

"Yep." We followed the bellman out into the steamy afternoon air. It smelled sweetly of frangipani blossoms.

"A client of mine treated me to a shelling trip here a couple of years back. Fascinating place. They still believe in magic, and it's-"

McClung shook his head impatiently. "Spare me the travelogue, Palmer." He waved a Palauan guidebook at me. "Bought my own travelogue in the gift shop."

I hadn't been about to go into a magic-of-the-tropical-nights rapture. There was magic here, all right, including widely-practiced "death magic," which specialized in arcane ways to kill people. I'd heard this from my bellman on my previous visit, a wizened old Palauan who was reputed to be a retired – or maybe not so retired – priest of magic. Taking no chances, I had tipped him way beyond average and sensed that I had made a friend.

"Here's my stop," McClung said as the bellman pulled the luggage dolly to the door of one of the cottages. "See you at dinner."

The bellman and I pushed further into the lush landscaping. On impulse, I asked him, "The old man, the old bellman when I was here before – I haven't seen him. He isn't – he hasn't-"

"He retired, sir." Ten yards later, the bellman stopped dead on the pathway between cottages. "You are the so generous American!" He still speaks of you! Oh, I tell him. Welcome, sir!"

Well, at least someone out here liked me.

The resort's beach faced west, and sunset behind the islands that dotted the seascape was going to be glorious. After I'd settled in a bit, I stepped back into the warm-as-soup afternoon. I ambled southward, then out on the long finger of sand and shell that the Japanese Navy had built as a breakwater for their seaplane anchorage. Aside from encountering a dozen or so black-and-white sea snakes idling at water's edge, my walk was a relaxing break from the tensions of the moment.

Said tensions, though, set in all over again at dinner. Tonight's feature was Mongolian buffet. McClung, Sennett and I opted for that. But Belnap, ever the extrovert, ordered fruit bat soup.

"Belnap," I said, "I'm not sure you'll-"

He cut me off with a phony grin. "You squares are afraid of adventure."

His grin faded when in came his big bowl of clear, quite evil-smelling soup. "Christ!" he exploded. "What's that floating in it?"

"The bat, sir," said our soft-spoken Micronesian waitress.

What I'd tried to tell him was that fruit bat soup, a Palauan specialty, was exactly that - served with the entire bat afloat therein. Palauan fruit bats are not bite-sized little fellows. They're big guys with fox-like heads and impressive wingspans. This one looked to be almost Piper Cub class.

The soup went back in a hurry. Belnap, for once considerably subdued, settled for the buffet.

Jack McClung, though, was as assertive as ever. "Let's review the situation, Palmer," he suggested with just a hint of strain in his basso-profundo. "Your report, we gather, is not going to be exactly a thousand percent for the expansion. If that's an accurate assessment, might you tell us why?"

I paused while the waitress refilled our iced tea glasses.

"Vietnam is a communist state. The government's attitude toward private enterprise is unclear. There are less risky possibilities elsewhere," I told him. And you three sons of bitches appear to be already running by remote control an illegal and revolting racket there. I didn't tell him that. But I wondered if they had somehow heard that I'd heard. Unsubstantiated rumor, but why risk my client's reputation?

The rest of the meal's conversation was sparse and cool. Evidently too cool for Belnap. Or he was suffering fruit bat soup flashbacks. He excused himself before dessert and walked out into the dusk.

Then McClung had at me again.

"After investing major money in this little junket, Palmer, the company is not going to be delighted with a negative report."

Ever the obedient puppet, Sennett nodded, fingering his lip décor. "You're aware that the CEO himself proposed the Viet expansion?" he tossed at me.

"Look, Sennett, I don't care whose pet project it is. I would be one lousy consultant if I didn't call it like I see it. That's what Prime Global hired me for."

We went on in that mode for nearly another hour. Thrust and parry with neither side budging a centimeter. I finally had enough.

"Good night, gentlemen," I said in the middle of a McClung rebuttal to one of my rebuttals, and I stomped out into the darkness.

In my isolated cottage room, I forced myself to dash off a postcard to my wife back in L.A. Couldn't concentrate. Left it on the table half written. Took a shower, pulled on pajamas, climbed into bed. Reached for the bed lamp –

My feet had found something. A tube of cool, yielding plastic?

Then it moved.

No one has ever leaped out of bed faster. I tore back the blanket and sheet. Stood staring – shivering. And not because of the air conditioning.

It was about 10 inches long, with black and white bands toward its flattened tail. A sea snake – a banded laticauda. Tiny fangs, I knew, but their venom was more potent than a cobra's.

I'm no snake handler, but I stripped off the pillowcase, wadded it up in my hands like a crude glove, grabbed the snake behind its head and tossed it out the door.

Then I checked every inch of that room, got back into bed and spent the rest of the night staring at the ceiling – with the lights on. Like a kid who'd just had the scare of his life.

Sea snakes don't crawl into hotel beds. Somebody had put it there. I was sure I knew who, but where was any proof?

What a great spot to be in.

The three of them were at breakfast when I walked into the dining room. Were those guilty expressions of surprise at my being alive – or relatively innocent glares of continued antipathy toward my forthcoming report? I barely nodded at the triumvirate seated at the window and breakfasted alone at a secluded table far removed.

As they were leaving, Sennett veered over to me. "Take-off will be at two p.m." He stroked his mustache. "Ah…"

"Yes?"

"Nothing, Palmer." And he joined the others.

Surely the prank-loving Palauan hadn't bribed one of the housekeepers to let him into my room to plant the deadly laticauda in my bed. Who else but my corporate clientele in an evil little conspiracy of which I had not one shred of proof? And I wasn't about to call in the Arakebesang chief of police to tie me up in international political convolutions. There was no love of Americans here. During their WWII occupation, the Japanese had built a serviceable infrastructure for the Palauans. Then in 1944, we arrived and blew much of it to hell.

Maybe a quiet walk would help me organize my jumbled thought processes. I wandered out on the beach again. The sun was dazzling, the air warm and soft as only tropical air can be. The edge of the Philippine Sea lapped peacefully at the shoreline. Maybe I was totally wrong about all this. Maybe the snake somehow…

A distant dot had grown into PR Director Marty Belnap, his smile back in place. He was casually flipping something into the air and catching it, like a playful kid.

I nodded, barely. The American equivalent of the Japanese mini-bow to one unworthy of a deeper dip. Instinct told me that this fatuously grinning young exec was megamiles away from trustworthy. But, again, not a whiff of proof.

He stopped and held out a nice, big seashell. Cone-shaped, a beautiful thing like ebony china overlaid with a pattern of arrowhead-shaped white splotches. Conus mamoreus, I recalled from my shelling trip here. The Marbled Cone.

"A real honey," Belnap crowed. "And still alive. You can see the meat in there."

I hesitated, then my conscience prodded me. "Let me tell you something about-"

"Ought to find yourself one for Mitzi."

"Belnap, listen to me, will you. That cone-"

"See you at take-off, Palmer." He tossed the shell into the air again, caught it and trotted down the beach.

"Belnap!" I called after him. "You'd better not-"

Then it hit me. Mitzi, he'd said! Nobody in the world but me and my wife Michelle herself know about my pet name for her. How in hell had Marty Belnap known–

The postcard I had left unfinished in my room! Lying on the table under the light I'd left on. The nosey bastard had read it on his way to the bed with the sea snake he'd so craftily picked up on the beach after dinner while the other two stalled me in the dining room. As I was sure McClung's guidebook had told him, the laticauda was a placid snake to handle. Unless it was molested, like having a foot bang down on it in my bed.

Belnap, you son of a bitch!

I started after him. Then an odd feeling swept over me. I heard my heart thumping. Like a drum, muffled by distance. My legs felt heavy as iron. I stopped. And that made me a son of a bitch, too. Then I shook off the alien feeling and turned to walk the other way.

The Learjet didn't take off that afternoon. It didn't take off until 24 hours later. When it did, there were only three passengers aboard: Jack McClung, Tom Sennett, and Marty Belnap. Two of them were no doubt discussing what to report to Prime Global's higher brass. Marty Belnap surely wasn't saying anything because he was in a coffin secured in the rear of the cabin.

The Marbled Cone is one of the most appealing and one of the deadliest of the cone shell family. It has an extendable proboscis with a harpoon-like tooth on its tip and a supply of paralyzing venom. There is no specific anti-venom for cone shell stings. After coma comes cardiac arrest.

Apparently, Belnap's cone had gotten tired of the rough treatment and zapped him. Belnap had made it back to his room but died on the bed.

Before they took off in the Lear, I shook hands with the two surviving execs, muttered appropriate sympathies, then boarded the next available Continental shuttle to Guam. Damned if I was going to finish this trip aboard a plane with those two murderous co-conspirators.

Had I, the intended victim, become in fact the murderer in our little group? Perhaps, even though a high-priced defense team could surely produce a verdict of reasonable doubt.

Someday though, if you really press me, I might tell you about an old bellman I knew. The rumor was that he had "all-seeing eyes" and was no amateur at Palauan death magic.

FUGU

Managing Editor Charlie Lovett wore a little smirk. "You got any idea what fugu is, Forrest?"

"Pufferfish," Dan told him. All of Charlie's two hundred forty pounds sagged in disappointment.

"Damn! I thought I had you. How about a Kaiseki ryori?"

"Got me there, Charlie."

He grinned smugly. "It's a Japanese formal dinner. And you're invited."

"What do you mean, I'm invited?" Japanese cuisine wasn't Dan's favorite. "I'm NewsLeak's crime reporter, not the roving food critic. Give it to Blauvelt."

"He's on another assignment. You're the winner of this one."

Charlie ran sausage fingers through his thatch of meringue hair. A signal, Dan had learned, that he wasn't about to back down. Having boozed his way to the bottom of the journalistic food chain, Dan was in no position to challenge. Dry as he had been for the past several years, he knew he was on perpetual probation. Hell of a position to be in for a Columbia grad who had cut his professional teeth on *The New York Times*. Now in his mid-forties, he had sunk to tabloid bottom-feeding.

"Charlie, what's a Japanese dinner got to do with crime reporting – Wait a minute. You said something about fugu."

Charlie's eyes rolled ceilingward. "Thank you, God. There's hope after all." His watery blues skewered Dan. "You know that pufferfish is a Japanese delicacy? You know that if it's not prepared by a chef who knows exactly what he's doing, fugu can kill you? Well, they're serving fugu at this Kaiseki rigatoni-"

"Ryori, I thought you said."

"Whatever, Forrest. You get yourself over to the Golden Tory-"

"I think that's Tor-ee-ee, Charlie, as in T-O-R-I-I."

"That's what I said. Up on 57th. It's Hiroki Tanaka's eightieth birthday, and you're the lucky guy who's going to represent me."

"Who's Hiroki Tanaka?"

"Guy I worked with in Japan back in the '40s. The Occupation. I was a sergeant, he was a civilian clerk."

"You were friends?"

"More or less. I nearly married his sister."

"Nearly?"

"Yeah." A distant look crept into Charlie's gaze. "Hiroki wasn't exactly for it. Their old man for sure wasn't. Fact is, I had to get myself shipped out of Tokyo."

He lumbered to his feet, walked around his battered swivel and leaned on its back. "When Tanaka moved here in the '60s, I talked to him on the phone a few times; we sort of let things fade. Never could quite read how he felt about me."

"And now he's asked you to his birthday fugufest. To embrace you or erase you?"

"Forrest, he was sort of a buddy, except for the sister thing." Charlie shrugged meaty shoulders. "I'd go myself, if I didn't-"

"-have so much to do here. Yeah, Charlie."

"Besides, Daniel, you could get a story out of 'BIRTHDAY STUFFER IS DEADLY PUFFER.'"

"You're a born wordsmith, Charlie. Maybe I'd better put in a call to Cousin Roy to stand by." Sometimes Dan suspected his cousinship with Detective Lieutenant Roy Forrest at Manhattan Homicide was the reason Charlie kept him around when he occasionally bobbled a story. Couldn't hurt NewsLeak to have a pipeline into the NYPD.

"Up to 57th tomorrow at noon, Forrest. And tell old Tanaka I wish him happy birthday. I told him you'd be there in my place."

"I hope he doesn't believe in killing the messenger."

Before Dan joined the festivities up on 57th, he spent some time in the New York Public Library boning up on fugu. If the Cardiff Giant - NewsLeak's cost-cutting Welsh owner - would let the staff spring for just one computer, saved taxi fares alone would pay for the thing, Dan thought as he delved into an ichthyological tome.

The fugu was a swell little pufferfish with something called tetrodotoxin in its intestines, liver and ovaries. Nice stuff, 275 times more deadly than cyanide. But fugu-eating was a craze in Japan. A restaurant could net $200 per puffer, but an experienced fugu chef had to prepare it. The puffer eaters' death rate had averaged 20 per year through the last decade. A mere dab of puffer poison killed you by shutting down the nervous system – on one milligram dab, the amount that would cover the letter "o" in a standard newspaper copy. One average-sized fugu carried enough toxin to do in 30 gourmets. Nice stuff, and no known antidote.

The author had been considerate enough to include a dandy little Japanese ditty about this off-putting fish:

Last night he and I ate fugu;

Today, I helped carry his coffin.

Charlie, thanks a heap.

Five aged Japanese gentlemen sat cross-legged and shoeless on straw mats around a low rectangular table. Dan shucked off his loafers and stepped into the private room in the rear of the Golden Torrii.

The sixth man greeted him at the sliding door with a medium bow – not overly formal, but not exactly warm, either.

"Mr. Daniel Forrest? I am Hiroki Tanaka. So pleased to meet you."

"Mr. Lovett sends birthday congratulations." Dan tried to mask his bothersome tad of apprehension. "And he wishes you many more."

Tanaka smiled. "So pleased."

He looked like a Japanese Gregory Peck, surprisingly tall, matching Dan's six feet. Dignified, well-preserved at four-score. He wore a long purple robe tied in the middle with an orange sash.

The others wore coats and ties. They looked like board members of the Tokyo National Bank. As one, they rose. As

Dan was introduced, each bowed pleasantly. He bowed back, feeling hugely out of place. Then they all sank together with popping knees. Dan's place was adjacent to the foot of the table, well below the sake. He was a guest at this exclusive dinner, but far from the guest of honor.

Using a word association gimmick, Dan had made an effort to remember all their names during the mass intro. To his immediate right was Mr. Yoho ("and a bottle of rum"), a heavyset fellow with thinning white hair. In his sixties, Dan guessed. Except for Dan, Yoho was the youngest man here.

Between Yoho and their host at the end of the table sat Mr. Shoyu ("I'll show you"). A rangy man in his seventies, Dan judged, with near bronze skin. Shoyu was the talker of the group, in a flood of impenetrable Japanese.

No one was at the foot of the table. Directly across from Dan sat a glowering Mr. Matsui ("Mott Street Suey"). Beneath a hairless scalp, his face appeared carved of beige soapstone. Matsui squatted wordless with an expression impossible to read.

To his left crouched Mr. Hojo ("Howard Johnson," a gimme), elderly like the others but with a full head of ink-black hair, dyed or a toupee.

The remaining guest, to Hojo's left and in the place of honor at Tanaka's immediate right, was Mr. Robun ("keeps boh-bo-bohbbin along"). He was an attractive fellow with long strands of ebony hair combed from just over his right ear across his shiny scalp. He couldn't sit still, even when he wasn't slipping in a word or two when the garrulous Mr. Shoyu paused for breath.

Their host coughed discreetly for silence, then said a few words in Japanese. Formal greeting, thanks for coming, Dan guessed when he caught a couple of arigatos. His Japanese was gleaned from World War II movie reruns.

Tanaka clapped his hands. The paper screen door slid

open. In walked two of the prettiest Japanese women Dan had ever seen. Their waitresses. One was tiny with a precise bob; the other was tall with lustrous blue-black hair to her shoulders – and startlingly brilliant green eyes. All around the table Dan heard sudden intakes of breath, well short of the reaction these two gorgeous women would have generated from groups of more typical New York geezers. But the male appreciation was there, all right – from everyone except the silent soapstone carving directly across the table: Mr. Matsui glowered.

The decorative duo worked around the table, setting in front of each diner dishes and cups from the stacks in the table's center then distributing pairs of paper-sheathed chopsticks. A fork for Dan. While ensuring he would eat, that seemed something of a put-down.

The two lovely waitresses poured the initial round of sake from the two porcelain pitchers on the table. Mr. Shoyu, the talker, made a toast. Dan raised his cup, but faked a sip. Even the rice wine's faint bouquet was a threat.

Then came a bewildering succession of beautifully prepared and arranged appetizers. Amazing how good raw fish looked. On Dan's right, Mr. Yoho caught his hesitation and pointed to something on the tray in front of them, something on a skewer. Dan tried it. Barbequed chicken. He gave Mr. Yoho a smile and a nod of thanks. Yoho beamed.

Next arrived a clear soup, a touch on the briny side but not bad at all. Then a round of raw fish without Dan's chicken escape. He tried it. Tasted like…raw fish.

The attentive waitresses cleared used dishes yet again and reappeared with platters of what looked like pork, rice and cabbage. "Tonkatsu," Mr. Yoho whispered helpfully. It was pork, rice and cabbage. All right, so far.

Following the next table clearance, all conversation ceased in dramatic anticipation. The paper doorway slid wide. In walked the taller of the attendants carrying a large, blue lacquered platter. When she lowered it to the table, Dan was taken aback by the beauty of what was on it: A large crane in full flight, all of it made of delicate slices of something pinkly translucent. Surely they weren't intended to eat this work of art.

Mr. Tanaka cleared his throat. He said something in a reverent sing-song that brought understanding nods from everyone but Dan.

"It is a traditional verse, Mr. Forrest," Tanaka explained in English. "'Those who eat fugu are stupid. But,'" he raised a forefinger, "'those who do not eat fugu are also stupid.'"

So this exquisitely sculptured crane was the fugu!

It looked benign enough. The platter was passed to the guest of honor. Skillfully, Mr. Robun flicked several slices onto his plate. Next, Mr. Hojo took his serving. And Mr. Matsui, then Matsui thrust the platter across the table to Dan.

There was no way out of this. Using his alien fork, he extracted a couple of innocent-looking slices from the crane's outstretched right wing, and he passed the platter to Mr. Yoho.

Dan suppressed a shiver. *Today I helped carry his coffin...* Had to read all about it, didn't you, Forrest?

Six pairs of eyes were focused on him. He offered a weak smile. And he nibbled a slice.

Crow, Dan had read, tasted like chicken. Rattlesnake tasted like chicken. Damned if fugu didn't taste like fishy chicken. Smooth and rich, but no body to it. But he had to admit there was a certain weird thrill at eating something with such a horrendous reputation.

What the hell. He ate the second slice. All around the table he saw approving smiles. Especially from the hyperactive Mr. Robun. He was boh-boh-bohbbing along, all right.

Then he wasn't. He froze in mid-bohb. His eyes fixed on the wall over Mr. Shoyu's bronze stare. Then all eyes were riveted on Mr. Robun.

Dan had read that a fugu victim's arms and legs turned numb. The vocal cords were paralyzed. The brain stayed clear, then breathing stopped.

Mr. Robun seemed to be working on that scenario. His mouth dropped open. His breath came faster and faster. Then stopped. His eyes rolled toward the ceiling.

And he toppled over backward.

Dan's first reaction was a reporter's cynical one. Oh, come on, gents. All this for my benefit? He waited for Mr. Robun to bob up again as the room dissolved into laughter at this elaborate Nipponese practical joke on the naïve Westerner.

Mr. Robun stayed put on the matting.

Dan's next thought, crass tabloid scribe that he was, centered on what a great NewsLeak story this was going to be.

The restaurant manager called the ambulance. Dan called Cousin Roy. Both arrived at the same time. The late Mr. Robun ("Dead, all right," the chunky Lt. Roy astutely observed) was micro-checked by the next-arriving medical examiner, photographed, then toted out in a zippered body pouch.

One at a time, Roy brought the luncheon guests back to their secluded dining alcove, Mr. Tanaka first.

When Mr. Tanaka emerged and strode past Dan with a grim, "So very sorry," Mr. Yoho was next summoned. A moment later, Roy stuck his head through the sliding door and bawled, "Anybody here who can interpret?"

A busboy in the middle of the restaurant confusion shouted, "Okay, I do it." He trotted into the private room.

Mr. Yoho emerged pale and shaken. In went – at ten-minute intervals – Messrs. Shoyu, Matsui, and Hojo, each stepping back out and back into his shoes stonefaced. Then it was Dan's turn. He slid off his Thom McAns and strode in. Cross-legging it on the mats again was more than he could hack at this point, and he was sure that Roy hadn't even considered it. They both stood and kind of ambled around. With his brogans still uncouthly on his feet, Roy mercilessly crunched the matting. He was built like a Rottweiler—big-boned, a touch squatty, but agile enough. In the height department, Dan had him by four inches.

"So," Roy said, "how've you been?"

"Getting along, Cousin. Getting along."

"No problem with…" Roy left that hanging.

"Dry as the proverbial bone." Dan gestured around the table, which had been cleared. "What's happened to the evidence?"

"I've had every dish, bowl, and all utensils impounded for Forensics. What do you make of all of this?"

"The obvious conclusion is that the fugu-" He looked at Roy questioningly. "You're up to speed on-"

"Got the fugu background from Tanaka. Go ahead."

"Looks like the chef wasn't as qualified as our host assumed. The platter went around, and the unlucky gourmet snared the poisoned fillet."

"Writers," Roy muttered. "So that's what you think? Botched preparation and an accident?"

"That might be what we're supposed to think."

Roy stuffed his hands in the pockets of his baggy trousers. The matting crackled destructively as he paced. "Supposed to think?"

"The set-up seems too pat for me. Tanaka invites a newspaper editor to his eightieth birthday party after being out of touch with him for years. Then-"

"Editor? You got a promotion?"

"I was a stand-in for Charlie. Tanaka was a buddy of his back in McArthur's Tokyo."

"You think he wanted Charlie here to witness an 'accident' that was really a murder?"

"Charlie thought Tanaka wanted him here maybe to get even with him for supposedly dishonoring Tanaka's sister back in the '40s."

"You said they were buddies."

"Aside from the sister thing." Dan began to do some pacing of his own on the opposite side of the shin-high table. "If that was the case, though, and I showed up instead of Charlie, I'd expect Tanaka to call off anything unsavory he'd planned for Charlie. I don't think doing me in would give Tanaka quite the same satisfaction."

"Sure would have focused Charlie's attention, though. Insulted Colombians have been known to wipe out entire families in revenge against one member. The Oriental idea of satisfaction might be a hell of a lot trickier than a simple punch in the jaw. Say the poisoned fish got past you somehow and Robun gobbled it by mistake."

"Won't wash, Roy. The waitresses didn't serve the stuff individually. We passed the plate ourselves, and it went to Robun first."

Roy started to lean against the partition near the door, realized it was paper and resumed his pacing.

"What did you get out of the other four guests?" Dan wondered.

Roy shrugged. "Whatever the busboy wanted to tell me. I'll have to interview them all again with a department interpreter. All four either spoke no English at all, or they decided they wouldn't speak it to a homicide cop."

He stopped at the head of the table. "Let's reconstruct the set-up here. Tanaka, the host, sat where I'm standing. You were down there at the end on the left. In between you and Tanaka was-" He flipped open his pocket notebook. "Yoho on your right, then Shoyu. Along the other side were Matsui across from you, then Hojo. Robun, the deceased, sat between Hojo and Tanaka, the host."

Roy slapped his notebook shut. "Can't make much out of that except that Robun was sitting in a handy spot for Tanaka to slip him a fugu mickey, if that's what he had in mind."

"What about Robun's relationship with Tanaka?"

"According to Tanaka, Robun was the old boy's investment advisor."

"Interesting possibilities there," Dan suggested.

"Except that Tanaka's a multimillionaire and doing very well, according to the busboy's translation of what Yoho told me. Yoho said he's Tanaka's trust officer at Mercantile."

"You find out what the rest of them do?"

Roy consulted his notebook again. "Shoyu is an old friend of Tanaka's from Tokyo days. The guy who sat next to Robun – Minoru Hojo, the one with the dyed hair – he's Tanaka's insurance advisor. And the fella who sat across from you, Shiga Matsui, he's a cabinetmaker."

"A cabinetmaker? Kind of out of his depth in that group, wasn't he?"

Roy nodded. "Thought so myself, but it turns out he's not your run-of-the-mill saw-and-sand man. He's a master cabinetmaker, high-respect category in Japan. Tanaka just finished doing over his Fifth Avenue condo, and Matsui had a big piece of the decorating contract."

"What's Tanaka's line?"

"Damn, Cousin, I'm supposed to be questioning you. He made his pile importing Oriental art for retailers all over the U.S." Roy frowned. "You see the problem? So far nothing that points to anything as a motive."

"Maybe Robun was done in by mistake. By Tanaka trying for somebody else, nailing Robun as an unlucky bysitter."

"I hope not. It's murky enough with Robun as the intended victim." Roy brightened. "Hey, maybe I'll luck out, and it'll turn out to be a heart attack."

A day later, back in his little plywood cell in NewsLeak's gritty 4th-floor office on 7th Avenue, Dan pondered the imponderable. There had been no way a murderer could have delivered a lethal dose of tetrodotoxin to a selected victim via the edible crane on its lacquered platter. So if it hadn't been a heart attack, it was a tragic accident.

Had to be. Except for Robun's dropping dead, had there been anything remarkably remarkable at that extraordinary get-together?

Accidental poisoning. Or maybe, after all, it was a laughingly termed "natural causes." Heart attack, like Roy hoped.

That idea was scotched when Roy called around 4:30. "Prelim report from the ME, Cuz. It was no heart attack."

"The forensics people are pretty fast down there on 30th Street."

"Slow week, plus computer analysis. Looks like fish poison, all right. Lucky more of you didn't get hit."

"You're saying it was accidental poisoning, Roy?"

"I'm saying I filed my DD-5, and that's what I was told to put on it. Case closed, if you know what I mean. Helps with the caseload mountain here." Roy was silent a moment, then he said, "But, Cuz, you're a free agent."

"Got you, Roy." They had an understanding; used each other now and then to get around certain obstacles. Roy's subliminal message: "I'm not sold on the accident theory, but I'm stymied by departmental bureaucracy."

Dan hung up and went back to musing about aberration at that now-infamous party. ...And Shiga Matsui's glower during the moment of otherwise universal appreciation for the two striking attendants. Was he only an aging grouch, or had that sourball grimace meant something?

On impulse, Dan picked up the phone again and dialed Hiroki Tanaka's residence. The old man's personal assistant with a youthful, polite voice left the line to consult his employer. Then he told that Dan Tanaka would be pleased to "receive" him tomorrow at 2:00 p.m.

Grabbing a quick lunch at Nedick's, Dan walked the three long blocks east to the IRT and subwayed up to the East Seventies. The Gold Coast. Three shorter blocks westward, he found the building. Brick with concrete trim and a number in gold. No name.

After an ID check and a verifying call, Security let him take one of the mahogany-lined elevators to the fourteenth floor. The entrance to Tanaka's unit was just a few strides down the plush hallway runner.

The houseman, in pinstriped vest and trousers, ushered him in with a precisely correct medium bow. The word "unit" was an insult to this spread. It was right out of the Japanese version of Architectural Digest, all brocade hangings and lustrous, hand-rubbed woodwork. Master cabinetmaker Matsui's work, no doubt.

The houseman cleared his throat discreetly and nodded at Dan's loafers. Dan pulled them off and followed the trim little man across a half-acre of ivory-mellow carpeting lush as lamb's wool.

Tanaka rose from a low sofa that faced an immense floor-to-ceiling picture window overlooking Central Park. A real breathtaker, that Cineramic view. As if they floated in mid-air two hundred feet above one of America's most beautiful expanses of urban acreage.

Incongruously, the old man wore bright green plaid and gold slacks and an eye-dazzling saffron cardigan.

"So pleasant to see you again, Mr. Forrest." He offered a dry claw of a hand. "My deep apologies for the terrible incident yesterday. Most regrettable. Most regrettable, indeed."

"Mr. Lovett was... surprised at your invitation," Dan told him. "He wasn't sure about your intentions."

"Honorable intentions," the old man said, indicating the plush gold sofa facing the huge window. For a moment they sat in silence, contemplating the panoramic view.

"After a long life in America," Tanaka said, "I have come to realize that what happened between Charles and me was simply a clash of culture. Not an insult to my family. But apology does not come easily in Japan. There has not yet been an apology for Nanking. Not even for Pearl Harbor. It has taken me decades to realize I should apologize to Charles."

"That's why he was invited?"

"Yes. When he could not accept, it would have been a true insult not to welcome his representative. You, Mr. Forrest."

"You were very gracious, Mr. Tanaka." Dan paused. "The, uh, unfortunate poisoning of Mr. Robun, of course, is what I'm here about."

Tanaka eyed the pocket notebook Dan had flipped open. "I am now speaking, I assume, 'on the record,' Mr. Forrest?"

For a NewsLeak reporter, nothing was ever off the record.

"I'm afraid so, sir, but I'm not here to build a sensational plot around what may have been an unfortunate mistake." (Forgive me, Charlie.)

"Ah," Tanaka said softly, "but it was not a mistake."

That had to be the last thing Dan had expected him to say.

"You aren't actually admitting-"

Tanaka held up a frail hand. "It was not a mistake because Mr. Kanagawa does not make mistakes."

"Mr. Kanagawa?"

"The fugu chef I had flown in from San Francisco for the occasion. He does not make mistakes."

"But the lab tests. I got the final report from the police this morning. Mr. Robun's death was from fugu poisoning."

"Obviously." Tanaka appeared totally unruffled. "I do not need tests to tell me that. I have seen death from fugu."

"What are you telling me, Mr. Tanaka?" This interview wasn't going at all as Dan had expected.

"I offer no conclusion. A friend whom I valued is dead of fugu poisoning. But such a tragic event cannot be the fault of Mr. Kanagawa."

"Any chef can make a mistake."

The old man's chin came up, and in the crackly parchment of his face, his mouth tightened. "Not," he insisted, "Master Chef Yukichi Kanagawa."

Dan tried another tack. "When the waitresses first entered the room, there was a general appreciation. Except for Mr. Matsui. I couldn't help notice his, well, apparent resentment."

"You are very observant, Mr. Forrest." Tanaka smiled thinly, showing the edges of ivory-tinted teeth. "But that incident is not difficult to understand. The taller of the two women, the one with the long hair, is Mr. Matsui's niece."

Well, well.

"He is very protective of her since her Caucasian mother died and her father – Mr. Matsui's brother – returned to Japan, leaving Nikko in her uncle's care.

Ah hah! A Caucasian mother, eh? Hence the green eyes. And Matsui is her uncle. But then, so what? Perhaps that was no more than an interesting sidelight to that strange luncheon.

"Assuming you are right about Chef Kanagawa's abilities, Mr. Tanaka, might you have any idea how Mr. Robun could possibly have eaten a piece of poisoned fugu?"

"No, Mr. Forrest, I have not."

"He was sitting between you and Mr..." Dan checked his notes. Howard Johnson. "Mr. Hojo."

"So Detective Forrest-" Tanaka frowned. "Curious. Two Misters Forrest."

"He's my cousin."

"Ah. Convenient."

"Sometimes."

Beneath wispy white eyebrows, Tanaka's sharp little eyes held Dan's. "Yes, Mr. Hojo and I were in arm's reach of Mr.

Robun's plate. But do you seriously believe that if either of us wished to do away with Mr. Robun, we would have chosen such an obvious opportunity?"

He crossed his stiff legs in their dazzling golfer's green. "And the opportunity was not as great as you may believe. You will recall there were no individual servings, only a single platter from which we chose our own portion."

He plucked absently at an invisible something on his knee. "The Western mind often leaps to the apparent obvious. Do I assume your cousin, the police lieutenant, has made such a leap?"

"Not at all, Mr. Tanaka." Dan decided there was no need to tell him Roy's superior had made a leap to the apparently obvious conclusion the poisoning had been accidental. Dan also didn't tell Tanaka that he had just decided to pay a visit to Mr. Matsui.

"Tea, gentlemen?" asked Tanaka's natty aide from the distant entrance of this palatial sitting area. And the rest of Dan's time high over Central Park's green splendor was spent listening to quite a touching reminiscence of a far younger Hiroki Tanaka's friendship with youthful Sergeant Charles Lovett (had Charlie ever been young?) in post-V-J Day Tokyo.

Back on the IRT, Dan barreled beneath Park Avenue then under Lafayette to the Spring Street Station. Manhattan was not as pretty way down here as it had been from Tanaka's cloud tower. He found Matsui's Cabinetry a couple short blocks east in one of New York's gritty pockets.

On the rattling ride south, he'd had time to do some constructive thinking. As an old Tanaka had pointed out, everything served at the deadly luncheon had been "family style." All the platters had been placed on the table, then the guests had helped themselves in rotation. That had made it impossible to poison just one diner out of seven.

Except for – Dan had sat straight up on the hard subway seat. But what was the motive?

Now he cupped his hands against Matsui Cabinetry's clouded plate glass. The interior was murky with just a hint of light far in the back. There was no bell button. He rapped on the glass.

"Matsui not hear that," said a quavery voice behind him. An aged Oriental stood on the sidewalk, hands on hips, chin jutting forward. "You friend of Matsui?"

"No, I'm a reporter."

"Reporter? You write story 'bout that son bitch, you write he killed my cat."

"Your cat?" What was going on here?

"I'm Tenno. I own wholesale place next door. There." Mr. Tenno pointed. "I sell good line of Ukiyo-ye copies."

Dan's blank look distressed him. "Woodblock, woodblock prints. Copies of Harunobu, Sharaku, Kitonage – old master. You interested?"

"Sorry, no. What's this about your cat?"

"Matsui put out garbage, cat eat garbage. Dead cat. Son bitch Matsui. You write that."

Dan peered back through the dirty glass storefront. "I don't think he's in there."

"In there, all right." Tenno stepped up to the adjacent door and flailed it with both fists. Dan was sure that barrage could be heard over on the Bowery, a block away.

Way back in the cabinet shop, he detected motion. So did Mr. Tenno.

"I go now," he muttered. "I do not talk to Matsui until he apologize for death of cat."

When Shiga Matsui unshackled his door and peered up at Dan with all the warmth of a pit bull, Mr. Tenno had silently evaporated. At that point, Dan realized Matsui had not spoken a word of English during the ill-fated birthday party. Here stood Dan armed with a three-word Japanese vocabulary.

"Ohayo," he said.

"I'm busy," muttered the glowering Mr. Matsui in accentless English. "Whatever you want, get it out then get lost."

Dan groped for English of his own. "I, uh, want to ask a couple of questions about the party yesterday."

"Most unfortunate," said Matsui without a trace of regret in his hard soapstone expression. "But 'those who eat fugu'-"

"Are stupid," Dan finished for him. "May I come in?"

"No, thank you. You are not police. As I recall, you are a reporter for a disreputable newspaper."

He was a foot shorter than Dan, but his Telly Savalas coiffure and his Mr. Five-by-Five stature had real presence.

"Okay," Dan said. "I'll get right to the point. Did you know Mr. Robun?"

"Hai, I knew him." There seemed a touch of bitterness in his from-the-belly tone.

"He was a friend?"

Matsui said nothing.

Dan tried a long shot. "I just left Mr. Tanaka. He spoke very warmly of Mr. Robun."

Matsui's eyes narrowed to slits. His voice took on a flinty edge. "The late Mr. Robun is not worthy of discussion."

Oh, ho. "Why do you say that, Mr. Matsui?"

"It is personal. Do not quote me in what you write, but in my opinion, the gods justly sentenced him."

Not a bad line.

"I'm not sure I follow that," Dan said. "You mean it was a fatal accident Mr. Robun deserved?"

Matsui bowed, just slightly, an ironic little gesture. "'Today we carry his coffin.'"

"You're going to his funeral?"

"A figure of speech. I will have nothing to do with his funeral."

"Somehow that seems, well, not in keeping with-"

"Japanese custom? What can you know of Japanese custom?"

"An assumption." Dan decided to throw him a curve. "Do you eat in your shop, Mr. Matsui?"

The cabinetmaker frowned. "No, I walk down to Little Italy. Why do you ask?"

Now Dan tried a change-up. "You don't show much regret at the death of a respected countryman."

"Respected!" Matsui's voice was near a squeak. His saffron complexion turned purple. That had obviously hit him where he lived. "Respected! He was an animal!"

"How so?"

"Nikko-" Then he shut up.

"What about Nikko, Mr. Matsui?"

"Good day, sir." Name, rank and serial number time.

"What about Mr. Tenno's cat, Mr. Matsui?"

But Matsui was already behind the door. Which he slammed in Dan's face.

Back up to midtown on the good old IRT. Dan was beginning to feel like the Phantom of the Subway. Off at 60th Street Station, he backtracked to 57th and found Nikko Matsui on duty at the Golden Torii setting tables for the early supper crowd.

"Dan Forrest from NewsLeak, Ms. Matsui. A word with you, please?"

Beneath the soft ivory of her cheeks, he saw her blanch a bit. My God, he realized all over again, this is one truly beautiful woman.

She glanced at him nervously. For the manager who might object to this interruption, or because a NewsLeak interview wasn't exactly a soothing prospect under the circumstances? Said circumstances were beginning to point in an interesting direction.

"I just left your uncle," he told Nikko, "and I got the impression that you and Mr. Robun were not exactly buddies."

Her startling emerald-green eyes flashed. "He was a–. No, we were not friends."

"You are not sorry he served himself the poisoned part of the fugu?"

She was visibly relieved at that. "To be honest, Mr… Forrest, isn't it? No, I am not mourning Mr. Robun. He was… He was…" Her voice trailed off.

"He was a financial advisor. Did you have any dealings with him?"

"He was my uncle's investment counselor."

"And he stole money from him?" that seemed a distinct possibility.

"No, no. He was very honest. Uncle Shiga made money through his advice."

"Then what–"

Her lovely face suddenly glowed crimson. Shame?

"It was between Robun and you, wasn't it?" Dan said. "Something personal."

She stood very straight, and her mouth compressed to a thin line. She said almost in a whisper, "One day last month, Mr. Robun came when my uncle was not at home. He would not leave. Then he–" The green eyes flared. "You cannot put this in your paper, Mr. Forrest. Rape is extremely personal."

She shut up and turned away, a Matsui family trait. Dan found a pay phone back near the restrooms and put in a call to Roy.

They met at the Golden Torii at 11:00 the next morning, the time the manager had told Dan Nikko Matsui came on duty. Conscientious woman that she was, Nikko showed up precisely on time. Not showing would have been futile, anyway. Roy had put a man on watch all night at her apartment building.

He and Nikko and Dan sat at a table in the secluded corner. Roy gave Dan a nod, and Dan ran with it.

"There was no way the food or the tea or the sake could have been tampered with so that only Mr. Robun was poisoned. It had to be delivered just to him. Even the plates and cups were set out from stacks on the table. It finally hit me there had been just one exception."

Nikko lowered her head. Her long, blue-black hair fell forward to frame her delicate face.

"Then there was Mr. Tenno's cat. It died from eating food in your uncle's cabinetry trash. But he told me he always ate out. What was food doing in his shop? Roy?"

"Tenno just couldn't get himself to put his pet cat's body in the trash. He still had it. We picked it up after your call yesterday, Dan. Had it tested. Fugu killed the cat." Roy turned to Nikko. "Your uncle had bought his own puffer."

"And he bought it," Dan put in, "to do a little fancy woodworking."

Nikko stared at the tablecloth.

"Roy, your turn again."

"You were there, Dan. Go ahead."

"The only items handed out individually at the luncheon were the chopsticks. I watched you set them around the table, Nikko. I watched you give Mr. Robun his pair. Chopsticks especially treated by your uncle the day before."

Roy sat back and folded his bulky arms. "We'd bagged and tagged all the dishes and sticks by individual users. When Dan called me yesterday, it wasn't any trick to find Robun's sticks. This morning, Forensics reported tetrodotoxin in microscopic grooves at the ends of Robun's chopsticks. By the time the fugu was passed around, whappo! Down he goes. Obvious goof-up by the chef. An accident."

"And only you and Uncle Matsui knew," Dan added. Or did you know, Nikko? You took a set of chopsticks from here, gave them to your uncle. He returned them and told you to give them to Robun. But did you know what was on them?"

At that instant, Roy broke in with what Dan thought was either ultimate political correctness – or unexpected chivalry.

"'You have the right to remain silent,'" he boomed. "'You are not required to say anything to us at any time or to answer any questions.'"

As he went on with the rest of the Miranda warning, Nikko looked up at him. A smile slowly spread across her elegant face.

TORRENT

Drilling the blast hole with hammer and rod was slow going. But maybe Mr. Llewellyn was right, Giovanni thought, as he slammed down the oversized hammer against the edge of the steel rod Stefan held in place. With each blow, the blast hole in the ebony anthracite face deepened only a quarter inch, but the dynamite charge would loosen a lot more coal than his and Stefan's and Yanek's hard going with their picks.

"My two Polacks and a Dago," Mr. Llewellyn called them, right to Giovanni's face. A Welsh bastardo. But Mr. Llewellyn gave the three of them work, even if it was illegal in this deserted slope mine; deserted, Giovanni knew, not only because the market for Pennsylvania anthracite had slackened off right after the war, but also because this mine had been closed for safety. No doubt because two years ago 11 miners had been crushed in a cave-in just a quarter-mile up one of the many side tunnels behind where Giovanni, Stefan, and Yanek now worked. And also maybe because the workings were so near the Susquehanna River. Now, in 1947, the mine was officially closed, its entrance boarded up.

None of that appeared to concern Mr. Llewellyn. Six days a week, skinny Giovanni Sivestro, Stefan "Worrier Bull" Popoweski, and "No Talk" Yanek Belinski squeezed through the entrance boards to pick and shovel all day in underground gloom. Then at dusk, Carlo Illuzi would rumble his truck into the cut just below the entrance. The boards were pried loose, and Mr. Llewellyn's two Polacks and a Dago would trundle load after load along the rickety narrow gauge track to the mine opening. There they would tip the laden tram car into the truck.

Everyone was sworn to secrecy. The vein was still rich, and it was there for the stealing. All that bothered Mr. Llewellyn was the slowness of their work. If he would just one time come down here with them, he would see how sudore – how much sweat – it took to load that little-abandoned mine car just one time.

But Mr. Llewellyn did pay promptly every week. Fifteen dollars cash for each mine car load they chipped from the coal face with hand-stinging pick blows, shoveled into the little tram, then shoved along the rattly track to Carlo's truck, waiting in the night at the tumbledown mine entrance. The loading of his truck done in the dark to reduce Mr. Llewellyn's risk. But nothing reduces our risk, Giovanni thought as he banged his rhythmic blows against the drilling rod. He took care to hit it squarely. That was not easy in the swaying circles of light from the electric lamps on their hard hats, and Stefan's big hands were only inches from the top of the rod.

They had worked without speaking for a quarter-hour when Stefan suddenly said in the flat silence between hammer blows, "I do not like this."

"The work, I am doing it," Giovanni pointed out. "You only holding the rod."

"Not the work I don't like. The dynamite. We have not used dynamite before. We are not – how do you say – powder monkeys. Do you know how much to use?"

"Enough to break up this maledetto coal face," Giovanni said as he swung the hammer again. Stefan was always big with the agitazione – with worry.

"But we are not even sure where we are."

"We are in this cursed hole, that's where we are."

"But," said Stefan, The Worrier Bull, "we do not know what is above. We should have a survey."

"If you are worrying about the river," Giovanni said, "I have paced from the entrance to here. Seven hundred steps. The river is one thousand two hundred. I paced that, too, up there on Saturday."

One thousand two hundred paces through October-chilled brambles and mountain laurel and leathery rhododendrons. He had been tired, bones aching, and the hilly walk to the river was also strewn with boulders. It had been 1,200 long paces. He was sure. Certo. Stefan was always full of agitazione grande.

Giovanni slammed the end of the drilling rod six more times. More than deep enough into the coal face for a stick of the brown paraffin-wrapped dynamite. He hadn't realized how hard he had been hammering. "Deep enough for two sticks."

"Two?" Stefan asked. In the wobbly light of Giovanni's headlamp, Stefan's broad, black-streaked face peered up like that of an uncertain child."

"Yanek, the cap, and fuse." The silent Pole – in a rare burst of words when Giovanni told them Mr. Llewellyn could get them dynamite – had claimed he'd done some blasting work in a New Jersey quarry.

As he slid one end of the yard-long orange fuse into the cap then pushed the cap into the end of one of the explosive sticks, Yanek did look like he knew what he was doing. He slipped the primed stick into the hole, thrust it all the way in with the rod, then turned to Giovanni.

"Two sticks, Yanek."

The Pole looked at Stefan, who glanced at Giovanni then shrugged. Yanek shrugged too, and slipped the second stick of 65% Du Pont "Extra" into the hole, careful not to dislodge the already placed fuse. He tamped loose coal into the remaining space then stood and nodded.

They gathered their shovels and picks, tossed them into the empty tram then trundled it a hundred yards down the tunnel to where there was a bend. The tram always pushed easier out than in, even when it was loaded. Which told Giovanni the tunnel sloped upward as it penetrated the bowels of the mountain.

"You wait here," he told them, and he trotted back to the loaded face. His first match went out. The second flared against the little exposed black O of powder in the end of the fuse. It sputtered then caught with the hiss of an angry serpent. Giovanni dropped the flaring end of the fuse and raced back to the bend in the tunnel.

They huddled behind the tram. From here they could not see the flaming fuse or hear its eager sizzle. They heard nothing at all, not even each other's breathing. The tunnel's gassy air closed over them in a stifling blanket.

Then Stefan, the Worrier Bull, said in a voice that startled everyone, "Did it go out?"

"Mr. Llewellyn said two minutes per yard of fuse. It is a yard-"

Giovanni's next word was swallowed in a ball of air and stinging coal dust that flew down the tunnel to slam them like something solid. Then the thunderclap of the explosion made his ears ring. He smelled the acrid odor of raw coal mingled with the explosion smoke.

As they began to shove the tram back up the tunnel's track, the Worrier Bull jerked straight up.

"What is that?"

They all stopped pushing. Over the ringing in his ears, he heard it too. A trickling. Water in this tunnel that had stayed dry as a bone even in last month's hard rains?

The chilling trickle sound suddenly swelled into a frightening rush. In a single second, Giovanni knew: His pacing of the distance had been imperfetto. The dynamite – 65% nitro – had been too powerful. The–

From the shattered coal face burst a roar as the tunnel roof began to collapse. In the beams of their headlamps, a glittering black wall surged down the tunnel straight at them.

"Jesus God!" Stefan shouted.

They were in the act of crossing themselves when the inrushing flood slammed them backward. The impact rammed the air from Giovanni's lungs. Angelica, I–

In seconds, irresistible tons of filthy water filled the tunnel. Anyone standing near the mine's entrance would have been astounded to see a thick black jet propel three mangled bodies and a shattered tram car from the hole near the foot of the mountain. But no one was there when the silence of early evening was broken by the outrush of water and its grisly burden.

The small valley below quickly filled with the dirty flow gushing from the mine until a sizeable lake formed where there had been only scrubby brush and a winding gravel road. The inky torrent swiftly drowned Stefan's old Chevy; then only when the valley's water level had reached well above the top of the mine entrance did the flow slacken. In twilight silence, the three bodies floated like bundles of filthy rags in a lake of black licorice.

The silence of the newly-formed lake was deceptive. When its level reached the level of the river on the other side of the mountain, the flow into the lake stopped. But deep underground, incoming water now snaked into side tunnels, broke open narrow walls between adjacent abandoned diggings, raced through the network of old mines that honeycombed the earth beneath Neshamong township and the Borough of Neshamong itself.

The water's hungry search for underground space was insatiable, and the Susquehanna River fed it. It was the Susquehanna River. The three bootleg miners had blown a hole in the riverbed 30 feet from shore. Now it roared an inexhaustible rush of water that had its origins a hundred miles away in the Finger Lakes.

At 8:15 p.m., Davis Llewellyn received a panicky telephone call from his truck driver.

"The mine, Mr. Llewellyn, she's gone!"

"Gone? What in hell's name do you mean, Carlo?"

"No mine. Only a lake."

"You drunk?"

"No, no Mr. Llewellyn. The Number Four mine, she's gone. The road, she's gone. The vallata, the...the valley, she's full of water."

Llewellyn was non-plussed but in control. "Go home then," he ordered the lumpish Carlo. "And you keep your mouth shut, you hear me?"

He hung up and sank heavily into his overstuffed reading chair by the parlor's front window. More interested in making his fortune than making a family, he lived alone at the dead end of West Carbon Street. His house was not big, yet not as small as the houses that lined both sides of the winding street. He planned to buy these houses one by one at forced sale prices as their idled mortgagees left Neshamong for the factories of Philadelphia or Camden. One day he would own the whole street, and he was certain it would only be a matter of time until the mountain resort of nearby Shannon Ridge would expand to acquire all available land this side of the borough.

For an out-of-work mine manager, he was doing all right. His bootleggers steadily chipped enough coal out of the area's closed but still-rich diggings to build him a nice bank account – quietly and steadily enlarged by mail deposits to a bank in distant California. The new paint on the house? His housekeeper who came five days a week to clean and cook for him? The townspeople had accepted his story about a well-to-do grandmother dying in far-off Cardiff, Wales, and leaving him a generous annual income.

He pressed his fingertips to his broad temples. A lake, for God's sake, where there had been a secluded valley…

Then his 230 pounds of idle-soft flesh quivered beneath his Irish tweed trousers and wool shirt. This morning, his two Polacks and the Dago had been given dynamite. The dumb bastards must have blown out the roof, and the roof was the bottom of the river. Great God Almighty!

He slumped in his chair, fingers pinching his doughy chin. Surely those three were dead now. Who else knew what they had been doing? Carlo, of course, but Carlo was in this too deep to say anything to anybody. There was no one else. Llewellyn had purposely kept his crooked operation as small as possible, not only for economy's sake, but for a situation like this.

He sat straighter now. The two big Poles and the little Dago he'd assigned to Number Four had been productive, but he could hire other desperate ex-miners looking for a dollar. And there were plenty more boarded-up but still-workable diggings he could plunder.

Davis Llewellyn, determined to be a rich man before he hit 50, smiled to himself. Aside from him and Carlo, no one else knew. When the bodies were found, the blame would fall on them, not him.

He picked up the evening paper and concentrated on the financial pages while black water began its rush through the abandoned workings beneath the Borough of Neshamong.

No one else knew.

But someone else did know. One night when Giovanni had returned blackened and weary, and again telling Angelica that he had a late shift at the mattress factory, she told him that was a lie. She knew coal dust from lint. He was working a mine, si?

"You accuse your husband of a lie?"

"When he does not tell the truth."

Angelica had more going for her than simple confrontation. For a full month, pleading various excuses, she had not let Giovanni touch her. Now she softened.

"Caro mio, I will be honest with you. Tonight, I want you. But you must be honest with me. I cannot make love with a dishonest man."

So when they were as one in their warm bed, he told her.

This very morning, before he left with the two others, he had told her more of it. He had told her of the dynamite, and his fear of it. When midnight passed and he had not returned, she felt all alone and frightened. In eight years of marriage, she'd had no children. All of her relatives were in the old country. She had only Giovanni. Now ice in her heart told her something terrible had happened to him.

Just after dawn, she heard it on their scratchy Philco radio. The river had broken through and was flooding the old mine workings. The dynamite? Giovanni had feared the dynamite. Now Angelica knew.

She ran to the nearby house of Katrin Popowski, Stefan's wife. She learned that Katrin also knew about the bootleg mining, and Katrin told Angelica about Yanek Belinski's part in it. Together they ran to the house of Yanek Belinski, and it turned out his wife also knew. All three wives knew about the secret mining of their husbands. But only Angelica had been told the full story – Mr. Llewellyn's part in it.

"He is such a big man in Neshamong," blonde little Stani Belinski pointed out, "no one would believe this. If we tell, then what will happen to us?"

"What will happen to us anyway?" asked Katrin Popowski, defiantly planting her big hands on her copious hips.

Yet, in the end, they decided there was no use in an accusation no one would believe.

Then Angelica, her brown eyes flashing anger, said, "I know who can do something."

"Who?" Katrin asked.

"Signora Miracolosa."

"Who is she?" asked Katrin and Stani together.

Angelica told them.

The day after the mine flooding, David Llewellyn drove his Studebaker to the end of the pitted macadam pavement near the riverbank. He locked the shiny green car and walked the rest of the way.

He was surprised by the size of the crowd that had already gathered on the steep, rocky bank to stare into the current where a whirlpool dented the slatelike surface. The network of mines that spread from here for miles under the township was sucking the river in through that spinning hole.

Down the river floated a half-submerged tree limb as long as his car, its branches sticking up like dead fingers. It drifted slowly in the current until it neared the whirlpool. Then it moved faster. The huge limb veered toward the sucking hole in the water, flipped into it. And in the blink of an eye, it was gone.

From the crowd arose a long "Oohhh!"

Llewellyn, standing away from the rest of them, had seen enough. He stomped back through the weeds and brush to his car. "God damn those three thick foreign bastards!" he muttered as he opened the Studebaker's door. Thank God they were dead now. No story to tell. At first light, their bodies had been discovered at the edge of the awesome new lake by a horrified Neshamong man hunting rabbits out-of-season to feed his hungry family.

The township police had accurately determined the three dead men had been bootleg mining and had broken through the riverbed. Sharp police theory, but without a hint of a Llewellyn connection.

On the third day after the disaster, two unusual things happened. The first was so dramatic that films of it appeared on every fluttery black-and-white Pathe television box that David Llewellyn had bought just last month, the first person in Neshamong to own such a device. The broadcast wobbled up the valley from Wilkes-Barre, and Llewellyn was able to fiddle with the horizontal hold control so the picture stayed fairly steady.

And what a picture it was. The Pennsylvania Bureau of Mines had managed to slap together a short spur line from the nearby Lackawanna RR tracks to the edge of the riverbank overlooking the whirlpool. The mine safety engineers somehow assembled a string of dilapidated freight cars. On the pulsing television screen, a small engine shoved the snake of empty boxcars onto the spur then over the riverbank.

One by one the huge boxcars toppled from the end of the improvised spur and crashed into the whirlpool. And each was instantly whisked from sight as if it were of no more consequence than a matchbox.

Now everyone knew the river's cascade into the vast underground web of mine workings could not be staunched. It would only stop when the township's honeycombed underpinnings were gorged with black water.

Not a pretty outlook. Yet, Llewellyn told himself, all he had to do was keep his mouth shut. He was in the clear.

Then the second unusual thing happened that day. When he walked out his front door to drive to the post office to mail this week's bank deposit – obviously the last one until he could come up with another scheme – he noticed a woman standing on the sidewalk a hundred feet up West Carbon Street. The woman looked vulturelike in her long black dress, her face obscured by a dark shawl she wore as a hood. As he drove past her, she stared straight at him, even turning to keep facing him as he rolled past.

When he returned a half hour later, she still stood there.

His housekeeper – "Just another Dago woman named Maria," he'd told the boys at O'Sheen's Tavern – had a strange reaction to the creepy old woman. After Maria nodded a goodbye to Llewellyn that afternoon, he saw her stop dead on his front walk, hurriedly cross herself, then walk up the opposite side of the street. He knew she lived a quarter mile up the other side.

When he pushed the lace curtain apart an inch and peered out just before sitting down to the supper Maria had made for him, the woman was gone. He shrugged and muttered, "Takes all kinds."

The next morning, she was back in the same place. Unmoving as stone, staring at the house. When Maria pushed open the door and shucked off her threadbare coat, he was waiting in the hallway.

"Who in the hell is that hanging around out there?"

She didn't answer.

"I asked you a question, woman!"

Again, Maria was silent, not even facing him.

His face flushed. He felt like slapping her. "Answer me!"

The little housekeeper turned to him slowly, her angular face pale and hard as granite. "She is Signora Miracolosa."

"'Mrs. Miracle?'" His bray of laughter made Maria's thin blue lips tighten. "What's her claim to fame?"

Maria muttered something he didn't catch.

"What? What did you say?"

Maria's voice was a near-whisper. "The Eye."

"The what?"

"The Evil Eye."

"Oh, for God's sake!" Llewellyn exploded. "Go on with your work."

Bunch of damned superstitious Sicilians infested this burg. Took a smart Welshman to make a real buck here.

The next morning, he stormed out his front door and strode right up to this "Mrs. Miracle." He was surprised to find that under the shadow of her hood she was frail and not nearly as tall as she had appeared from his parlor window. In fact, she seemed dead already, her face like wrinkled parchment. Except for her eyes. Something like blue anthracite flames danced in those eyes. He forgot what he had planned to say.

"Go home, dammit!"

Her feisty, unblinking stare cut right into him.

He spun around and stomped back to the house. Back inside, he decided that weird stare seemed so only because Maria had told him the old woman has the Evil Eye. He snorted. Never listen to anything servants tell you. Maybe the two of them were working together to give him a scare.

Why? No one but Carlo knew about the cause of the mine disaster.

The following day, the old woman was out there again. He began to wonder if somehow there really could be a connection between her and what had happened at Number Four mine. That didn't seem possible, but might Carlo have let his tongue get away from him after too many beers at O'Sheen's?

No, there'd be a lynch mob outside by now, not just one old woman. He looked through the slit in the curtains again. She stood there like Death without a scythe.

Damned if he'd let this get to him. Go about your business, Davis Llewellyn. He was beginning to understand how the so-called Evil Eye worked. It ate from the inside. Signora

Miracolosa just stood out there, really doing nothing at all until you ripped yourself apart with a heart attack or maybe collapsed from just plain worry. Like the voodoo stuff he'd read about. Neat trick. But he wasn't having any.

The week dragged on, and the impact of the mine collapse and the river's invasion dulled a bit. The fuzzy television news pictures had moved on to a national story concerning a suspected subversive curiously named Hiss.

Now that he knew what her game was, Llewellyn could laugh at the persistent old woman. Life went on. The Bureau of Mines people argued in the paper over what to do with all the water sloshing around deep beneath the township. Carlo delivered the last of the bootleg coal sales money, minus his commissions, and promised to be ready for whatever lucrative scheme might be next. Davis Llewellyn relaxed.

Until Saturday evening, just before supper. He heaved out of his chair to take a quick look through the parlor window. Still out there, now in the wan glow of a streetlight. With her dumb, useless stare. Talk about a waste of ti—

What the hell was that! The floor had just vibrated. He grabbed the back of his chair. An earthquake here, in Northern Pennsylvania?

The floor shuddered again. He heard a muffled rumble right beneath his feet. In the cellar. Had one of the floor joists given way?

He bounded into the kitchen, tore open the cellar door and flicked on the light switch. No light. Both bulbs blown? More likely a fuse. He banged down the long flight of wooden steps, sinking into darkness as he groped for the fuse box.

He felt a whoosh of cold air whirl up around him. Heard a noise like tons of earth falling. Froze in mid-step. Too late. The stair collapsed under his feet. He slid downward, the splintery handrail tearing his scrabbling palms.

His panic-stricken throat cut his scream to a strangled squeak. Frozen-voiced, Davis Llewellyn plummeted through a hundred feet of black space as he followed his cement floor into the torrent of river water that had undermined his house. The last sound he heard was the shriek of twisting timber, so very much like a woman's victorious cry.

FALLOUT

In the quiet Northeastern Pennsylvania August afternoon not even a hint of tragedy. Then the airport's low-winged, single-engined PT-19 howled in from the west, yawning and pitching as if a panicky pilot were at the controls. But Joe Pritchet was Hardington Municipal Airport's steadiest flight instructor.

The lemon yellow army surplus trainer nosed down in a straight-in landing approach – downwind. No heed at all to the windsock or the airport's mandatory traffic pattern. The plane bounced hard, settled, then swung off the runway and taxied hell-for-leather for the concrete apron. A bunch of us instructors and G.I. Bill students stood there wondering just what was going on with Chief Instructor Pritchet and the student he'd taken off with a half-hour ago.

As the plane taxied onto the apron and the engine died, I saw only the forward open cockpit was occupied. Or was Pritchet hunched down in the rear seat to fix something? Or maybe sick?

He had taken off with student Alec Wharton in the front cockpit. But only Wharton scrambled out. The rear cockpit that instructor Pritchet had buckled himself into on take-off was empty. Had Pritchet landed them at some other airport then sent Wharton back here alone? That would be enough of an infraction to get him at least a serious reprimand from our discipline-obsessed airport manager.

One look at Wharton as he yanked off his goggles and helmet told me – told all of us – that Pritchet's student was in a state of panic.

"My God! Oh, my God!" His screech sent an icy wave straight up my spine.

I raced toward him, trailed by everyone else.

"Where's Pritchet?" I yelled.

"He's gone."

"Gone? What do you mean, gone?"

"He... Pritchet..."

"Calm down," I told him. "What the hell happened?"

"Let me handle this," a gritty voice ordered. Marty Meehan had plowed through the growing crowd behind me. I stood aside for our bulldog of an airport manager.

"It was horrible," Alec Wharton babbled. Sweat matted his dark hair. His lanky, six-foot frame jittered in his khaki flight coveralls. "I can't believe it happened."

"Get a grip on yourself," Meehan ordered, his jowly face jutting into Wharton's sheet-white grimace of disbelief. "Exactly what happened?"

Wharton ran a hand through his sweaty mop and sucked in a shaky breath. "We were practicing acrobatics-"

"So where's your parachute?" Meehan demanded. "Airport rule. No acrobatics without parachutes. Pritchet have one?"

In the dead silence, I could hear the drone of one of the airport's Piper Cubs down in the south practice area five miles away.

"Neither of us had chutes," Wharton said in a near whisper.

Meehan's exhale was close to a groan.

"We were practicing stall recoveries," Wharton rushed on, "but Pritchet decided to demonstrate a loop. We nosed down, picked up speed, then up, over – and that's when it happened."

"Exactly what, dammit!" Meehan yelled.

"Right at the top, he... he fell out! Gone. I still can't believe it."

Meehan – all of us – stared at him.

"How high were you?" Meehan finally managed to get out, as if that made any difference.

"Three thousand."

Silence. I heard the distant Cub's engine noise rise and fade. The heat radiating from the concrete apron felt as if someone had suddenly thrown open a blast furnace door.

Meehan blew out a ragged sigh, and all of his bluster went with it. "Where?" he almost whispered.

"West practice area. Over those big cornfields just below Lonesome Pond."

To my surprise, Meehan – usually as warm as wood – put an arm around Wharton's shoulders. "Cripes, kid, what a hell of a thing to go through. Good job bringing the plane back in yourself. How many hours you got in it?"

"Three."

"Just three. Look, try to pull yourself together, go upstairs and wait in my office."

Meehan motioned to Bill Collins, our gloom-faced string bean chief mechanic, edging through the crowd.

"Check it out, Bill. I want to know what the hell happened up there." Meehan turned to me. "Looks like you're chief instructor now, George."

"Lousy way to get a promotion," I muttered.

"Yeah." You come upstairs, too. I want you in on this."

In Meehan's sparse office, he asked Sally Taylor, his middle-aged secretary, to brew a fresh pot of coffee. This was 1948, when it was okay to ask secretaries to make coffee. Silex in hand, she left us. Meehan shut the office door. For a long moment, he stood at the big window, his back to us, staring out at the hangar apron and the airport's two paved runways.

Alec Wharton hunched in a chair near the window, both hands knuckle-white on its arms. I sat on the edge of the chair by the door. Marty Meehan finally sank into his creaky swivel behind the desk with yet another ragged sigh.

"Holy Lord," he rumbled. "I don't need this."

He pulled a file folder from his desk drawer. Opened it. Took out a pair of horn-rimmed glasses I'd never seen him wear before. Studied the file. "Okay," he said to Wharton, "you got your private ticket last month. Joe Pritchet was your instructor for the commercial course, which you're three hours into at the moment. So you've logged about forty-five, fifty flying hours. Right?"

"Forty-seven, counting today."

"Pritchet checked you out in the PT-19 after one hour of dual."

"Yes."

"Come to think of it, didn't I see you take off solo in that plane sometime before noon?"

"Right. At 11. Pritchet sent me out to practice power-on and power-off stalls. He said to come back in forty-five minutes, pick him up and he was to check on how well I'd done."

"And three thousand feet over the west practice area, Pritchet decided, for some damn reason, to show you a loop?"

Wharton stared at the floor. "That's right."

"Then he-" A knock on the door stopped him. "Yeah?"

Mechanic Bill Collins's horsey face peered in. "Thought you oughta know, Marty. The seat belt in the PT-19's rear cockpit broke."

"Broke! Jesus, why?"

"Frayed where it rubbed on the left edge of the metal bucket seat."

Meehan sat back, elbow on the chair arm, hand cupping his chin and his fingers over his mouth as if he just didn't want to say anything more. But he had to.

"Bill, don't you check seat belts?"

"Hell, Marty, I check engines, airframes, controls, oil and fuel systems." He flared red. "Never heard of a seat belt needing maintenance. Who checks seat belts?"

Meehan stared at him. Then he muttered, "That'll be all, Bill. Thanks."

Collins left, and now Meehan looked at me. I could see him crumpling inside.

"I gotta call the CAA," he groaned, "and the State Aviation Authority and the State Police. When the police get here, George, I want you and Wharton to go out in one of the Cubs and help locate Pritchet's body. Unless somebody finds him and calls in before the cops show up. Or calls them. Or-" He realized he was rambling. "Hell, just stand by until I get this mess in hand."

Nobody called in the discovery of a body out there in the west practice area. Twenty minutes after Meehan phoned the Hardington Barracks, two gray Pennsylvania State Police cars pulled up to the airport fence. One of the dark-gray uniformed troopers stayed at the airport to interview Meehan – and for sure, mechanic Bill Collins. The other trooper headed west. He would keep an eye on the Cub I would pilot with Wharton as my spotter in the rear seat of the cramped, tandem two-place–

"I'm not going," Wharton announced. "I'm never going to fly again."

Oh, fine. Here we stood in the flight line at the edge of the hangar apron, about to search for Pritchet's body, and the only one who knew where it was had a case of flight jitters. Not that I blamed him. I didn't like this assignment either. But the thought of former P-51 fighter pilot Joe Pritchet moldering away in the August heat overcame any hesitation on my part. I'd been a co-pilot on B-24 bombers in Italy, and P-51 fighter cover had been the primary reason I was still alive.

"Joe Pritchet flew 68 missions, some of them in support of ground troops," I told Wharton. "I heard you were with Patton. You ever get any help from '51 pilots, Alec?"

"Coupla times," he murmured.

"Then get in this damn airplane." That was harsh, but I was finding Alex Wharton to be not the most likeable of our student pilots. Struck me that he was a tad more concerned about himself than about the pilot who had died trying to teach him. He had been my student through his private pilot training. I'd found him introverted, humorless, but fanatically devoted to earning his private ticket so he could move up to the commercial course. I'd had him tagged as a career pilot in the making, but now his resolve had collapsed.

With a long, hard glance at me, he climbed into the little yellow monoplane and strapped himself into the rear seat. I spun the prop. The engine caught, ticked over. I wedged into the front seat and closed the top and bottom halves of the split door. We took off into the light west wind.

In a few minutes, Wharton tapped my shoulder and pointed a few degrees to the left.

"It happened over those cornfields just past the pond," he shouted over the Cub's engine racket.

I swung left. Somewhere behind me, the police unit was picking its way through the rural roads, following the best it could.

Five minutes later, on my fourth 500-foot-high pass over the corn rows, I spotted what had to be Pritchet's crumpled body. A khaki-clad sprawl between rows. Nobody else anywhere in sight. The nearest farmhouse was a good mile and a half north. I circled until the cop car caught up, turned off the nearby country road into the dirt farm lane and stopped. The trooper stepped out and began to make his way into the field. I headed back to the airport.

"That's it," Wharton said in my ear as we trundled toward the hangar apron. "As of right now, I'm done with flying."

I swung the Cub into the tie-down line and cut the switch. "Listen to me, Alec," I told him. "You came here all the way from – where was it?"

"Ludlum, Indiana."

"From Indiana to earn yourself a flying career. And, damn it, you were my best private student. Soloed in just six hours of dual. Most everybody takes eight. Why throw it all away because of-"

"You weren't up there seeing him fall out."

"I've seen a whole damn bomber blow up and everybody fall out. I flew the next day."

"That was combat. You had to."

He had me there. "Look. Give it some thought, will you?"

"I've given it all the thought I need to. I'm-"

Knuckles rapped on the plexiglass upper half of the door I hadn't opened yet. The trooper who'd stayed at the airport bent down. "Alec Wharton? I need to talk to you."

The six-foot-three trooper, his broad-brimmed campaign hat tipped aggressively forward, took him upstairs to Mary Meehan's office. I heard the door shut, then Meehan clumped down the steps.

"Go in the hangar and take a look at the seat belt, George. Tell me what you think."

I found Bill Collins up on the right wing, leaning into the rear cockpit.

"Must be the tenth time I've checked this belt," he muttered. "I still don't believe it." He held up the buckle strap. About a foot of the other strap was still tightly in place. "Take a look a the busted end, George."

The belt had broken where it had been pulled over the left edge of the metal bucket seat. The broken end showed a lot of fraying for an inch or so from the ragged break.

I reached down and fished up the stump of the broken piece. It, too, was badly frayed.

The other trooper directed the county coroner to Pritchet's body. Then, since Weston Township had no police of its own, he interviewed the few farmers who could have possibly witnessed the accident. However, it had taken place at midday when the several farmers close enough to have seen Pritchet fall were home eating lunch. One, though, had seen a low-winged plane make a pass over the vicinity of Lonesome Pond, but he was certain that had been at 11:30 a.m., not around noon. The next day, a CAA investigator interviewed that same farmer. He stuck to his story.

No one had witnessed Pritchet's deadly fall. No one had to. The facts spoke for themselves.

Bill Collins, of course, lost his job. He was taken to court, but his war record got him a hung jury. Bill had won the bronze star defending Henderson Field on Guadalcanal against a Japanese suicide assault. Killed five of them with a borrowed carbine; not bad for a Marine aircraft mechanic. The county prosecutor decided against a re-trial, but the CAA pulled Bill's mechanic license.

The airport's spirit faltered and began to die. The G.I. Bill student flow dwindled to a trickle. I saw no future as an instructor on commission. Three bucks was not a bad hourly rate in those days, but instructors were paid only for increasingly sparse flying hours. I took a shot at selling home air conditioners for a new Hardington company a decade ahead of itself. It was the wrong time, and Pennsylvania was the wrong place. The girl I'd hoped to marry left me for a stockbroker. I left town for greener pastures.

My aborted A/C salesman career gave me a certain glibness. I talked my way into a PR slot for a Philadelphia-based shopping center developer.

In the summer of 1954, I was driving west on U.S. 40 toward Indianapolis to set up a press party announcing our proposed shopping mall there. Around noon that sun-drenched July day, I was ready for a lunch stop. Out of the shimmering distance emerged a little sign: LUDLUM 4 MILES. Hope they have a restaurant there, I thought. Then my subconscious twanged. Ludlum? Where had I heard something about Ludlum? Got it. My old flight student Alec Wharton had come from Ludlum, Indiana.

He hadn't come from much of a town. A scatter of houses, then a skinny business district flanked both sides of Route 40 as it arrowed through on its way to the state capital another 30 dead-straight miles out there beyond the heat waves. On the right, though, I spotted blue letters on a small white marquee. I slowed down then angle-parked in front of the Kosy Kafe, the only out-of-state license in the whole Hoosier row.

The Kosy Kafe looked small-town-drab, but it smelled fine: home fries and fresh baking. The eight or so tables along the left side of the hole-in-the-wall eatery were occupied. The counter to the right had seats open. I slid onto a red-cushioned stool near the door. The counter was serviced by a chunky, middle-aged woman in a pale green uniform. Big hairpins piled her too-yellow hair on top of her head. Stitched above her left breast in dark green thread: "Mavis." She looked hard, but her voice was soft.

"Hi. Welcome to Ludlum. What can I get you?"

I ordered a cheeseburger, fries, banana cream pie and coffee. No conscience twinge at all; the nation's appetite-withering food police were decades in the future.

We bantered about the steamy weather, Pennsylvania versus Indiana as great places to live, why I was driving to

Indianapolis. Then I mentioned Alec Wharton. "Told me he was from here. You ever heard of him?"

Mavis rolled her brown eyes. "Who hasn't? Pretty wild story there."

"Oh? How so?"

"Well, actually it was more about his sister." She leaned close. I'd struck a chord with a gossip.

"His sister?"

"Yeah. She was Corn Queen back in 1945. Or was it '46? Anyway, she was-" Mavis dropped her voice to a near-whisper- "raped."

I gave her a blank stare. Such frank gossiping wasn't exactly commonplace in the 1950s. Especially to strangers. Or was it because I was a transient stranger that she felt free to impress me with local scandal?

"That's what she swore happened to her. Done by one of them crop duster pilots. Come here in the spring for the bug season, gone by late summer. Anyway, it really set Alec wild, his sister - a married woman - treated like a common...a common I-don't-know-what."

"So what happened to the duster pilot?"

"Him? He claimed it was consequen—conse—"

"Consensual?"

"That's it. Sure kicked off the town's motormouths. Next day, he bugged out. Never seen again. Alec was away somewhere. When he got back a couple days later, I never seen him in such a swivet. Rammed around town like a crazy man for a couple weeks. Then he just up and left Ludlum. I reckon he couldn't take all the talk."

"But he'd had nothing to do with what happened."

"Yeah," Mavis agreed, "but you don't know small towns."

"Did they ever nail the duster pilot?"

"Not that I heard. He was gypsy, worked for himself. He could be anywhere - anyway, it woulda been his word against hers. And you know what they do to the woman in a trial like that." She gave me a warm smile. "You gonna be in town long?"

Now she was getting a bit more buddy-buddy than I wanted to be. I asked for the check, left her a good-sized tip and headed for the door. Then I stopped. Walked back to the counter where she was picking up the check and money. A really disturbing thought had hit me. I hesitated. But I had to ask.

"What was the duster pilot's name, Mavis?"

"Richard."

Now I felt better.

"No, wait a minute," she said. "That was his last name. First name was Joe. Joe Richard. Or maybe Richards."

"Or-" my mouth went dry. "Or maybe...Pritchet?"

"Oh, yeah! That was it. Joe Pritchet."

In Indianapolis, I registered at the same mid-town hotel where, through a dozen phone calls during the past three weeks, I'd arranged for the announcement party. Now I checked out the meeting room, consulted with the h'ors d'oeuvres chef, called the local graphics company one more time. Everything was in order. But all through my logistical checkout, I was preoccupied with what I'd heard back in that obscure Ludlum eatery.

After a London broil in the hotel grill room, I went back to my fourth floor single and called Hardington, PA information. Held my breath. Yes, William Collins still lived there. Got him on the third ring.

"Who? George Nichols? Oh, my God, of course! You were chief instructor after Pritchet was... After Pritchet."

His voice wasn't as confident as I'd remembered.

"I'd like to sit down with you, Bill. I've learned something you'll want to hear."

"I'm available. Too damned available. Name the time and place."

"I can make it to Hardington late afternoon the day after tomorrow. Say around 6 p.m. You name the place."

I expected his home address, but he gave me directions to the Anthracite Tavern on Spruce Street.

"Sounds fine, Bill. Supper on me."

The company brass arrived in Indianapolis at noon — in a chartered Piper Apache. No 500-mile Chevy chug for those four. My non-event event went off like greased clockwork, a highly attended demonstration that you can buy a lot of media coverage with a few good graphics, a mound of lobster paté and free-flowing hooch. I reveled in corporate congratulations, lavishly tipped the help with company largess, and was eastbound on U.S. 40 by 5 p.m.

The stress of the Indianapolis do, combined with the hideous 1948 scenario my mind was spinning, did me in just east of Columbus, Ohio. I pulled past a sputtering neon MOTEL MODERNE sign, parked and signed in. Slept late, had rock-hard fried eggs, scorched toast but surprisingly good coffee and hit the road again around 10 a.m.

I'd underestimated the time it would take me to go almost the entire loopy length of the Pennsylvania Turnpike before I cut northeast on U.S. 11 through Wilkes-Barre then up the long valley beyond. A blood-red sunset tinted the valley's rim as I bumped through the dismal outskirts of Hardington. I didn't find the Anthracite Tavern until a few minutes after 7:00. A lost cause, by now. Bill Collins surely would have given up and gone home wondering just what I'd thought was so important.

But there, in the beery, cigarette-hazed murk, he sat, alone in a dark-stained booth for four, nursing a bottle of Pabst. He looked a lot like more than half a decade older. Stubbly chin, sunken eyes. The face of a man in defeat.

But he brightened when he saw me pushing past the crowd at the bar. Not a noisy crowd; just a mutter. All older guys. A spiritless clientele swallowing numbness, knowing King Coal would never rule again.

I thanked Bill profusely for waiting me out.

"Figured you might have got hung up somewhere. Anyways, I didn't have nothing else planned tonight."

Or any night, I suspected.

"How's the wife?"

He shrugged. "Left me two years ago."

"Sorry to hear that."

"My fault. She couldn't-"

"You fellas need anything?" Our waitress, a skinny brunette, wore a skimpy black dress and a red checkerboard apron.

"Bring my friend another Pabst," I told her. "And I'll have a grilled cheese, fries, and a beer of the same name." I turned back to Bill. "You want to eat?"

"Grilled cheese and fries sounds fine."

The waitress disappeared into the cigarette smog.

"You working?" I asked Bill, then felt an embarrassed flush at the unintended cruelty.

"Here and there. Auto repairs mostly. Never went back to aviation. The CAA's lifting my license killed that."

"I've always felt you were had, Bill."

"Good of you to say that, but naw, I did myself in with that smart-ass comment to Meehan about 'who checks seat belts.' I shouldn't have said it, but he pissed me off questioning me like that."

"He was kinda panicked, Bill. We all were."

"Yeah. Well, after that, it was all downhill for me. What bugs me is that it was just flip talk. Too late I remembered I had checked that seat belt the day before. It was okay. But nobody at the trial believed that."

"I do, Bill." Then I told him about my conversation in Ludlum's Kosy Kafe.

"Sweet Jesus," he breathed when I finished. "That backs up something I've stumbled onto."

"And what might that be?"

Bill's rheumy eyes held mine then broke away when the waitress came back to clunk down our order.

He took a swallow from the fresh bottle, set it down with exaggerated care, swept an imaginary crumb off the cracked pink plastic tabletop.

"I brought something to show you, then I decided not to. Afraid you'd think I was just an old has-been pitying himself about a lost past. But after what you just told me, I think you'll find it kinda interesting."

He reached into his shirt pocket and pulled out a newspaper clipping. "This is outta the Philadelphia Inquirer. They carry a section on news from the rest of the state. Ran this a couple months ago."

He handed me the clip, heavily creased as if he'd re-read it a dozen times.

10-YEAR-OLD SAVES HER
OLDER BROTHER

Weston Township, April 22 – Ten-year-old Melissa Brighton saved her brother Terrence, 15, from drowning yesterday in tiny Lonesome Pond when his air hose separated from his makeshift diving mask. These two children were trying out an underwater "treasure magnet" Terrence had built, using a surplus WWII mine detector.

"I was in big trouble," Terrence admitted, "until Melissa swam down and stuck the air hose back on."

"The boy had become confused," Weston volunteer fireman, Cecil Norton, stated, "and I don't doubt that he would've drowned except for Melissa's help."

"It wasn't worth it," Terrence admitted later. "All we brought up was a couple rusty tin cans and an old rasp file."

I set the clipping on the table and stared at Bill.

"Trouble is," he said, "none of what you told me or this-" he gestured at the clipping – "would hold up in court. It's too late, anyway. The airport closed last year."

"I heard."

"I don't even know where Marty Meehan might be. It's too late for anything to be done."

"Not quite," I told him. "Could I somehow get a photostat made of this?"

"You can have it. I'll just try to forget the whole thing. Nobody can do anything now. It's over."

"Not quite, Bill." I reached out and shook his hand.

"Not quite."

It took a while, but I found Alec Wharton. After a whole lot of phone calls – the Veterans Administration was the most help – and a bit of dumb luck, I located him in New Jersey. No record of marriage; still a loner.

I had a week's vacation coming, took it, and drove due east across the Garden State.

I crossed Barnegat Bay on a rainy September afternoon, then drove along the arrow-straight highway up the middle of that long, 40-mile spit of land that separates the bay from the Atlantic. Around 5 p.m., I spotted the water tower marked LAVALLETTE. This was a summer season town, now mostly deserted, but I figured Wharton would still be here. I'd learned he was a draftsman in Lavallette's minuscule planning department.

The address I had put him in a little cedar-shingled beach cottage. I pulled up at the sandy end of the macadam side road, parked next to the low-slung green Studebaker, walked in the rain along the duckboards to the weather-bleached front door. No bell. I knocked. Nothing. Knocked louder. He should have been home from work by now. Wasn't that his car out—

The door creaked open.

"Yeah? What can I — Hell, you can't be, uh, George... Nichols, wasn't it?"

"Still is, Alec. You're looking tanned and fit. A little gray, though. I shouldn't wonder."

"What's that mean?"

"Ask me in, and I'll tell you."

"Uh, sure."

We sat in front of a big window that looked out on the beach and the surf beyond, wind-spumed and ominous. A perfect setting for what I was about to do. He hadn't offered me a drink, just a chair. Grudgingly.

"What in God's name brings you to Lavallette, of all places?"

"You do, Alec."

"I don't follow."

"I think you will. You had everyone fooled. Cost Joe Pritchet his life. Cost Bill Collins his career and probably his wife. And, damn it, I was never the same after that day, myself. Been haunted by it for years."

"Yeah, me too. I can't forget it." He stared out at the thrashing waves. "Can't forget it," he repeated.

"And I'm here to make sure you never will, Alec."

Now he looked at me with some sixth sense warning him I wasn't here on any mercy mission.

"Let me get straight to the point. After the incident with your sister-"

Now I really had his attention.

" -you tracked Joe Pritchet to Hardington, probably through the CAA licensing division. Then you blitzed through the private pilot course with me so you could get to fly with him in the open cockpit PT-19."

"I don't see where any of this-"

"Check me on this: Students flew solo in the rear cockpit of that plane, but in the front cockpit with an instructor. The instructor sat aft."

"I know all that. What are you-"

"The day Pritchet died, you took off solo in the rear cockpit, knowing Pritchet would be in that cockpit on your next flight. And when he was-"

"He looped the plane and the seat belt broke, and he fell out. Everybody knows what happened, Nichols. It was an accident."

"I don't think so. One, Pritchet was a disciplined flight instructor. He wouldn't have suddenly decided to play loop-the-loop with a student and no chutes. Two, Collins checked the rear seat belt the day before, and it was fine."

"In Meehan's office, he said-"

"He thought better of that too late. Let me tell you my take on this. You flew off solo to practice stalls. You didn't practice any stall, Alec. You spent that time sawing away at your seat belt – which would be Pritchet's seat belt on your next flight."

"Ridiculous! How would I know he was going to try a loop?"

"I doubt there was even a loop. At 3,000 feet, you whipped the plane inverted, probably gave it a shot of forward stick to treat Joe to heavy Gs, and the strain popped the weakened belt."

Alec smiled, but his eyes weren't in it. "So what did I do with that 'saw'? You know I had nothing on me when I came back alone."

"It wasn't a saw, Alec. And you were too slick to bring it back. You remember that one farmer who saw the PT-19 make a low pass over Lonesome Pond?"

"That was me, looking for Pritchet's body."

"It was you, all right, but you weren't looking for Pritchet. He didn't fall out until after mid-day. The farmer swore you flew low over Lonesome Pond at 11:30."

"Why would I do that?"

I reached in my jacket pocket and handed him the clipping Bill Collins had saved. Watched Alec Wharton's tanned face drain to sickly gray.

"You flew low over Lonesome Pond to throw out that rasp."

"Everything you're saying... It's nothing but a guess," he managed.

"Yeah," I said. "Better than your guess, though, that Joe was guilty. Maybe he was, but how closely did you question your sister?"

I didn't wait for an answer. I stood up and leaned over him." You can keep the clipping. Put it in your scrapbook."

"What are you going to-"

"I think it's up to you, Alec."

"What the hell do you expect me to do?"

I walked to the door then turned back. "What do I expect you to do? Sweat, Alec. I expect you to sweat."

TURKEY DURKIN AND THE CATFISH

The moment Alexander Khreel stepped off the little river steamer onto the research station's floating dock, Durkin knew the man was not going to fit in. Up to now, Durkin had only suspected Khreel would be a problem. After all, it was highly unlikely the untrained nephew of the Khreel Foundation's chairman would be a scientific asset here at Research Station 4, halfway up the Amazon. Now that Durkin saw Khreel in the flesh, his suspicion hardened into realization that scrambling up the bank, followed by one of the deck hands laden with two glossy leather suitcases, was trouble.

To Durkin, Khreel looked as if he had been transported to the middle of the Amazon directly from a Broad Street sporting goods store. He arrived sweating at the bank's crest, in now-soiled safari chinos and a ridiculous pith helmet. He towered over Durkin and said, "Why in the hell don't you build some steps up from the dock?"

"Because the six-month rainy season floods the river nearly up to this level," Durkin said. "Alexander Khreel, I presume."

"Yeah. Where can I find Durkin? I'm supposed to-" begrudged enlightenment seeped across Khreel's precisely chiseled features. "Could you be him?"

Durkin knew he looked unprepossessing in his grubby khakis, but sure not that unprepossessing.

"I am he." He stuck out an unenthusiastic hand. He hadn't asked for help. He didn't need help. Yet here in the guise of an assistant stood Chairman Oliver Khreel's dim-bulb nephew, exiled to mitigate the Philadelphia fallout of a scandal involving Alex Khreel with some married Main Line socialite. So had come the rumor in a letter from one of Felicia's Upper Darby friends. Uncle Oliver had alleviated the family problem by making Nephew Alexander a problem for Durkin now.

The man had no marine biology background at all, Durkin noted. "Alex is a Cornell man," the chairman had written. "I believe his major was hotel management."

Hotel management. Maybe here among the rag-tag frame structures of this Amazon Astoria, he could see that Durkin's little cadre of Bororo Indians turned down the sheets on the cots at night and left a fresh orchid on each pillow.

"Take him under your wing," the chairman's letter had directed. "Teach him what you can."

Teach him what you can? A key phrase. Not, "teach him everything," but "what you can." A tip-off this bronzed giant now recovering from his huff-puff up the riverbank was of limited mental prowess. The huffing and puffing told Durkin something more: The man's ruddy glow had probably been acquired in a Philadelphia health club – amplified by more recent lounging on the steamer's gritty little deck during its 500-mile ramble upriver from Belem.

Despite the pith helmet's broad brim, Khreel dramatically shaded his eyes. "Now that I'm here, exactly where am I?"

"Roughly between Oriximina and Terra Santa," Durkin rattled off with a touch of pleasure at Khreel's wince.

"God. What is there to do around here besides whatever you do for the foundation?"

Durkin smiled. "There's an opera house in Manaus, the closest city of any size."

"Where's Manaus?"

"By river, three hundred miles west."

"Jesus."

The deckhand plunked down the bags and gave Khreel a burlesque salute, a lopsided grin, and muttered something that didn't sound complimentary.

"What did he say? I don't speak Spanish."

"Neither does he. That was the Portuguese equivalent of 'have a nice day.'"

Khreel looked around as if he were expecting to summon a bellman, then he gave a whistling sigh, bent down and hefted his two bags. Durkin in the lead, Khreel puffing behind, they walked down the path from the riverbank.

"Jesus!" Khreel said again, this time with more vehemence. Durkin knew his unasked-for assistant had just gotten his first real look at Station 4.

"This is all there is to it? This clearing at the edge of the jungle?"

"Research building on the right, mess hut and housekeeper's quarters straight ahead, storage and generator buildings back there."

Durkin nodded at the weather-faded clapboard building to their left, a long narrow structure. "Living quarters. Felicia and I are in the near end. You'll be at the far end."

"I heard your wife is here with you. When do I meet the 'little woman'?"

That struck Durkin as just about the patronizing limit. He'd already had it with this Philadelphia philanderer, had it at first glance. He instinctively disliked anyone that much taller than Durkin's own five-foot-seven. Moreover, Khreel had the good looks of a men's sleepwear model, a distressing contrast to Durkin's sallow boniness. Even in his soiled safari suit, Khreel managed to project a debonair aura, an effect peculiarly enhanced by his hard-traveled appearance. Durkin's slacks and shirtsleeves flapped around his skinny limbs.

Mingling with the compound's deep rot aura, a faint odor of spice trailed in Khreel's wake. Shaving lotion, for God's sake, and this late in the day.

"The little woman," Khreel had said, as if the likes of Durkin would attract only the kind of mousy, vapid work-a-day wife that trite expression anticipated.

"Felicia will join us at supper. Right now, it's siesta time for her."

The whole station, in fact, was dozing: Felicia, the two solid male Bororo Indians (Durkin thought they were Bororos, but in a country that had encouraged racial intermarriage for decades, it was hard to be precise) and Agata, the young, almost pretty, mixed-breed girl in her twenties – the best worker of the three.

Employer to employee, Durkin showed Khreel to his barren quarters, pointed out the screened-off tank that served as their bathtub when the run-off from the roof was enough to fill it, and left the man to settle in until suppertime.

"I thought I heard the steamer leaving," Felicia murmured sleepily from inside the mosquito netting over her cot. "Is he here?"

"He's here."

"Is he what you expected?'

"Exactly."

Durkin sat back in one of the creaky wooden chairs and watched her doze again. When he had literally run into her at the University of Florida during his graduate studies, she had looked like an English Lit major – which she had turned out to be, with an IQ way up there. That had appealed to him only minutes after they had clashed cafeteria trays. He saw right past the bee-sting breasts and bony hips beneath her bag of a dress. He liked her for her brain. That electrified her. And that was why, when he asked her two months later to marry him, she had breathed a fervent, "Oh, yes!"

Intimacy was new to Durkin. He liked its novelty but not the mental strain that went with it. Felicia Noonan Durkin was not an easy coupler. She wanted her moments of culmination to be bracketed by persuasive fore-happenings and lengthy afterglows. All of which paled for Durkin after only a few months. He loved her, sure, but... He was aware that she lamented the fast fade of their initial bliss.

Then, one year to the day from the date of their marriage, they found themselves up the Amazon. Literally. Five hundred miles from Brazil's northeast coast.

"And six hundred miles south of Paramaribo. A thousand miles from Rio," she had muttered when the asthmatic river steamer had bumped them ashore. The research station's frame structures would have failed the lowest of the Pocono Mountain summer camp standards. The two Indian men were "day workers" who had the good sense to return each afternoon to their no doubt more comfortable village a mile southward – along a rank trail Durkin was never to have the slightest impulse to explore.

The Durkins replaced a scraggly-bearded skeleton named Warnowski, a wreck of a Ph.D. who had been sent here by the foundation the year before. His specialty was supposed to have been freshwater stingray, but observation told Durkin it was now the pinch bottle. Not long after the steamer, with Warnowski aboard, chugged out of sight along the sharp bend to the east, they found an unopened bottle of Haig & Haig behind the tattered linens in the residency cupboard. Durkin poured the Scotch onto the spongy ground behind the building.

A year here had changed them both. With little to do in the oppressive climate, Felicia grew lethargic. At the same time, she blossomed like a tropical flower. The bony hips filled out. The pathetic little breast buds blossomed. Unexpectedly, Durkin found himself drawn to a soft, warm, compelling female. He liked the surprising excitement of that, and he liked his work for the foundation. After he learned something of the ways of the Bororos and Agata, he liked them, too. Everything here had fallen satisfyingly into place.

Now the heavy hand of nepotism in far-off Pennsylvania threatened to... well, screw it up with the mandated arrival of Alexander Khreel.

The big man from Philadelphia ambled into the mess hut fifteen minutes after Agata, slender and sleek in brightly-dyed homespun, had served a thin fish soup.

"I thought in South America, you ate late," were his first words.

"We eat while it's still light. Saves generator fuel," Durkin informed him. But Khreel was not listening.

"So this is the missus. Well, well, well. A pleasure to meet you, Mrs. Durkin."

"Please, Felicia, Mr. Khreel."

"And I would be most happy if you will call me Alex." He seemed to be undergoing a transition to smooth civility as Durkin watched.

"The menu for tonight?" Khreel asked her.

"Fish broth and-" Felicia spoke with the hovering Agata in rapid Portuguese that she had picked up with little difficulty.

She turned back to Khreel. "Roast pork and manioc. With papaya for dessert."

"Impressive, here in the middle of nowhere."

Felicia smiled at Khreel's compliment, obviously enjoying her unaccustomed gracious hostess role. "Agata spent a few years in Manaus. She was a chef's assistant at the Restaurante Palhoca. We're very fortunate."

The delicious aroma of roast pork loin, carved from a wild boar the two Indian men had speared in honor of the occasion, provided a veneer of civilization in the raw hut. It was abruptly shattered by a hair-raising screech across the broad river.

"Jaguar. Getting ready for the hunt. They hardly ever get over to this side." Durkin said that perfunctorily. He had just realized something a lot more disturbing than a jaguar's evening scream. He was struck by the fact that after Khreel entered the mess hut, his speculative slate blue gaze had never once wavered from Felicia until the jaguar's shriek had split the outside silence.

"Breakfast at seven," Durkin said coldly as they finished eating. "In the lab at seven-thirty. I'll teach you what I can."

Khreel was not a morning person, Durkin decided. At breakfast, the man met Durkin's "Good morning" with no more than a surly nod. In silence, he downed two cups of Agata's excellent Arabica coffee in an apparent effort to jolt himself awake. Then he leaned back in his camp chair and stared up at the underside of the thatched roof.

"God," he muttered in disgust. "There are lizards crawling up there."

"We stay in our part of this little world, the anoles stay in theirs." Incorrigibly task-oriented, Durkin glanced at his watch. "Time to get to work, Khreel."

The research building was the best-constructed in the compound. Its corrugated metal roof protected the lab area at one end. The rest of the large interior was occupied by rows of bubbling aquariums and their ceaselessly humming air pumps. The pumps, the electrical outlets and lights here and in the other buildings, and the emergency radio all were powered by the throbbing gasoline-fueled generator in the rear of the clearing. So Durkin informed Khreel as he toured his superfluous assistant through the lab then into the area holding the tanks.

"That was the damned thrum-thrum-thrum that woke me up this morning," Khreel said with a grimace.

"After you've been here awhile, you won't notice the generator. Now in this first tank-"

"Felicia doesn't join us for breakfast?"

"Seven's too early for her." To focus Khreel's wandering attention, Durkin tapped his forefinger on the edge of a murky tank. "In here is an impressive example of Electrophorus electricus. Notice the two fine wires leading to the voltmeter on the side of the tank. The purpose-"

"Wait a minute, Professor. In English, okay? Electro-for-what?"

"I thought the technical name was self-evident, along with your keen observation."

"Looks like a fat watersnake to me."

"It's an Amazon electric eel, capable of a discharge up to five hundred fifty volts. Enough to stun a horse."

"Why him?"

"I don't follow you, Khreel."

"What are you doing with this guy?"

At least that crude question showed a flicker of interest.

"I'm tabulating precise measurements of its discharge rates, voltage peaks and eventually, its controllability."

Khreel shrugged. "Why?"

"There may be certain medical, even military applications. The latter is classified," he said with a degree of satisfaction. "Next we have three tanks of Sphaeroides annulatus."

"Uh huh. Look like fish to me."

"They are fish. Not native here, they're west coast Gulf puffers. Saltwater fish, but the foundation has no facility in that area, so they're here. The flesh is edible, even delicious. But the intestines, liver, gonads and skin contain tetrodotoxin, a deadly poison."

Durkin was in lecture mode now, a status he enjoyed. "The victim first notices tingling of the lips and tongue. That develops into numbness of the entire body, respiratory difficulty, hemorrhages of the skin, muscle twitches, tremors, then convulsions. There's no antidote and only a forty percent survival rate. The foundation is interested in the puffer's pharmacological possibilities."

"Swell."

They moved on to an outsized tank of brownish water that seemed paved with large, fleshy discs.

"Stingrays," Khreel offered, apparently unimpressed by a creature so commonplace.

"Potamotrygon motoro, the Amazon variety of freshwater stingray. The venomous stinging barb on this variety is situated well out of the tail instead of at its base."

"So?"

"So that weapon near the end of the long whip of a tail makes the Potamotrygon among the most dangerous of the species. The wound is hugely painful, of course, and stings in the upper body areas have been known to be fatal. Again, there is no specific antidote."

Khreel bent to peer into the tank, shrugged and straightened. Durkin waited for his obvious question, but he said nothing.

"The purpose of the rays' being here is the simple extraction of venom for shipment to a Miami research lab in search of an antidote."

Sweat began to stain Khreel's shirt, not from the impact of this little hall of aquatic horrors, Durkin surmised, but from the oppressive humidity.

"Next we come to Urinophilu erythrurus, members of the catfish family, known locally as 'candiru.'" Durkin crouched to observe the dozens of tiny fish hovering near the bottom of the brackish tank. "Barely two inches long – some of them not even that – and pencil-lead thin, these are one of the most fascinating animals of the dangerous marine animals. They may have military applications if-"

But Khreel wasn't listening. His attention had wandered upward through the lab hut's screening and beyond to the woman who ambled across the compound toward the mess hut. Lithe in blue slacks and a white blouse, Felicia was on her way to breakfast.

"Khreel? Khreel!"

"Yeah, what?"

"Your first duty is to take that broom over there and sweep this place clean." Agata would be happy, Durkin thought, to be relieved of her research building cleaning duties. Dynamic balance, in a way, since she was now cooking for another mouth.

"Sweep? Hell, this is a dirt floor."

"All the more reason to keep it swept. After that, there are housecleaning opportunities in the lab area as well."

That should take care of Mr. Alexander Khreel for today. Durkin strode into the lab portion of the building, satisfied he had properly fitted the man into the scheme of things. At the bottom.

But at lunch, with Felicia joining them briefly, Khreel appeared newly energized.

"Quite a little chamber of horrors your hubby has there." He nodded over his shoulder in the direction of the research hut. "Convinced me to stay out of the river at all costs."

At least I made some inroad into that pudding of a brain, Durkin felt, but he still didn't like the way Khreel's eyes addressed Felicia alone.

"Back to work," he ordered as Agata cleared away the remains of her version of caleirada, a fish stew thickened with farina and doused with a peppery sauce.

In the afternoon, Durkin instructed the two Bororo men to repair the siding on the generator shed, and he sent Khreel to help them. That ought to complete stage one of the useless fellow's basic training. The Indians were not delighted to spend the steamy afternoon replacing warped boards with newer ones from the lumber stockpile, but they stuck at it. Which was more than Khreel did. At 3:45, Durkin discovered he was missing.

...And found him sprawled on the little veranda behind the residence, a glass of lemonade in hand, Felicia seated nearby.

"I was under the impression I'd told you-"

"Enough, enough, professor. Seems to me we have a minimum to do and all the time in the world to do it."

"The foundation is expecting-"

"Oh, Emmett," Felicia broke in. "It's his first day. Besides, I haven't had anyone from the outside to talk to since we've come here."

Thus dismissing Durkin, she turned back to Khreel. "The Turners in Bryn Mawr, do you know them, too?"

That night after supper ("Fish again?" Khreel had snorted as if the chef at this resort had lost all imagination), Durkin found his patience further stressed as he and Felicia prepared for bed.

"He has no interest in what we're doing here," he grumped. "And the man didn't finish what I told him to do. So endeth the day with Mister Khreel."

"But he is amusing in a way." In the dim light from the naked 25-watt bulb overhead, Felicia's sea-green eyes were more alive than Durkin had noticed in weeks. Months, his heart stuttered.

"Amusing?"

"He's brought all the latest Main Line gossip."

"Including the little incident concerning himself?"

"Well, that may have been her doing as much as his. Those things are never totally one-sided. It takes two, doesn't it?"

"You're defending the man."

"I'm being impartial. Go to sleep."

Through the following week, Durkin assigned Khreel to a succession of minor tasks that Khreel performed in his lackadaisical fashion, or in one instance, not at all. That one involved the mealworms in a covered tray in a corner of the aquarium area. The worms were propagated as food, primarily for the puffers and candiru.

"Damned if I'll touch those squirmy things," Khreel announced, and he stalked out of the building.

"You'll do as I say!" Durkin shouted after him. But the big man walked on as if Durkin had said nothing at all. A half-hour later, Durkin spotted the two of them, Khreel and Felicia, strolling along the riverbank.

"You, sir," he assailed Khreel at dinner, "are a disgrace to the work of your uncle's foundation."

Khreel smiled. "But here I am, Durkin. And Uncle Oliver says here I stay. For a whole goddamn year." His smile had begun as one of mirth at Durkin's impotent railing. Now it was one of mockery.

In their quarters, after a long silence, Durkin said quietly into the darkness, "He's trouble, Felicia, and you're... not helping matters."

From her side of the muggy room, he heard nothing.

"Felicia?"

He felt her weight on the edge of his creaky cot.

"He's just a boy in a man's body, Emmett. Try to understand him."

She thrust the mosquito netting aside. "He amuses me, but you're my husband." Which struck Durkin as a peculiar way to put it, and what ensued seemed more palliative than passionate.

"You will bear in mind," Durkin told Khreel in the lab a week later, "she is my wife." As soon as he had said that, he realized how ludicrous it must have sounded to this hulking playboy. If Durkin had been the six-foot-one, 200-pounder, and if he had snarled, "She is my wife!" at a 140-pound, chicken-boned Khreel, it would have come off as dramatic. But the actuality of Khreel towering over him while he squawked up at the man made the threat toothless. Even comical.

"Don't scare me, prof." A grin displayed Khreel's beautifully capped teeth. "Hey, listen, I'm not going to sweep, saw or pick worms today, okay. Time for a day off. Mind if I borrow the canoe or dugout or whatever that thing is down there on the dock?"

"Yes, I do mind."

"I thought you would," Khreel said amiably, and he walked out.

"Come back here!" Durkin fumed. Another couple minutes and Khreel would have had him shaking his finger and stamping his foot. To hell with the man. Maybe the best way to handle this was to live and let live. Surely he could trust Felicia to... Not to... Hadn't she called Khreel a mere boy?

He went about his lab work with more equanimity than he had felt for days. When Khreel had not reappeared by lunchtime, he didn't find that disturbing. With luck, the man had fallen out of the dugout and piranhas had picked him to the bone. Except that Durkin had never seen a trace of that deadly little scavenger in this vicinity.

When Felicia also failed to appear at the mess hut, Durkin decided to take a not-so-casual stroll along the riverbank. Just as he reached the drop-off, he spotted them exiting the dugout. He stepped back as he was hidden from below, feeling a twinge of guilt. The man's got me spying on my own wife.

Then his guilt burned into futile anger. Felicia's bright frock (where did that come from?) had merged with Khreel's suntans. They were embracing down there!

Through lunch, Khreel and Felicia acted like two adolescents trying very hard to cover an amusing indiscretion. Durkin was assailed with anger, frustration, and disillusionment – with Felicia, and with his own sense of leadership. He was in charge here. Yet Khreel – an inferior example of manhood if ever there was one – and his own wife, whose superior intellect had captivated Durkin in the first place, showed signs of running amok. In the face of Khreel's arrogant disregard of station procedures and even common decency, Durkin found himself powerless.

Worse. That afternoon he sensed the Indians knew what was afoot here. Even when they had been hard at work and he approached, they would manage to face him respectfully until he nodded and passed by. Now, except when he directly addressed them, he found himself ignored.

Agata had been less subservient than they, but she had managed to convey respect through a tiny, ever-present smile. Now she erased that pleasantry. Her bittersweet chocolate eyes seemed to pierce his, to spear straight into his brain and find cravenness there.

He was a marine biologist, not an expert in complex human relations. He had no idea what to do. So he did nothing.

Next, Khreel failed to appear in the research building at all. He sunbathed on the rustic veranda. He strolled about the compound. He disappeared for hours, and Durkin noticed more and more frequently, so did Felicia. Along the river in the dugout? Down the path that led to the Bororo village? Where they went remained a mystery because Durkin refused to lower himself to searching for them.

He asked Agata to return to her former additional chore of cleaning the research building and was gratified that she accepted without protest.

Felicia didn't seem to care whether Durkin noticed her barely suppressed state of new-found excitement, her frequently flushed face, her often-rumpled clothing. The two of them surely knew he knew. He was further depressed because they obviously didn't care.

He felt he faced two dismal choices: confrontation, which he would undoubtedly lose; in fact, already had. Or endurance. Surely Felicia's innate intelligence would surmount her infatuation with this physically attractive – to her – novelty who had enlivened her monotonous existence here. Durkin could even relate to that. He had his absorbing work. She'd had... what? An abortive try at writing a novel that now mildewed somewhere in a residence building storage closet. Then she had begun to catalog fauna she observed in the clearing. That, too, died in the endless days of heat and sudden drenching rainfalls. Now she had Alexander Khreel. Another fad, Durkin could hope.

For two more weeks, Station 4 endured a balance of tensions. Durkin's gripping anger was mitigated by the interesting fact that Felicia still came to him occasionally, and he even found quirky stimulation for that apparent atonement for her fascination with Khreel.

Further offsetting Durkin's hatred of Khreel was the man's obvious physical superiority. In bare-knuckled conflict, Heaven forbid, Durkin knew he would quickly be reduced to mincemeat.

Perhaps he could conceivably devise some non-confrontational means of settling with his now detested "assistant." A slice of gulf puffer liver slipped into Khreel's fish stew? But murder was not in Durkin's soul.

The Indians now pointedly faced away whenever he neared. They took his orders, they did their work, but they would not show him their faces. Agata could hardly work the mess hut without facing its diners, but her little smile had suffered an apparently permanent death. Her expression was now one of stone.

He could live with that. He could live with the backs of the Bororos giving him what constituted a version of continuous jungle "mooning." He could even live with Khreel's refusal to do anything at all by way of useful work. He would survive Felicia's fling and Khreel's high-handed relationship with her. Because he had to, and because this wasn't Philadelphia.

It was the Amazon outback, 500 miles from anything real, and they all had become jungle-stressed. Isolation-warped. Crazy.

Then Khreel did something that shattered the uneasy dynamics of Station 4. He did it one evening at dinner after he and Felicia had been missing more of the afternoon. What he did probably did not seem to him more meaningful than adolescent teasing. But to Durkin, it was an unpardonable bombshell.

Khreel wiped his mouth, settled back in his groaning wood-slat chair. Chuckled to himself.

And he said to Durkin, "I understand they used to call you 'Turkey.' Haw-haw-haw."

Durkin felt his blood rise over his limp shirt collar, race along his jaw and suffuse his cheeks crimson.

"Haw-haw! Gotcha, Turkey," Khreel blathered. "Has a nice ring: 'Turkey Durkin.'"

Durkin glanced at Felicia. She smiled at Khreel. She had told Khreel.

God, how Durkin hated that nickname. All nicknames. In private grade school, a nine-year-old lump had called him "Emmy." Durkin was undersized, with a piping little voice. The more he protested, the worse it got until the whole school was chanting, "Emmy, Emmy, your name is femmy!"

In high school, he was for a time free of the taunts of what he considered the snobbish rich kids. Then some wag came up with "Spider," all too appropriate for a skinny runt with toothpick arms and legs. He lived miserably with that all the way to graduation.

Then he left it behind with a sense of relief when he entered U. of P. whereupon another mental Visigoth struck upon the euphonious "Turkey." "Turkey Durkin" did have a catchy ring. It stuck with him all four years; followed him through graduate studies. Then he'd thought he'd left it at the University of Florida – where he had met Felicia Noonan, coincidentally from Philadelphia. She had never once used that horrible nickname.

Yet now she had told Khreel, and they had unified to ridicule him. Durkin felt as if an icicle had plunged straight down his gullet to explode frigid shards in his gut.

But as his hands gripped his chair arms in a rictus of fury, he realized he was as incapable of standing up to this chortling lout as he had been of confronting his tormentors from the age of nine.

Perhaps Felicia was putting him to the test, something she may have concocted from equal parts of boredom, Durkin's gradual transfer of passion from her to his work – then the flattering attentions of Khreel. She had escalated the challenge by increasing intimacy with the idiot, and Durkin had done nothing. Now she was employing, through Khreel, raw derision. At long last, Durkin found that unbearable.

But though he now seethed with fury, he was still the same man behind it, a man unable to assail Khreel head-on, and just as incapable of waylaying him along the Station's latrine path and firing a bullet into his heart. In fact, there was no firearm available. Durkin wouldn't hear of it.

A spear? Surely one of the Indians would be able to provide one. But the thought of even the likes of Khreel twisting on the end of a length of hardwood pole turned Durkin's blood cold.

Now Felicia and Khreel flaunted their *affaire Amazonia*, as Durkin bitterly termed it to himself. One late afternoon, when he trudged across the compound from the research building, he heard laughter. Felicia's giggles, then Khreel's deeper chuckle. This from behind the screening of the rain cistern, their clothing hung over worn panels like defiant flags. They were in the thing together.

A surge of hot fury made Durkin's head thunder. Unendurable. And that mocking laughter. Simply unendurable. His fists knotted, his throat threatened to close. Yet he strode away.

At supper, she clung to Khreel's arm, all pretense now dissolved in the rain forest's fetid oppression.

"What's for dinner, Turkey?" Khreel boomed, and they were shaken with helpless laughter, drunk on each other. She had passed over the line, out of Durkin's world into Khreel's. If life had a way of balancing inequities, Durkin thought, surely such a balance was long overdue.

Then the evening rains, as predictable as sunset in this post-flood season month, stopped. The water in the run-off cistern that served as their jungle hot tub grew algae-ridden and dank. On Durkin's order, the Indians drained it.

Yet, several afternoons later, Durkin heard splashing and mirth behind the screening.

"Had the Indians fill it with buckets from the river," Khreel blithely told him at supper. Now the man had even taken over compound management; ordered the Bororos to fill the tank with river water...

When he heard Felicia's first shrill scream, Durkin looked up from the voltmeter on the Electophorus aquarium. When Khreel's hoarse yell joined in, and the Indians loped across the compound toward the rear of the residence building, Durkin set down his notes and trotted out of the lab.

By the time he reached the run-off cistern, both Bororos had crowded inside, between the tank and the screening, jabbering wildly but uncertain as to what to do about the naked, panic-stricken white man and woman thrashing in the murky water.

"God Almighty!" Khreel screeched at Durkin, "get us out of here!" The man's face contorted in a grimace of terror. His words were overridden by Felicia's hysterical screams.

On Durkin's order, the two Indians began to hoist Khreel from the tank. As he emerged, the shouts of the Bororos merged into an eerie chant, three syllables, over and over.

"What..." Khreel managed through clenched teeth, "what's 'candy-roo'?" then he pawed himself frantically. "Oh, God!"

"'Candiru,' they're saying," Durkin told over Felicia's cries. "The little catfish I tried to explain to you in the lab. They burrow straight into any body opening, and because of their rear-facing barbs, they can be removed only by surgery."

"Jesus! In this tank? How-" Khreel's question disintegrated into a pain-wracked moan.

"Incredible," Durkin said. "To all of us, I'm sure."

The two of them were hauled out, naked and writhing, wrapped in blankets and carried into the residence. A day later, summoned by the emergency radio, a seaplane from Oriximina picked them up to fly them to Belem. With prompt surgical attention there, they would at least live.

In a week, perhaps several, the State of Para would send an investigator. Durkin could almost hear the conversation now.

"You say, senor, the Bororos filled the tank from the river. Very careless."

"They did as they were ordered."

"By you, Senor Durkin?"

"No, by Mr. Khreel."

"I see. Unfortunate that the Bororos did not notice the candiru in their buckets."

"The river is always muddy here. See for yourself."

"Si, you are right." The inspector would shrug. "An accident. And Senor Khreel seems to have brought it about by his ignorance."

And that would be that.

The day after the seaplane had rushed Khreel and Felicia eastward, the compound seemed to exist in suspended animation. Agata arrived glum-faced to clean the research building, strode past Durkin as if he didn't exist, seized the broom and began to work her way along the row of aquariums.

Then she stopped and bent down to peer into the candiru tank.

In her accented English, she said, "Empty? Empty tank?"

Durkin gazed at her, his face as impassive as that of either of the Bororos. Shortly she left to prepare his lunch. When he walked to the mess hut an hour later, both Bororos suddenly turned from their chopping away at an invasive root, stood and faced him respectfully.

That was a welcome change.

In the mess hut, when Agata brought his broiled fish, her smile had returned. As she leaned down to set the plate at his place, her breast softly brushed his shoulder. Something that had never happened before. He found that quite heart-warming.

Even exciting.

HAMADRYAD

Ten miles north of Fort Myers – where the Tamiami Trail arrowed through miles of scrub and sand and the fringes of Punta Gorda hadn't shown up yet – Sammy "Little Shot" Pippitone pushed himself straighter behind the wheel of his rented Ford Taurus. According to the info he'd been given yesterday, the Garden of Serpents should be coming up soon. Out here in the Southwest Florida boondocks, he ought to be able to make the hit Q & E – quick and easy – then zip back down to Southwest Florida International and catch a red-eye back north in time for an early breakfast in Manhattan.

Sammy's nickname hadn't come from his smallness, though he wasn't a lot bigger than an oversized jockey. They called him "Little Shot" because he was at the bottom end of the caliber scale from Orlo "Big Shot" Orsini. The Big Shot packed one of the new .50-cal Desert Eagles, a monster hand-cannon with huge half-inch diameter Spear Lawman ammo that would stop a charging rhino if there'd been one up in Queens to try it on. It also made a gut-jarring bang you could've heard from Borden Avenue all the way up to 44th, even with heavy traffic.

Sammy Little Shot hated Orlo's kind of slam-bang service. Sammy considered himself an artist at what he did. No big boom. He used a sweet little Sterling Model 300, a six-shot automatic only four and a half inches overall – not much more than eight inches with its fat steel carrot of a noise suppressor threaded to its muzzle. Sammy never called the fat carrot a "silencer." There was no such thing as a "silencer," but the suppressor cut the Sterling's normal bark to no more than a sput. Sammy always placed that little sput just an inch from the mark's skull just behind the ear. The neat, quiet work of an artist.

He'd gotten Sterling here in the bag he'd checked through from JFK. The airlines didn't often x-ray checked baggage. If they did, his bag carried a phony name and address tag that matched his phony driver's license. And he was always careful to case the crowd at baggage pick-up, willing to let the bag stay on the conveyor if he spotted any security waiting. At Southwest Florida International, nobody looked suspicious about anything. A holiday crowd.

There the place was, maybe a mile ahead on the right, a one-story pink stucco building done in Spanish hacienda style. Sammy let the speedometer slip back from 75. The speed limit here was 65, but everybody was topping that. A cream and brown RV blared past his left as he pulled off the highway and crunched to a space in the sand-and-shell parking lot.

The target's name was Lester Biorkin. Or had been. According to Sammy's briefing phone call yesterday, now the Federal Witness Program called him "Louis Burke." As far as The Family was concerned, the FWP was a great help. The Family had a mole there, and the mole could turn up just about anything they wanted. At the moment, they wanted Biorkin, who had done three hateful things to upset them.

First, a year ago he had witnessed from his taxi up in Harlem the disposal by gunshot of Don Dominic Giovanchi. That wouldn't have been bad if Giovanchi's recycling had been handled by one of the Family's routine disposers. But it had been made personally by Don Edmundo Carli himself. "I owe him that honor," Don Carli himself had explained to his worried security pros. Anyway, who'd've thought such a gutsy and thoroughly stupid taxi driver would be wandering along Lennox Avenue just as Don Carli's .45 brightened the night? Who'd've thought its driver would recognize the distinguished shooter? But worst of all, who'd've thought the hack driver would do the second hateful thing: be dumb enough to testify and put Don Carli himself up the Hudson in Ossining for 25 to 35?

Worse. When word from Don Carli himself came down out of Sing Sing, a worker shooter named Skagg had been sent to Miami to take care of Biorkin. Dancing through Biscayne Boulevard traffic a couple feet behind Biorkin, Skagg went under a gravel truck – or so the story went. That was the third hateful thing. Biorkin made it across the highway, Skagg was roadkill. At that point, the Family decided a worker shooter had been a bad choice. They contacted a specialist shooter: Sammy Little Shot.

Now here Sammy was, sliding one slender polished black Thom McAn out of the Taurus to the gritty parking surface, then the other. Wrong shoes, he knew, but he hadn't had much time to put his wardrobe together for this urgent swing south. It had been "Ten Gs and leave now, or be picky, wait for the next one and hope you don't starve in between." Nice way the Family had of putting things.

So here he was. The blue and white seersucker pants would be okay. The button-down white shirt would pass. The blue poplin jacket was already too hot, but he couldn't take it off because that would expose the handgrip of the Sterling and its suppressor stuck in his waistband.

He left the car unlocked in case he'd need to make a speedy exit, shaded his eyes and looked up at the façade of the Spanish hacienda. And that was when he felt a prickle of icy slivers. All through the plane trip down to Fort Myers then back up here by rental, he had pushed to the back of his brain just where he had to go to find Biorkin-Burke. The Garden of Serpents was a tourist attraction, a goddamn snakeatarium. If there was anything he hated enough to send cold slithers through him, it was a snake. Hated them even worse than bats, and he hated bats enough to stay inside after dark – even in Midtown in winter. The bat hate came from his mother, when he'd been a kid back in Jersey City. One of them had gotten into her bedroom, and she'd gone bonkers, rolling on the floor, screaming it was going to get in her hair and strangle her. When he was older, he knew that probably wouldn't have happened, but it never stopped giving him the shakes. Even now, he couldn't make it all the way through a Dracula movie.

The snake business had started when he was ten. He and a buddy had chased a grass snake under a fence. The buddy ran around the other side, screamed, "I got it!" and stepped on it just as Sammy leaned down with his mouth open. Something green and sour and vile squirted out of the snake's mouth straight into his. He spit and gagged and spit until he thought he was going to die.

As Sammy stared up at the big green and pink lettering across the whole front of the Garden of Serpents, he felt that same gagging urge begin to throb in his throat. The letters were decorated with vines – until a closer look showed him the vines were snakes, holding each other's tails in their mouths. The sun, low on the horizon behind him, made the intertwined lettering seem to writhe in its brassy glare. He swallowed his revulsion and walked into the building.

A few tourists fingered the gaudy souvenir display racks that flanked a sales counter on the left side of the beige-tinted lobby. On the right were a pair of restroom doors labeled "Hiss' and "Herss." The entrance to the exhibit area was center rear, a heavy solid wood door with a ticket cage just to its left.

He realized he was stalling, hoping that somehow Biorkin would magically appear, walk out to the parking lot and make things easy. Sammy didn't want to go into the exhibit area. But Biorkin worked here. He had to be doing something or other in there. To avoid the guy's leaving through a back door while he stood here wondering about it, Sammy had to make himself do what he desperately didn't want to do.

Careful not to expose the black gun butt, he yanked out his wallet and handed five bucks to the bored-looking platinum-haired babe behind the screened ticket window. Then he faced the entrance door, took a long, deep breath, and pulled it open.

Years ago he'd read that snakes smell like cucumbers. That might have been a lot of horse hockey, but he could swear as he stepped through the door, all of a sudden he smelled cucumbers. And there wasn't a snake in sight. He'd expected a big room with rows and rows of cages. It wasn't like that at all.

He was outdoors again, in a big courtyard open to the darkening sky. The central area was crisscrossed by two concrete walks. The walks intersected in the middle, cutting the high-walled courtyard into four sections. In each section was a – what? Some kind of cinderblock ring. Sammy walked over to the nearest one, his shoes scuffing through tanbark mulch.

He peered into a big, 15-foot-diameter wall. His blood turned to instant ice. Down there in the bottom of the six-foot-deep pit was a writhing tangle of fat black snakes. Christ, there must be hundreds of them, Sammy realized.

He stumbled backward until his feet found concrete again. A wave of black dots began to block out his vision. He fought it off. Okay. He was okay now. But he sure didn't want to see what horrors must be in the other three wells.

A roofed hallway that ran along four sides of the courtyard was formed by the windowless outside wall and a low parapet around the inside. Widely-spaced concrete columns jutted up from the parapet to support the inside edge of the hallway's tilted roof. All along the outside wall of this open hallway, Sammy made out rows of glass cages. He was glad the light was getting so bad he couldn't see what was in them.

In a distant corner, a knot of people had gathered around some guy in a white coat. Sammy couldn't spot anybody anywhere else in here, so he walked across the courtyard toward the gathering. He was careful not to look into the two wells he passed on the way.

Standing at the edge of the little crowd down here in the corner, he could see a short guy in a white coat working with something on the edge of the knee-high parapet. When a big-butted citizen moved aside, he saw what was going on. The white-coat had a damned snake right out here with everybody. Only his little pole with a hook at the end was between him and the snake.

Sammy actually knew what kind of snake it was. The flaring hood was a dead giveaway. This skinny little snake man with brush-cut gray hair was diddling around with a cobra. A couple of feet of cobra and the snake was getting tired of it. It made a lunge for the guy's hand. Just as it did, the guy whipped in his other hand and the bony little snake charmer had the thing by the back of its neck. Sammy was goggle-eyed.

"You going to show us the hamadryad this afternoon, Doctor Grovenor?" The speaker was a brainy-looking teenager crowding right in on the cobra act.

"Afraid not, son." The snake doctor had a voice as dry as scales on leaves. "We bring him out only on Sundays."

Sammy wondered vaguely what the hell a "hammer dry head" was, but his attention came back to the matter at hand in a hurry. From the shadows behind the parapet, an arm reached out to give the snake wrestler a glass jar with rubber stretched across its mouth. The guy with a handful of cobra brought the jar up to the snake. It snapped its fangs deep in the rubber top. Sammy was revolted, but he couldn't make himself look away as the yellowish venom drooled down the inside of the jar. The snake's glittery little eyes looked like he was having a fine old time sinking his fangs into something.

Sammy shook his head to break the tight string of horror that had tied him to the cobra. And he got a look at the guy who handed out the jar.

He was tall with neatly-styled black hair and sharp green eyes in the kind of face Sammy had seen as Mercenary of the Month in *Soldiers for Hire* magazine. Biorkin. Sammy recognized him from the photo the Family had thoughtfully provided. Just the kind of good-looking, overconfident guy Sammy liked to whack. "Gives me a lot of satisfaction," he had relayed back to Don Carli up there in Sing Sing. Whacking a tall guy like Biorkin here made up for Sammy's being so little that everybody was always looking down at the top of his head.

While the spidery snake doctor went on with his show for the tourist trade, Sammy edged over to the parapet where the glass jar supply man, also in a white coat, was idling.

He felt so pleased with the way this was working out, he smiled at the target and said quietly, "Hi, Biorkin." Call it bravado or whatever, it was his trademark. The murmured greeting with a big smile just before the whack. It confused them, and a confused target was an easy target. He waited for the inevitable panicky reaction.

Biorkin didn't react at all. That wasn't so pleasing because Sammy's edge was gone now. The rest of this would be nothing more than mechanics.

Dr. Brushcut was folding up his act now. Sammy stayed on the fringe of the crowd as it ambled back toward the lobby door. Near the door, though, he drifted off to the left and fitted himself neatly behind the roof column in the southwest corner of the yard.

In a few minutes, everybody was out of the place except the snake charmer and Biorkin - who was obviously his assistant. Having the two of them in here was dicey. Then Sammy heard the doc call out, "Good night, Lou." The little snake expert walked up the hallway on the other side of the courtyard.

The light was getting really bad. Sammy watched the guy turn the corner and come straight down the west hallway toward him. But, as Sammy had figured, the snake doctor stopped at the lobby door, pushed it open and stepped out of the exhibit yard.

Beautiful, Sammy realized. Only he and "Lou" Biorkin were in here now. Couldn't have engineered a better set-up if he'd planned it himself.

The courtyard was deadly silent. Had Biorkin somehow slipped out? Was there a backdoor Sammy hadn't noticed?

Then he heard a rattle. A rattle! Come on, calm down. Rattlesnakes don't make door noises. There was a door back there, and son of a bitch Biorkin was going through it!

Sammy sprinted down the south hallway, first running flat out, then getting a lot more careful as he realized he was racing along only a foot from the snake cages that lined the outside wall.

He skittered around the southeast corner of the corridor, raced along the east side – and hell, here it was. A rear door. He shoved down the panic bar. The door wouldn't budge. It was locked by a key-operated deadbolt. Biorkin had gone out this way. Now Sammy had to run all the way back to the main entrance where he –

What was that?

He turned, held his breath and listened. Footsteps. Sounded like they were going up the north hallway toward the door. The guy was still in here. He must have locked this rear door from the inside, and he was still futzing around in here.

Then Sammy heard the footsteps pause; heard a grating noise, like wood sliding on concrete. Biorkin's paddling steps picked up again, headed for the main entrance.

Sammy launched himself straight up the middle of the courtyard. Biorkin was still over on the north side. If Sammy was quick enough, he could reach the main door the same time Biorkin did.

At the mid-point, where the walkways intersected, Sammy's leather shoes slipped. He went down on one knee, cracking it painfully against the concrete. He'd told himself he ought to start wearing rubber soles, but he hadn't found a pair that looked decent. He bounded up again, but the slip had cost him. He caught a glimpse of Biorkin's white coat as the big main door opened. Saw a flash of lobby lighting. The door slammed shut again.

Biorkin was in the lobby, no doubt racing for his car. Now Sammy would have to go out there, scramble into the Taurus, tail Biorkin until he pulled into his driveway or stopped at some store on the way home. From that point, Sammy would have to improvise. This thing was getting more complicated than he liked.

He reached the end of the main hallway and lunged for the door.

Locked. He shook the handle. Locked with a keyed deadbolt like the other door.

This was crazy. Him, Sammy Little Shot Pippitone, the world's greatest snake hater, locked in with a world-class snake population. He sagged against the door, pulled great ragged breaths and tried not to go onto giggle-sob hysterics. If Big Shot Orsini were ever to hear about this, there'd be no end to the ragging Sammy would have to take.

He tried to concentrate on that funny side of it, but there was no getting around what was going on. He had let a dumb-ass taxi jock outflank him and lock him in here with hundreds of –

A hot needle of panic speared through him. He banged on the door with both fists. "Let me outta here! I'm locked in. Let me OUT!"

He put his ear to the door. Nothing. Biorkin must have been the last person in the place, and now he was gone.

Sammy slowly turned and faced the courtyard. Silence. Silence blanketed by darkness thick as a quilt. He could barely make out the rim of the courtyard wall against the overcast night sky. To his right, almost at his elbow it seemed, he heard a faint jitter of scales against something dry. A snake, just a couple of feet away, was shifting around in his cage. A tremor skittered down Sammy's spine.

A flicker of blue silhouetted the east wall of the courtyard. What could – Then distant thunder rumbled. He felt its vibration through the thin soles of his city shoes. Did the snakes feel it, too? All around him, he heard uneasy rustlings.

He didn't belong in here, for Chrissake! Not here in snake city, Florida, ten miles from nowhere.

Out on the Tamiami Trail, a truck howled past. There were people going by not a hundred yards away, but he might as well be on the moon.

Come on, Sammy. Think.

He backed tightly against the door. Climb outta here maybe? The only access to the roof over the perimeter hallway was up one of the supporting columns. If they'd been narrow enough to get a grip on, he might be able to shimmy up to the hallway roof. Two problems with that. The top of the courtyard wall was another good eight feet further up, and the columns were too thick to try climbing in the first place.

Lightning flickered again. The seconds between flash and rumble were fewer. Damned storm was moving closer. Like he needed that on top of his immediate problems.

Slow down, Sammy. There were only two problems: Get out of here. Then whack Biorkin. He wasn't too worried about the Biorkin part. He had a line on where the guy lived, and the Family had feelers everywhere if he skipped before Sammy could get at him tonight.

The big problem was right now – getting out of this hellhole before he went… batty.

He would have to think of that. And this place was worse than Dracula's castle. There you'd only have to worry about the Count. Here he was surrounded by hundreds of creepy fang-bearers. The image of a cobra biting into the rubber-topped jar flashed vividly to mind. How could the snake doctor get himself to even touch the damned cobra? How many cobras were in here with him? What was in the other three walls? Did the snakes out there crawl out of their pits at night–

Jesus, what was that?

Over to his left, he'd heard a grating noise, long and loud. Like somebody pulling a fire hose around a corner. That sure hadn't been a snake in a cage. Whatever it was, it was right out here.

Forked lightning straight overhead strobed the courtyard dead white. Seconds after darkness fell back in, he could still see the courtyard burning in his eyeballs. Empty, thank God, with the walkways a giant cross.

That could keep old Dracula away, he thought.

Thunder exploded like a ton of TNT going off.

His ears sizzled. No, that wasn't in his ears. It was a hiss. He had definitely heard a hiss. And damned close. Just to his left.

He was out of here!

As Sammy leaped over the hallway parapet into the courtyard mulch, he felt something hit his right knee. Then his left shoulder. Soft impacts, but terrifying. When his face was struck, he almost laughed through his panic. Raindrops, that's what was hitting him. Big fat raindrops.

He stumbled to the center of the courtyard as the scattered drops merged into a deluge. The cascading sheets were shot through with lightning that threw the walkways and cinderblock serpent wells into brilliance that blinded him for seconds afterward.

Hunched against the storm's beating downpour, soaked and shivering, Sammy shoved his right hand under his sopping sports jacket and jerked out the automatic. Something was damn sure loose in here, something more terrifying than anything he'd seen in the cages. He didn't know what it was, didn't even want to imagine. But he knew it was here because he could feel it, just like he would have felt the deadly threat of a hidden shooter from a rival Giovanchi Family.

He knew there was something worse than a Giovanchi shooter in here, something that made the hairs on his neck ripple. With the pistol in both hands, Sammy crouched, swung around in the inky blackness. What in hell could–

The lightning strobed twice, only a fraction of a second each time, but it etched into Sammy's retinas a sight so incredible, so terrifying that he froze tight.

The thing stood taller than Sammy in his shooting crouch. It swayed there, ghostly white with lidless eyes that stared down at Sammy like gleaming bronze marbles.

Dracula! Sammy thought wildly. The crossed sidewalks didn't mean a thing. For a frozen moment, he crouched motionless, praying what he'd seen had been an illusion, a figment of panic.

Then his stunned brain jerked him back on track. He pulled the trigger. He got off just one wild shot as the hellish apparition crashed over his extended arms and sank daggers deep in his neck.

"Found him just like that," Doctor of Herpetology Herman Grovenor told Charlotte County Sheriff Duncan Bosworth. They stood in the early morning's glare in the center of the courtyard flanking the body of the little man in the sodden blue jacket and seersucker trousers; the little man with two widely-spaced punctures in his neck.

Nearby, two of the sheriff's deputies were supposed to be checking for "clues," but mostly they stared into the snake wells with huge distaste.

"And the hama-whatever. You say you found him out of his big cage?" Sheriff Bosworth was a big man with a florid face, but Grovenor could see under his lacework of capillaries, the sheriff was pale as paste.

"Hamadryad," Dr. Grovenor amended. "When I got here, he was footloose and fancy-free. So to speak."

He looked down at the body. "I don't know who this unfortunate fellow is, or how he got himself locked up in here. Found him just like this when I opened up this morning."

"Who was the last person to leave last night?" the sheriff crouched and aimlessly fingered the deceased's neck.

"My assistant, Lou Burke. Oh, you mean could he have left the cage open? Not him. He's a detail man. It's more likely this fellow came in a misguided effort to steal the hamadryad, and it got out of hand. Literally."

No smile from the sheriff. "The thing's worth money?"

"Well up in five figures, Sheriff." Dr. Grovernor frowned. "Funny thing about Lou, though. He called in just after I called you, said an emergency had come up and he had to quit."

The sheriff looked up from his crouch. "Quit?"

"As of today. Said he'd be back in touch to tell me where to send his severance check."

"I'll check on him, but I can't say I blame anybody for giving up this kind of showbiz." Bosworth stood and gazed uneasily around the courtyard. "You sure you corralled that hama-whatever?"

"Hamadryad, Sheriff. Our king cobra. I can't imagine how he got loose, but he's safely back in his cage. All eighteen feet of him."

"That's some hell of a snake!"

Dr. Grovenor smiled like a proud parent. "The only snake, I like to say, that can rear up and look you straight in the eye."

NO CABS AFTER MIDNIGHT

A truly lousy day. The company's jolting order to fly to Houston to tackle a sudden shift in Lone Star Victuals' pending national contract. Thank the Lord, Marcia was able to come through with flight and hotel reservations. Then the rush home to pack a carry-on bag. Give Joanne a run-by kiss. Floor it to Philadelphia International. Screech into long-term parking. Squeeze into a middle seat with zilch legroom for hours of rough weather dips and bumps. Get here after midnight –

And not one damned cab at the Houston airport's taxi stand.

Christ! Then he spotted an airport shuttle bus. The only up in this whole down day. At 12:49 a.m., Paul Morrison, Boltman Development's third-ranked financial officer, dragged himself into the Star State Arms. His dejection was eased a bit by the fully-carpeted, plush lobby. Behind the mahogany registration desk, an impeccably-combed clerk – in coat and tie at this dismal hour – sharp-eyed his approach.

"Morrison, Paul. I have a reservation." He squinted at the brass nametag over the clerk's jacket pocket. Erwin Holt.

"Morrison," Holt muttered. He fingered through a box of file cards, turned to tap a computer keyboard, faced Paul. "I'm sorry, Mr. Morrison. I find no record of a reservation."

"It was made earlier today."

"My apologies, Mr. Morrison, but-" He shrugged.

"Hell! Just give me a room."

Holt frowned. "I'm afraid that is a problem, sir."

"A problem?"

"We are full up."

"I thought big hotels always held a couple of rooms in reserve."

"It's the Franchise Executives national convention, sir. We are entirely sold out."

"For God's sake! You've botched my reservation, and you don't have one damned room available. What in the hell do you expect me to do? Sleep over there in one of your lobby chairs?"

"I do have a suggestion, sir. The Lone Star Plaza. It's only four blocks from here. Let me check."

"Yeah. Damn it. You do that."

Holt picked up his phone, made the call, then turned back to Paul with a smile. "All set, sir."

"Thanks. Now you can get me a cab."

Holt gave him a frustrated glance. "I'm afraid we have a problem there, sir."

"Another prob-"

"No cabs after midnight."

"What the hell does that mean?"

"The city has had a series of late night robberies of cab drivers. The taxi companies have suspended service from midnight to six a.m. Sorry, sir."

"You're saying I have to walk it?"

"Only four blocks, sir. To your left as you leave the front entrance. That seems to be the situation, sir."

"Thanks for the Star State Arms' impressive service, Erwin." Paul grabbed his carry-on bag and clumped toward the entrance. "You will be hearing from my company," he snapped over his shoulder. And he pushed out the entrance into the night.

Dark as hell beyond the hotel marquee's halo. Paul swung left and peered into the damp gloom. Down there - 'way down there - he detected a glow. Had to be the Lone Star Plaza. The long, dark stretch between was punctuated by just three feeble streetlight glimmers. No headlights. Not a single car. Talk about isolation. Creepy.

He set out along the damp sidewalk. Behind him, the marquee light faded. He walked in darkness, unimpressive apartment and office buildings to his left, dark as the night. Great cover for lurking... Paul shuddered.

In the middle of the second block, he decided to step off the sidewalk to walk down the center of the deserted street. Out here, he might at least hear a threat coming.

He was wrong about that. He didn't hear a damned thing until hot breath exploded in his left ear. Excruciating pain in his side took his legs from under him. He crumpled to the pavement. Felt hands plundering his jacket and trouser pockets.

No need for a knife, you bastard. If you'd asked for it, I would have given you my wallet.

The pain eased. Disappeared. Then he died.

"Is this Private Detective Elrod Montgomery?" A tense female phone voice.

"This is Rod Montgomery, yes." I detest Elrod.

"This is Joanne Morrison, Mr. Montgomery. Lieutenant Phipps of the Philadelphia Police suggested I call you about my husband."

Uh oh. Another marital mess case. Hate these. But a guy has to eat. "Your husband," I echoed and braced for the incoming tide.

"Paul Morrison, Mr. Montgomery. He's... dead."

I gave her a noncommittal, "I am sorry, Mrs. Morrison."

"He was killed in Houston. A mugging, they told me. Dreadful word."

"Houston."

"Paul's company, Boltman Developers here in Philadelphia, sent him there. He was found on a city street, stabbed to death."

Now she had my attention. "When was this?"

"Three weeks ago. I've waited for something more from there or from the police up here. I'm tired of waiting for someone to do something."

"My sympathy, of course. But it sounds like-"

"I know exactly what you're going to say. Like an unfortunately all-too-common street crime. But I know my husband, Mr. Montgomery. I can't imagine him wandering around the streets at one in the morning."

I hesitated. Then I asked her, "Was he a-"

"A drinker? That's the first thing the police asked. No, he was not. Another thing, Mr. Montgomery. Before he got on the plane here, Paul told me he would be at the Star State Arms Hotel. After the Houston police called me with the horrible news, I phoned the hotel. They said he had a reservation, but he never appeared. Yet he was found sprawled in the street just two blocks away. Something is wrong about all this, really wrong. But the police down there and up here have written this off as nothing more than a-" Her voice broke.

"An ordinary street mugging." I finished for her.

"Lieutenant Phipps with the police up here said you might be... helpful."

That was Stan Phipps for you. Hated to let anybody down, but eager to lob hopeless knotty ones to me. I assumed he felt the Houston cops were right. Another midnight mugging in a big city. But if the vic's wife wanted to push it, I was available. An unofficial shoulder for widows to weep on.

"I'll be glad to help you in any way I can, Mrs. Morrison. Where are you?"

"I'd rather come to you. I need an excuse to get out of this house, all the memories..."

"I'm in Orchard Glade, ten miles southwest of the city. Just off Route 1 near Chester Heights."

"I'm in West Chester. I'll be there in twenty minutes."

I gave her my street and house number.

"A home office?"

"Not as off-putting as the traditional PI's bare-bones office down a creaky second-floor hallway, Mrs. Morrison."

"I'm leaving now."

"I'll be here."

Twenty minutes later, a gunmetal blue Lexus pulled into my driveway. Joanne Morrison was chestnut-haired, medium-tall in a trim navy pants suit. Green eyes like lasers. She gave me a firm but cold-fingered handshake, and I led the way down the steps from the living room to my lower-level office.

"Coffee?"

She shook her head and perched on one of the two chairs in front of my desk. I grabbed my clipboard and took the other chair, a set-up I'd found more productive than across-the-table interrogation.

"Fill me in, Mrs. Morrison. What did your husband do at Bolton Developers? What was his position?"

"Paul worked in Boltman's financial department."

"As?"

"As a 'number cruncher,' he called it."

"And he was sent down to Houston-"

"So suddenly. They hardly gave him time to pack a carry-on bag."

"Did he tell you why the rush?"

"He didn't know. Said something about a problem with one of the company's biggest shopping mall renters. He promised to call me after he checked in at the hotel."

I consulted the clipboard in my lap. "The Star State Arms, you told me."

She nodded. "But he never called me." Her cool look collapsed and her voice choked. "The Houston police did." Then she added, in a near-whisper, "At four in the morning. God, what a nightmare."

She needed a moment, then she said, "They told me Paul had been stabbed in the street two blocks from the hotel. He was found by someone driving home from a party, who reported it to the police."

"You remember who talked to you?"

"Sergeant Porter."

I made a clipboard note. "Did Porter say anything about checking with the Star State Arms?"

"He said Paul never appeared there. I called the hotel myself, and they told me Paul had a reservation but never appeared."

"So... Your husband is rushed to Houston, never shows up at the hotel, but his body is found two blocks away. Doesn't make sense, but I'm sure the police down there already have it pigeon-holed as another incidental street crime."

"That's why I hope you might be able to find out exactly what happened, Mr. Montgomery."

"I can't promise to find out 'exactly what happened,' Mrs. Morrison. But from what you've told me, I should be able to find out more than we know at the moment."

"'More' is better than what I know now, Mr. Montgomery."

"Please call me 'Rod,'" I said, and I gave her my daily rate plus a hopeful advance figure. I felt that I wouldn't cost her much. This sounded like an investigation-by-phone case.

Apparently less than impressed by my financial disclosure, she peered about, then nodded up the steps. "I haven't heard a sound from up there. Do you live alone?"

"Divorced." That admission generated trepidation in some, curiosity in others. Joanne Morrison showed no reaction at all. She opened her purse and pulled out a checkbook. "Five hundred in advance, you said."

She stepped into her Lexus, started the engine, frowned, then rolled down the window.

"Something I didn't mention to the police. It seemed irrelevant in what they assumed was a... mugging."

"Try me."

"Paul was worried about something at work. He never told me, but I could tell."

"Something at work?"

She shrugged. "I'm sorry. Guess I just can't accept such an inglorious way for Paul to-" her emerald eyes teared up. She rolled the window shut and backed out of my driveway.

The house was silent, all right. Nobody here but me since my marriage fell apart. Well, since Leahla had apologetically told me she was in love with Vance Monahan, a goateed charmer who lived six houses away. And where they both now lived. Hating them was more effort than I wanted to expend in that direction. So we all remained on nodding acquaintance. Détente, you could call it, if my Cold War memory serves.

In fact, Leahla's wife-to-neighbor transition bothered me less than the one the Philly PD shoved at me: take the blame for what one of the most revered captains had done, retire early with full benefits – or fight it out and lose anyway and everything. My craven practicality won out over windmill-jousting futility and put me where I now sat.

Brooding over the past keeps you out of the future. I grabbed my desk phone.

"Detective Sergeant Porter," the third Texas voice said, after I'd bullied my way past the first two.

"Rod Montgomery, Sergeant. I'm a Philadelphia PI investigating the death of Paul Morrison."

"Can't help you much. He was found dead in the street. No clue why he was out there."

"His wife tells me he was sent to Houston on short notice, had a reservation at the Star State Arms a couple blocks from where he was found. Any ideas how he got there?"

"First we had to check on who he was. Wallet was lifted, but he had a return flight ticket in his pocket. And the tag on the carry-on bag near the body had his name and business address on it. An early morning phone call to Philadelphia verified it was Morrison. He'd flown from Philadelphia International just after midnight. Checked the two hotels he was only a couple blocks away from. He had a reservation at the Star State Arms, but they say he never got there."

"What in the hell was he doing on the street on foot with his hotel only two blocks away, Sarge? Only thing I can think of might be an argument with a bad-tempered taxi driver who threw him out there. That's a stretch, but it's all that comes to mind."

"It's more than a stretch, Montgomery. We've had a rash of taxi hold-ups here, so at the moment, no cabs run between midnight and six a.m. Want to take another stab at your far-fetcher?"

"Tell you what. I find out anything worthwhile, I pass it on. You do the same?"

"You pass it on to me, not your local papers."

"Agreed. For the moment, though, I've got zero input."

I hung up and tapped fingers on my desktop. Morrison never checked in, but he was found only a couple blocks away. Assumedly stabbed while walking... No cabs after midnight.

Two days into the case – if there was a case – my only progress was that call to Sergeant Porter down in Texas. As I downed the dregs of my morning coffee, I was back on the phone. Porter, this time calling me.

"Didn't tell you this yesterday because it was such a long shot."

"I'll take anything I can get."

"The day after Morrison was killed, airport maintenance found his wallet in one of the concourse trash bins. Morrison's prints on it, of course. Plus another."

"His wife's?"

"Nope. An AFIS computer search turned up one Karl Lesch. Rap sheet shows violence against a stranger. We've put out an APB on him."

"I appreciate the update, but I wonder why you're being so neighborly?"

"Call it a favor."

"Or a maneuver to keep me from gumming up progress with some wild stunt of my own."

"That, too. We find this clod and that wraps it up...Rod. No need for you to spin wheels and maybe kick up some interfering gravel. We nail Lesch, I'll give you a victory call."

He hung up, and I sat there staring at my framed Marine Corps honorable discharge document hung on the opposite wall. Nothing heroic implied; I'd spent most of my hitch guarding our embassy in Moscow.

...Well, great. I had taken a five-hundred-buck retainer to crack a case the Houston cops had already split wide open. If I were the crooked cop now forever implanted in Philadelphia PD records, I could do nothing for a few days, then report my "findings" concerning Karl Lesch and wing it from there until he was found or cold-cased. Ride Houston's horse for a few days, then cash a check from a grateful Joanne Morrison.

At 3:10 p.m., that unworthy speculation crashed and burned.

"Got him!" Sergeant Porter exploded in my phone. "At his sister's house in Baltimore. Flying with a fake ID, the dumb bastard rushed up there like a homing pigeon. Thought her name changes through three marriages would lose her in the records. The computer scores again, so, my friend, that wraps it up."

"Baltimorean kills Philadelphian in Houston."

"You almost got it."

"Almost?"

"Lesch isn't from Baltimore. Last known address Camden,

New Jersey." Porter paused, then he said, "Anything you do now would be treadmill, Montgomery. Sorry, we've just reduced your gross income. But... have a nice day."

I cradled the receiver. Fine thing, I'd stepped into a cut-and-dried case with no need of outside expertise. I finger-drummed my desktop. Something about Porter's cold water call... Ah ha! One small overlook. He hadn't looked at the map. Rough, tough Camden is in New Jersey, Sergeant, but it is right across the Delaware River from Philadelphia.

Pretty thin, to be objective about it. But it was the only thread I had left to earn my fee. And I realized Porter hadn't said a word about why Paul Morrison had been wandering around two blocks from his hotel.

Near Willow Grove, north of central Philadelphia, I pulled off state route 611 into a big, crowded parking area. At its far edge stood a huge spaceship. That's what Sylvan Circle resembled. I parked as close to the alien-looking, two-level shopping center as I could find space, and walked to the broad entrance of this imposing architectural donut.

At ground level, a ring of shops, restaurants and a Starbucks encircled a park-like lawn planted with impeccably sculpted shrubbery. The mini-park was open to the overcast Southeastern Pennsylvania sky. The upper level of this mighty cruller was occupied by Boltman Development's headquarters, a ring of offices with its interior windows offering a supervisory view of the retailing bustle below.

Two staircases flanked the entrance. The one on the right was labeled EMPLOYEE ENTRANCE. On the left: BOLTMAN DEVELOPMENT. I climbed that one. Up top, a thirty-something receptionist with a helmet of closely-cropped, steel-colored hair gave me a mouth-only smile. "May I help you, sir?"

"I'd like to talk to the head of your finance department."

"That would be Vice President Vanoppen. Have you an appointment?"

I purposely had none such. I'd found unexpected walk-ins could produce helpful blurts from the unprepared.

"Tell Mr. Vanoppen Detective Montgomery is here investigating the Morrison case."

Her icy blue eyes shot me a long appraisal. She picked up her phone, gave Vanoppen my intro, word-for-word, clanked the phone down. "Fourth office on the left."

"Thank you, m'dear."

She threw me a viral glance. I strode down the curving hallway. Well, not exactly a hallway. Office doors on the left, open bullpens of departmental minions on the right. Most of their occupants busied themselves at computers. Quite a few of these otherwise busy bees seated by the big interior windows seemed unable to resist the retailing roil below.

The fourth elegantly-paneled door on the right bore a framed plaque:

G. WALTER VANOPPEN

CHIEF FINANCIAL OFFICER

I tapped and walked into a cubicle with a small desk and heavy-set, gray-haired fortyish woman in cool blue. She glanced up from her computer. "Detective Montgomery?"

"The very same."

She nodded at an inner door. "In there."

A huge picture window dominated the CFO's office, with a grand view of the parking lot and the still-undeveloped rolling acreage beyond. Finance mogul Vanoppen sat behind a behemoth of a desk, its top obscured by a deluge of paper. He looked up from a mass of computer spew, his long, narrow face a scowl beneath a possibly sixty-buck hair trim. Pretty self-indulgent, I thought, for a guy in his fifties, but it complimented his Armani suit coat and crimson power-tie. Who wore a suit coat and tie behind a desk in this day and age?

He affected a precisely trimmed little mustache that he stroked with thumb and forefinger before he said, "I assume you are from the Philadelphia Police, Detective."

Enough of the dupery, now that I was in here. "Nope, I'm a private investigator, hired by Mrs. Morrison."

"Joanne has hired a private detective? Why?"

"She's wondering why Paul was out in the street when he had a reservation at the hotel only a short distance from where his body was found. I'm wondering the same thing. Among some other things."

"Such as?"

Vanoppen hadn't stood to greet me or offered me one of the chairs near his imposing desk. I sat down in one anyway. "Such as, Mr. Vanoppen, he had a reservation at the Star State Arms, never showed up there, but his body was found not many feet away."

Pensive mustache stroke. Then, "We've all wondered about that, Detective."

"Any thoughts?"

"I'm a CFO, not a detective."

"What were Morrison's responsibilities here?"

"Computerization of all the company's financial operations."

"Not PR."

That got me an exasperated scowl. "Certainly not! Why that question?"

"He told his wife he was being sent to Houston to handle a problem with one of your mall tenants."

"A financial problem, Detective. He was one of our finance experts."

"How many others in your department?"

"Just two, now. Charles Davenport handles all billings and payments. Marsha Franklin is a paper pusher. Paul was our computer ace."

Vanoppen was more loquacious now, but we were going nowhere. How about a little shock treatment? "Ever heard of Karl Lesch?"

Did that damned little mustache caress falter just a bit?"

"Who's Karl Lesch?"

"He's the guy who killed Paul Morrison."

Vanoppen's dry-ice gaze gave way to a frown. "I haven't heard that. Where did you hear that?"

"From the Houston police. Lesch was arrested yesterday in Baltimore."

Was Vanoppen less surprised that I'd expected, or was his rigid attitude one of executive pride?

"So," he said, visibly pulling himself back to full composure, "case closed."

"Except for the bothersome details I mentioned."

"They would all seem obviated by the arrest in Baltimore."

That assumption was pronounced in a tone that told me I had gotten all I was going to get from G. Walter Vanoppen. I filed away his little falter at the mention of Lesch, and I stood.

"I thank you for your time, sir. If you think of anything more that might be of help, give me a call." I tossed one of my cards on his paper pile and walked out. But not away. Across from his forbidding office entrance, I strolled into the finance department's bullpen. Not abuzz with activity like the Promotion Department I'd walked past on my way here, the Finance pen had only three desks. The empty one, I assumed, had been Paul Morrison's. At the desk nearest the entrance in the hip-high separation wall sat a woman in her mid-twenties. With her hair in a severe bun, and wearing horn-rimmed (good Lord) glasses, she seemed to be disguising her prettiness. Her only jewelry, if I could call it that, was a red-topped straight pin in the white collar of her blouse.

"Marsha Franklin, no doubt." I nodded at the nameplate on her desk.

"Good observation," piped the other drone in this seemingly somnolent hive. "I'm Charley Davenport." He bent a thumb toward the other chair in front of his blond wood desk. "What can I do for a police detective? Yeah, the word has already gotten around."

"I'm not with the Philly police, Charley." I stuck out my hand. "Private investigator Rod Montgomery. I'm working with Joanne Morrison."

"Oy," he said in mock alarm. "A shamus!"

This guy had to have been his grade school's class clown. I went at him head-on. "You have any idea why somebody would want to kill Paul?"

"Sure. A street thief after his wallet." Charley grinned. "You could have figured that out without my help."

I saw Marsha's eyes roll ceilingward.

"You seem overly distraught, Charley."

"Hell, we're all distraught. Some of us cover it better. What happened is a damned shame, and nobody seems able to do a damned thing about it."

"That's not quite accurate, Charley. The Houston police have nailed the guy who did it."

Charley jovially dissolved. "You're kidding!"

"Guy named Lesch. He left a fingerprint behind."

"You're kidding," he said again.

"Caught him in Baltimore."

"Baltimore?"

"Yep. Nailed there for a killing in Houston, and he's from Camden."

"I'll be damned."

"That makes three of us, including Joanne Morrison."

"You found out anything more?"

"I don't know if there is anything more, Charley." I was getting nothing from this joker. I stood. "You think of anything helpful, give us a call." I tossed one of my cards on his desk and stepped back to Marsha.

...Who surprised me by reaching for my hand. "I'm so glad you're trying to help, Mr. Montgomery." She had a dry palm. Crinkly. Then I realized she was passing me a note.

Back in my car, I read her neat, prep school-like printing: Graber's Grill, ½ mile up 611. On the right. 20 minutes.

I pulled into the place in ten. Since she obviously wasn't looking for publicity on whatever she had in mind, I took a table in a secluded corner, ordered coffee, and kept an eye on the entrance. Nine minutes later she slipped in, surveyed the place with a quick glance, spotted me and hurried over.

"I can't take too long," she said, as the college-age waiter closed in. "Egg salad sandwich and iced tea," she told him.

"Ham and Swiss on rye." I waited until he was out of earshot. "You've got my total attention, Marsha."

"It's that I... that I..." She stopped. Then she leaned closer. "Through the past couple weeks, I could tell Paul was... nervous about something."

"You have any idea what?"

I studied her as our waiter arrived with Marsha's iced tea and a coffee refill for me. Her prim hairstyle and the damned dark-rimmed glasses told me she was a pretty woman who wanted to be taken seriously. And she was concerned about something beyond the street mugging theory.

I took a quick snort of coffee. Then we both sat silent as the waiter plunked down our sandwiches. When he left, I asked, "You think Paul was concerned about something he knew or something he did?"

"How would I tell?"

"Did he seem guilty or angry?"

She nibbled at one of her sandwich wedges. Sipped tea. Then peered at me. "I wish I'd been more observant. Best I can tell you is he looked... concerned." She frowned. "I guess that's no help at all."

"Don't underestimate yourself, Marsha. Let's go over what we know. First, did Paul definitely have a reservation at the Star State Arms?"

"Yes. I made the call myself."

"Do you know what the financial problem with that Houston company was?"

"Something Charley told Mr. Vanoppen about. Then Mr. Vanoppen told me to make the hotel reservation and arrange for Paul's airline ticket."

"But Paul never appeared at the hotel."

"That's what they told me when Mr. Vanoppen had me confirm what the police had told him."

"Who did you speak to at the hotel?"

"An Irving... No, wait, Erwin was his name. Erwin Holt, the night manager at the registration desk. He confirmed that Paul never appeared." She checked her wristwatch. "Oh, I've got to get back. I've told you what I know – which really isn't much. I just know it's unlike Paul to be wandering around in a strange street. He was such a precise, organized–" Her voice broke. She bounced to her feet. "Gotta go." She opened her purse.

"This is on me," I told her. "Then I'll see you to your car."

"No, don't. Somebody might spot us together."

"You're that worried?"

"Can't help it. Nothing that happened in Houston sounds right to me."

I watched her walk to the door. A nervous walk. More confirmation that I could be into something bigger than Sgt. Porter assured me it wasn't.

I signaled the waiter for the check. I'd made up my mind. I wasn't unraveling anything up here. Morrison had been sent to Houston and was killed there. If Joanne approved of the expense, I was flying to Houston.

A clever way to go about my Houston recon, I convinced myself, would be to duplicate Paul Morrison's trip there. So I called the Star State Arms for a reservation and boarded the same daily Philadelphia-Houston flight Morrison had flown. Turned out to be an uneventful flight, as the cliché goes, with plenty of time to mull over my theory that the rapid arrest of Lesch cleared the Houston cops' street crime case. Morrison's out-in-the-street location had been sidetracked in the departmental glory of such swift apprehension of his murderer. But to me, his wee-hours stroll made no sense at all.

The big Boeing touched down just before midnight, as his flight had. I avoided a baggage claim wait—I toted only a carry-on, as he had. But by the time I negotiated the walk through the terminal, I emerged out front significant minutes after midnight.

No cabs. Only an airport shuttle bus, which I boarded, along with three red-eyed business types. After they were dropped off at a Hyatt Regency near the airport, the weary-looking young driver peered at me over his shoulder. "Star State Arms, you said?"

"You got it."

"Couple weeks back, fella I left off there on this run was killed."

My God, what a coincidence! No, maybe it wasn't. This dismal, wee-hours haul on deserted streets surely couldn't be an eagerly sought-after assignment.

I leaned forward. "You let him out at the hotel entrance?"

"Hell, yeah. Where else would I let him out?"

"You see him walk in?"

"Nope. That was my last stop, and I wanted to get home. But where else would he go?"

"Good point." Maybe the point.

Ten minutes later, we pulled under the gleaming marquee of the Star State Arms. I left the driver gaping at a ten-dollar tip.

The guy behind the registration counter in the otherwise deserted lobby struck me as a version of a snotty chap in a cut-a-way and striped trousers, modernized here into a navy blue jacket with a star-shaped hotel logo patch on the pocket, a starched white shirt, and a sky-blue tie. In his mid-thirties, with neatly trimmed dark hair and a clean-shaven, narrow face, he gave me a cold appraisal as I neared his stronghold.

"Good evening, sir." No smile.

"Rod Montgomery. Mr.-" I peered at this little nameplate on the countertop – "Mr. Erwin Holt. I have a reservation."

Holt bent over a computer keyboard, clicked briefly, then straightened. "Yes, Mr. Montgomery. We can put you in a very nice room with an excellent view of the city."

"That'll be fine. When I made the reservation on such short notice, I was afraid you might be full up."

"We aren't at all crowded this time of year. And we always have several rooms set aside on emergency reserve." He twirled the registration pad toward me, and I signed in.

"Carry my own bag?"

"We have a bellman on call. Just a moment and I'll ring-"

"Hold a bit." I nodded toward the entrance. "Too bad what happened out there a while back."

Erwin's hand stopped an inch above what I assumed was the buzzer to summon the invisible bellman. "To what do you refer, sir?" He was giving me English butler phrasing deep in the heart of Texas.

"Paul Morrison. Stabbed in the street out there."

Holt's hazel eyes gave me a long, speculative look. "A tragedy. We were all shocked."

Casual conversation so far, but I needed to go a lot further. I moved against the counter, eye-to-eye with Holt. "I understand he had a reservation here."

"That is correct, but he never showed." I peered straight into Holt's eyes as he said that, and I detected something.

His pupils contracted enough to be discernable. A tell-tale sign of a lie.

"The driver of the shuttle I just got off told me he delivered Paul Morrison to your entrance right over there. You think he wandered away down the street?"

"Apparently, that is what happened." Holt's pupils contracted again. And he hid his now-restless hands behind the counter. Another liar's giveaway.

I assumed the Houston police interviewer – Sgt. Porter? – accepted Holt's assertion that Morrison never showed up here. At that point, everyone's attention had to be out there with the body, not in here with Holt's body language.

I shrugged. "I dunno, Erwin. Seems unlikely Paul would walk off into the night when he had a nice, safe reservation here. I'm told he did have a reservation."

Nervous nod from Holt. Now his eyes were anywhere but on mine. Liar sign number three. I had him, but I didn't want to push him into tight lippery. I'd found casual, friendly conversation unglued many a guilt-obsessed holdout.

"I'm sure what happened out there in the street really shook you up, Erwin. You had to wonder what in the hell he was doing out there. And could you have done anything that would have changed what happened? That's gotta be a hard thing to live with, Erwin. If it was me, I could see how-"

He fell apart right in front of me. Sagged against the counter. Shrugged hopelessly. "It was supposed to-" voice almost a whisper - "It was supposed to be a joke."

What the hell was this? I tried to sound warm and friendly. "A joke, Erwin?"

With his palms flat on the counter, he looked up at me. A face collapsed in misery. "I got a call. From one of Morrison's old fraternity brothers. A man with a grudge. Something Morrison had done to him back in their college days."

"Some of those frat tricks can be real mean," I said by way of keeping Erwin in confession mode.

"He told me he wanted to put Morrison on the spot like he'd been put in. He'd heard about no cabs after midnight in Houston. Making Morrison walk down the street to another hotel would even things up between them."

Holt's eyes rolled upwards in what I assumed was self-disgust as his part in a practical joke that went awry.

"You get a caller ID on that one?"

"No. It was blocked. 'Unknown name, unknown number.'"

"Yet you agreed to this dubious little caper."

"I wasn't sure I wanted to be part of it until he told me it was worth a lot to him. When the envelope arrived, it had a note to call him if I agreed, or send the money back."

"The money?"

"Ten one-hundred-dollar bills – for my small favor of denying Morrison's reservation."

"You notice a postmark on the envelope?"

"Ardmore, PA."

A Philadelphia suburb. Could be the sender wasn't as smart as he thought he was.

Holt's eyes finally met mine. "I swear it was supposed to be a joke."

"Why didn't you tell the Houston police?"

"I was in a panic. I felt I'd abetted a murder!"

"And now?"

"I'm the innocent bystander of a practical joke gone bad. You figured out I was lying to you. I figured out I was lying in front of a private investigator." He smiled at my surprise. "You've got cop written all over you, Montgomery. But if you were one, you would have had to ID yourself and tell me my rights. So I guessed PI."

I'd had him. Now he had me. "You're perceptive, Erwin."

He let out a long, pent-up sigh. "It was supposed to be a practical joke."

"Too bad you were so easily bribable, Erwin. Your conscience has kicked in too late for Paul Morrison."

I spent the night in a relaxingly plush room at the Star State Arms. Time to contemplate:

Erwin Holt's painful explanation of his part in a joke-gone-bad convinced me he had been taken in – quite willingly when the bribe arrived.

But the practical jokester would have to know well in advance that Morrison would go to Houston. Time was needed to send Holt the bribe, then wait a few days for it to be returned if Holt declined. That much was shaky enough, I thought. It got worse. Morrison himself didn't know about his Houston trip until the morning of the day it took place. Too many precise calls for some outsider to master. Logic told me whoever set up Morrison had to be close to, or in, the Boltman company. The answer wasn't down here; it was back up there in Boltman's magnificent glass and fieldstone donut. Specifically, in the finance department.

After a quick breakfast then departure with the cabs now running, I was back in the air heading northeast. And mulling again. As southwestern Texas morphed into Louisiana, I centered on the obvious: Paul Morrison's fatal Houston trip was an elaborate plan to silence him over something he knew about Boltman's four-person finance department.

Penetrating a big company's – hell, any company's – financial ops wasn't in my job description. I needed an inroad. And I thought I knew how to get one.

Marsha Franklin and I met at her apartment on Saturday, the day after my return to Philadelphia. On the second floor of a walk-up, she lived not in the splendor suburban Upper

Darby implied, but in tasteful, working-girl neatness. Living room, bedroom, kitchenette. I noted a computer and printer set-up in a corner near the kitchen entrance.

In mid-morning lavender slacks and short-sleeved white shirt, she perched apprehensively on the end of a flowered sofa. I took the adjacent armchair, put a mug of coffee she'd offered on a nearby end table, and gave her a reassuring smile.

"First, let me fill you in on what night manager Holt seemed convinced happened down there," I told her Erwin's fraternity joke confession. Took a sip of coffee while she pondered. "Sounds more than a touch nutso to me," I said, "but Erwin seemed sold on it. You happen to know Paul's college?"

"University of Pennsylvania, right here in Philadelphia."

"How about Charley Davenport."

"You think he-"

"He struck me as a jokester. So going along with Erwin's story, Charley's got to be the prime suspect."

"You can forget about Charley. He's a University of Maryland grad."

"Nobody else would have the info to pull it off, so trash the prankster theory. Unless-"

"Unless?"

"Unless it was laid on Erwin exactly as he described it, but used as a cover-up to an intricately plotted murder. Consider this: How would some old college buddy not associated with Boltman know Paul would fly to Houston? And when? Paul himself didn't know until the day he was sent. And why was he sent?"

She stared at me. "You're saying Charley set up Paul, wanted him killed? Why in the world would Charley- Oh! Because of what Paul found out."

"Spoken like a true Mensa member."

Her hand flicked to her collar. "You know about the red-headed pin. You're very observant, P.I. Montgomery."

"Noticed it when we met in your office. But you're not wearing it now."

"I wear it at work as a sort of defiance, I guess."

"'Ha, ha, you clods. I'm smarter than you think.'"

She smiled. "Precisely."

"OK, smartie, how am I doing so far?"

"You're leaving the tough part to me. Whatever obviously troubled Paul, something so serious it got him killed, has to be right there in our finance department."

"We're both on the same wavelength, Marsha. Problem now is, I have no way of probing further."

"And I do."

"I hope."

She pondered. Then she said, "You're looking for some aberration that-"

"That proves old-fashioned crookery with the accounts. My uninformed guess. But I have no way to unearth it."

"You're thinking: The department's computer data."

"Vanoppen calls you the department's 'paper pusher,' but I did note a computer on your desk. And..." I nodded toward her electronics' set-up.

"The paper I 'push' at work does come out of my computer there."

I took another drag of coffee. "Does your office computer give you access to Charley's and Paul's?"

"Not officially, but when they had computer hang-ups, they asked me for help. So, yes, I have their passwords. Gives me access even from here."

"Ah so. If you come across anything 'helpful,' let me be the first – hell, only one – to know."

I stood, thanked her for the coffee and impending expertise, and drove back to my split-level office.

Two days later, nothing. I phoned a "progress" report to client Joanne Morrison, summarizing my encounter with Erwin Holt down Texas way. It sounded like progress but not the kind that would lead to resolution. That, I hoped, would come from Marsha Franklin's after-hours computer probing.

At 10:30, three nights later, she called. "I've waded through a mountain of download from Charley's computer, and I've found a discrepancy."

"Discrepancies are gratefully received here. Whatchoo got, Marsha?"

"It's in the incoming billing from three big suppliers. Some of the payments going out from Boltman were slightly higher than the billings coming in."

"How slightly?"

"Give me a minute."

Several minutes and a spate of clicks later, she said, "Here's an example. Incoming bill from Rockhill Asphalt. This one's for paving a new Boltman mall in Ohio. The billing amount was $1,340,045. Outgoing payment from Boltman; $1,348,045."

"A misprinted 8 in place of the 0?"

"Or eight thousand bucks extracted by a crooked Rockhill bookkeeper who pockets half and sends the other half to-"

"Charley Davenport. No huge swindle. But carried on over some years, it could add up. How many of these 'adjustments' have you turned up?"

"Plowing through twelve months' worth of data, I've found eleven examples of such 'kiting,' I guess you'd call it. The most recent one was a biggie. A $40,000 boost on a $5,430,646 billing for structural steel. The total fraudulent additions for those twelve months is over $127,000."

"Split two ways, not a huge take for a high-risk crookery."

"But carried on at that rate for the five years Charley has been with the company, it could be a nice little salary amplifier."

"And," I said, "a helluva problem when Charley realized Paul had tumbled to what was going on. So Charley sets up Paul's demise. A thousand to Erwin Holt. Wonder how much

Charley paid Lesch for his part?" Another thought fired in my reeling brain. "What about Vanoppen?"

"I wonder about him, too." But he doesn't have an office computer, so we'll have to depend on what I'm sure the newspapers would, or will, call a 'widening investigation.'"

"I owe you one, Marsha."

"The big thank-me should come from Boltman. I could be the lonely heifer left standing in the pen when the bulls are gone. Could be worth a lot more hay than I'm getting now."

"Mensa, Mensa, Mensa. I still owe you one. But first, I'm calling the cops."

I wasn't sure who had police jurisdiction at Willow Grove, so I left that up to my lone friendly Philly contact, Lt. Stan Phipps.

"You've got the thing solved, and you're turning it over to me?"

"Like any P.I., I could make a citizen's arrest. But I don't even carry a gun, Stan. You know I'm more the researcher type. Whoever actually takes Charley Davenport in and gets him convicted gets the credit. I don't want publicity. It gets in my way."

"I'll be in touch."

And he was, two weeks later. The pinch was scheduled for 10:00 on a Wednesday morning at Boltman's finance office bullpen. I was invited.

I got there a few minutes early, greeted Marsha with a smile and a little nod.

Charley glanced over. "Ah, the shamus! You turn up anything new? Or are you hooked on Marsha's schoolmarm hair and horn rims?"

Then he peered past me. I looked around at a group of two plainclothes and two uniformed cops striding toward us around the corridor's curve.

Charley shoved back his chair, jumped to his feet, then made a rush for the hallway. And I finally contributed my one and only physically aggressive participation in this whole caper.

As Charley charged through the bullpen's opening, apparently making a panicky rush out of here, I stuck out my foot. Charley sprawled flat onto the hallway carpet and was yanked back up in handcuffs.

As the cops prodded Charley back down the hall, I told Marsha, "I still owe you."

"You don't owe-"

"At least dinner tonight."

"Well... OK."

In the short run, Vanoppen proved to be innocent of embezzlement but guilty of slipshod management. In the not much longer run, Marsha became his temporary then permanent replacement.

Swordfish steak for her, T-bone for me. And I found our dinner a treat well beyond the menu. For the occasion, Marsha literally let her hair down and shoved her klutzy glasses in her purse. Quite a breathtaking transformation. But she still wore her little red-topped Mensa pin, something of a don't-count-your-chickens message?

Well, who knows, I thought. The night was still young.

FLOATER

Whe he caught sight of the object in the canal behind his house, Sam Wolff thought it was a manatee, not an uncommon visitor this time of year on their Southwest Florida barrier island.

"I don't think so, Sammy," Myra Wolff said, her butterless melba toast arrested halfway to her mouth. "It's not moving."

They had been enjoying breakfast in the cool of early morning on the canalside upper deck of their piling house. Now their attention was on the large gray object nudging their dock down in the canal.

"Tide's coming in," Sam observed. "It's a dead manatee, drifted in from the bay."

He set down his coffee mug, pushed back from the glass-topped table and walked down the rear steps to the sparse lawn. Out on the dock, he felt like he'd been hit with a jolt of electric current. He stared down at a human body, face down, dressed in gray slacks and a long-sleeved shirt, its left shoulder gently bumping the corner dock piling.

"What is it, Sam?" Myra called up on the deck.

"Don't come down, Honeybun. It's a floater."

He was surprised at his word choice. Too much TV. "A body, Myra. Some unfortunate fellow drowned."

"Omigod!" Myra shrieked. "Should I call Nine-one-one?"

"Oh, yes indeed," Sam shouted back. "But use the regular police number. It's not an emergency now."

Thirteen minutes later, he had a yard full of people.

First to appear was Katherine "Kat" Curtci, promoted to detective just weeks ago. She had lucked out on this one. Assigned the undignified task of checking out a weenie wagger report at the lighthouse end of Malabar Island, she had been muttering to herself such a call should be a uniformed cop's job, when the radio erupted.

The island's thirty-person police department was normally concerned with toad-in-the-toilet and bare-bosom-on-the-beach complaints. A response to an I-found-a-body call was a detective's plum. When it came, Kat was only a quarter mile from the Wolffs' palm-shaded gray piling house.

Out back in the canal was a body, all right. Kat stripped off her shoes, hiked up her skirt and worked her way among the mangroves down the sandy bank to the right of the dock. She waded in ten feet, out to the corpse. The high tide water was warm as blood this overcast August day, but she shuddered as the gook on the canal bottom squeezed through the mesh of her pantyhose. The stench was impressive, but she knew that three minutes of bad odor numbs the olfactory nerves. She could hack it for those three minutes. Then the Wolffs would be admiring the macho lady cop.

For Sam Wolff's benefit up on the dock where he gagged into a handkerchief he'd clamped over his nose, she probed for a pulse. The body's neck felt like clammy chicken skin. Beneath its thick water-soaked black hair, the back of the skull appeared to have been battered inward. She checked the hip pockets of the work pants. Nothing.

Scavengers had already worked on the ears and fingertips. All she could determine at this point was that the body was male, black hair moderately long, and he was dressed in a gray work shirt and gray trousers. Reaching underwater around the hips, she forced her fingers into the front pockets. She felt a hard little object in the left one. A ring. She held it up against the overcast sky. Thin gold with a lilac-colored square-cut stone. About two carats of amethyst, she guessed. What a peculiar item to find in a dead man's pocket.

With the ring clenched in one hand, Kat stood, her five-feet-eleven elevating her to dock level.

"You said you spotted him just a few minutes ago, Mr. Wolff?"

"Yep. Myra and I had just started breakfast when I-"

The howl of multiple sirens drowned out the rest of what he said. The sirens cut off abruptly, doors slammed, and here came at least a third of Malabar Island's PD, all crowding onto the dock until there was no room for its owner.

"Come up out of there, Bela. This one is mine."

Kat glared up at the doughy face of Detective Sergeant Ellis Duckworth. Wouldn't you know he'd be the detective assigned? No love had been lost between them. When Duckworth had heard about her Transylvanian heritage, he'd chortled. "Don't go out on night patrol with Bela LuCurtci." She had surveyed his ballooning waistline and said brightly, "'Thar she blows!'" Thereafter he was known to the entire department as Moby Duck.

"I thought you were all tied up in the rash of burglaries we've been having, Moby." She stepped back from the body and waded toward shore.

"This obviously takes precedence," Duckworth said in a tone he usually reserved for ignorant civilians.

She climbed back up the canal bank, her neatly-trimmed raven hair in disarray. She pulled her shoes onto wet feet. Her navy skirt was water-soaked almost to the waist.

"'The policeman's lot is not a happy one,'" Sergeant Duckworth chortled. He thumbed back the brim of his straw planter's hat. "Cole Porter."

"Gilbert and Sullivan," she grumped, looking back at the corpse in the canal."

"Whatever. How deep is it down there?"

"No need to get your toes tainted, Moby. Male Cauc, about thirty-five-"

"Drowned."

"Nothing in his pockets except-"

"Robbed then drowned... Except what?"

She handed him the ring. He eyed it briefly and dropped it into a plastic evidence bag from his pocket.

"Except the back of the skull shows massive damage-" she managed to get out before Moby butted in again.

"Hit over the head, robbed then drowned-"

"For God's sake, Sergeant, stop hopping to conclusions and listen to me!"

His little eyes glittered. "Got to ya, didn't it? Go back to your unit and put in a call for the county ME."

"You put in the call, Moby; you already told me it's your case."

"C'mon, let's have a little teamwork."

"Yes," she agreed eagerly. "Let's. I want to work on it with you."

He snorted. "In a year, maybe. When you know something. I need-"

"Time of death? Two or three days ago."

He fanned himself with his wide-brimmed hat, exposing a lot of bald skull. Then his bright little eyes almost disappeared in a squint. "Based on what?"

"A body stinks 'til internal gasses form. It's summer here in the sub-tropics, and gas forms in two or three days. Up comes the body."

"Could have been floating for a couple days after it came up."

"Unobserved in a canal or out in the bay? Come on, Moby. It would have been spotted long before now by the daily geezer fishing armada. Huh uh, he came up last night, and the tide drifted him here."

"Call the ME," Duckworth growled, and he turned his back. Hadn't listened to a word she'd said, Kat thought. Then, as she walked back to the canal bank, she noticed he was furiously scrawling in his pocket notebook. Maybe he had listened.

When she returned to dockside a few minutes later, Duckworth had begun to clear the area of extraneous police uniforms. He talked the chalk-faced Wolffs back up to their rear deck, then turned to Kat.

"You, uh, might as well stick around, see what the ME has to say." That was offered in such an offhanded way that she half expected him to dig a self-conscious toe into the lawn and give her an "aw shucks" shrug. Instead, he glared at her, his wide mouth compressed to a razor slash. A body language, "Well?"

"Thanks," she said. "I will."

Cal Hewlett, the county medical examiner, looked up from the body he had rolled over then back again to its original face-down position. Kat noted the wiry little ME, feathers of white hair curling from under his Orioles baseball cap, had spent most of his time fingering the head wound.

"Typical floater," he announced. "Best guess, he's been dead two days, three at most. More likely three, considering the condition of the fingernails. 'Bout to fall off. No ID on him."

Duckworth gazed down from the dock. "Any chance of prints?"

"Nope. Scavengers have seen to that." Hewlett stripped off his latex gloves and dropped them in a plastic bag. He pulled off his cap and ran fingers through unruly white hair. "Mighty peculiar, that ding on the back of the head."

"How so?"

"The lacerations, Moby."

On the dock beside Duckworth, Kat suppressed a grin. The nickname had spread to the ME's office.

"Thought it was a blunt instrument job."

"I think it is, with an added attraction. Under all that hair, he's full of little cuts."

"Cuts?" Duckworth stepped to the edge of the dock and peered down.

Hewlett slapped his baseball cap back in place and pulled its long bill low over his eyes. "'Nuff said for the moment. Fax you my report tomorrow morning latest."

At his rubber-topped steel desk in Malabar Island Police HQ, Duckworth scowled at the fax that had just rolled out of the department's machine. Nursing her Styrofoam cup of dense coffee at the desk in front of his, Kat had swung her chair around.

"Well?" she prompted.

"Weird," Moby offered. He handed her the three-page fax. "You make anything of that?"

Death, she read, resulted from massive cranial trauma caused by two non-penetrating and 16 penetrating wounds.

What in the world...?

The ME had shaved the back of the head and found two parallel non-penetrating injuries, four and a quarter inches apart and three inches long. Each was depressed into the skull a quarter-inch.

Between them were four rows of incisions, four per row, each incision penetrating the skull 3/8 inch. The incisions were at approximately 1-inch intervals in one direction, ½ inch intervals in the other. All were within a 4-inch by 2-inch rectangular pattern.

"So, Bela, what do you make of that?"

"I can't even begin to guess."

He nodded. "Thought so."

"And you?"

"Same. Look, I'm going over to the mainland to check missing persons reports. You... do whatever you can here."

Funny. Kat had felt sublimely confident when she was verbally jousting with Moby Duck. But now that he had, in effect, put her on her own without him here to riposte her wit, she felt as if she were about to plunge face down in the sand. She had completed an exhausting house-to-house on both sides of the canal. Half the homes were owned by winter season residents and currently stood empty. The seven year-rounders whom she had caught at home stated they had neither seen nor heard anything useful.

The sky had cleared. Now the Southwest Florida sun beat down mercilessly. She walked from the last occupied house to her car. Dead end. Except for the peculiar configuration of the fatal wound. What could possibly inflict that geometrically perfect square of sixteen little stabs? Some New Age meat tenderizer mallet? The only such mallet she was familiar with had blunt knobs on its striking face.

She buckled her seat belt, turned the key, flipped the A/C to MAX and backed the Plymouth out of the sand-and-shell drive. Could the pattern have been carefully inflicted by a crazy perp with maybe an Xacto knife or scalpel? Were they dealing with a nutso model builder? A mad doctor?

But what about the two long parallel dents on either side of the recessed square of stab wounds? They sure put a damper on any specialized mallet theory.

Back at MIPD HQ, she pulled in just as Moby was dismounting his own unmarked unit. "Anything?" she called across the roof of the car between them.

"Only missing persons listed with the county sheriff are kids. You got anything?"

"Nope. Half the homeowners are north. The other half neither saw nor heard any evil."

"Not surprised," he said as they walked across the parking area. "Canal's too shallow for a body to be in for long before somebody spotting it. Had to drift in last night, and the Wolffs saw it as soon as they went out on their rear deck."

"We should check the tide tables," Kat suggested.

"Done that. High tide was at 7:40 a.m., just about when the Wolffs spotted the body. My guess is that it came up in the bay just as the tide was turning and drifted on into the canal.

"How far could he drift without being spotted?"

Duckworth grinned. "Checked on that, too. Over at the Coast Guard station on the mainland. If he'd been dropped on the other side of the bay or any real distance from this island, he would have been spotted easily between here and there when he came up. Their best guess is he was dumped on this side of the bay, somewhere between the canal and Lighthouse Point. I took a look over there. Couple docks go out right far into the bay, and most their houses are empty this time of year. My guess is he was dumped from one of them docks, say on Wednesday."

He tossed her a self-satisfied little smirk. "So what have you come up with?"

"Zilch." She hated to admit it, but so far Moby had done all the sleuthing.

They climbed the steps to the PD offices. He held the door for her, but she couldn't help feeling even that little courtesy was a backhanded way of showing her he was the prime mover on this case.

The coffee machine produced its quarter's-worth of bitter brew. She sipped the stuff absently, staring through the squad room's rear window at the little lake out back.

Okay, so he was the prime mover, but now that she really thought about it, what had he moved? The only new data was a best guess that the vic had been dumped in the bay off one of the docks between the canal and Lighthouse Point. That wasn't a whole lot of help, was it? They'd have been better off if-

"Hey, Bela," Duckworth grumped, "quit daydreaming and do something constructive. Way this thing stands now,

Chief McReady'll have us both on the carpet if we don't turn up something useful pretty quick."

She spun around. "Speak for yourself, Moby. What you've got isn't any-" Her voice trailed off. What he'd said had just twanged a subconscious memory. She made a lunge for the Yellow Pages directory in her desk drawer.

At nine the next morning, she drove across the causeway without telling Moby anything. He was still hung up on tidal currents and wasn't in a receptive mood anyway. Let him find his own leads.

All three establishments she had jotted down were on the mainland, normally out of her jurisdiction but not in the investigation of a murder that had taken place on Malabar Island. The first was a gray cinderblock building in a weedy corner of a failed industrial park along the Tamiami Trail. MCNAIR CARPET LAYERS read a florid red and yellow sign over the entrance.

She pulled open the squeaky plywood door and stepped straight into what looked like a semi-deserted supply room with a desk in one corner adjacent to a restroom door.

"Yo!" she shouted. "Anyone here?"

A toilet flushed, and shortly a chunky man with thin sandy hair and a really terrific sunburn emerged from the restroom drying his hands on a paper towel.

"Sorry," he muttered. "Damn boat broke down last weekend. I was out in the sun for hours before anybody came by. I think I've got radiation poisoning, f' Chris'sake." He chucked the wadded towel toward a wastebasket beside the desk and focused on her. "What can I do for you?"

"Detective Curtci, Malabar Island Police. Mr. McNair?"

"The same. You want a rug for your department or your apartment?" that, with a fleeting grin.

"I'd like to take a look at one of those things rug layers use. Pad at one end, kind of a gripper thing at the other."

"A knee-kicker. Sure, got one back here behind the desk."

He bumbled around back there then straightened up holding a device about 18 inches long, telescoping steel tubes with a padded square at right angles on one end. He handed it to her, and she studied the other end. Bingo! Four rows of four half-inch steel spines in a steel rectangle. Just as she'd remembered from the carpeting job she'd had done in her Maryland apartment before she moved down here last year. The carpet layer had slapped the protruding spines into the carpet near its edge then whammed the padded end with his knee. The sliding block of prongs stretched the carpet into place. She'd bet that Moby had never seen one of these. His little bayside house had tile floors.

She hefted the knee-kicker. Yes, it would make an efficient if clumsy murder weapon. She handed it back to McNair.

"How many companies in this area use these things?"

McNair scratched a shoulder and winced. "There's a bunch of carpet companies, but none of them have in-house layers. They all subcontract to one of us."

"I found Yellow Pages listings for just three carpet installers. There are only three?"

"That's right. There's me, there's A-One Carpets over on Gulf Road, and there's Redhen Layers up on Riveredge Street."

"Redhen Layers — are they for real?"

"Named after the owner, Gustave Redhen. Play on words gets him remembered, but it's the quality of work that counts."

"How is a carpet-laying job handled?"

"Teams of two. It's real specialized. I'm lucky to have three teams on the payroll."

"Have you had any contracts over on the island in the past week?"

"Huh-uh. Wish we had."

"None of your teams assigned over there?"

"Told you, no."

"Well, I thank you, Mr. McNair. You've been a help."

He squinted up at her. "What's this all about?"

"Just routine," she said with a smile. She loved delivering that vapid Hollywood exit line.

She found A-One Carpets in a more congested part of town, sandwiched between Kentucky Fried Chicken and Wendy's. The little clapboard one-story building had been painted a wretched flamingo pink with sea green trim. She parked in one of the spaces out front, not difficult since all six spaces were empty. The day's heat had reached simmer level as she read the typed notice stuck on the aluminum entrance door with masking tape: Closed for Vacation, August 15-31.

That took care of A-One Carpets, unless one of the company's teams was free-lancing. She'd try to check into that if Redhen Layers – Lord, what a name – didn't, uh, hatch out.

The place reeked of cigarette smoke. Gustave Redhen, as tall as she, looked a lot like... Well, he had a cockscomb of rust-colored hair, a scrawny neck, and he carried his beaked-nosed head thrust forward. In the corner of his mouth rested a king-sized smoke.

"What possible interest can the Malabar police have in my little operation?" His voice was high and scratchy. As he spoke, the cigarette bounced in syllable time.

"Maybe none, Mr. Redhen." Hard to say the name with a straight face. "How many teams of carpet layers do you employ?"

"Three. Wish I had more. Good layers are hard to find."

She glanced around the office. Walnut-framed 8-by-10 glossies adorned the stark white walls, photos of Redhen shaking hands with presumably satisfied customers. She recognized one of them as a former U.S. senator. Another was the current mayor.

"You have an illustrious clientele."

"I do all right." His beady little eyes stayed on her. "You are not here on carpet business."

"In a way, I am. Have your people done any work on Malabar Island in the past week, Mr. Redhen?"

"One job, four days ago. Big one. On Strangler Fig Road for a retired head of OT & T. had to send a helper along with them to carry the carpeting in. More than three thousand square feet of it."

"I'd appreciate the customer's name, Mr. Redhen."

He walked to a green steel desk, rifled through a box of file cards and handed one to her.

"May I use your phone?"

"Sure. Right there on the desk."

Beside the phone was a coffee can lid brimming over with stained butts. She pushed it to the farthest corner of the littered desk and dialed the number on the card.

"Mrs. Oliphant? This is Detective Katherine Curtci, Malabar Island Police."

"Yes, Detective?" Mrs. Oliphant's contralto voice was that of a woman not at all intimidated by a call from the police.

"I understand you had new carpeting laid several days ago."

"Yes, last Wednesday."

"By a crew of three men."

"There were three when they started. I went out for several hours, and when I returned, there were only two. They told me the third man had come along only to help them carry the new carpeting in and the old carpeting out. He wasn't needed for the actual installation."

"You left the crew in the house by themselves, Mrs. Oliphant?"

"Well, I hadn't planned to, but an emergency came up. My daughter lives here on the island, and her son had fallen and cut himself badly. I babysat her youngest while she took the boy to the doctor."

"And when you returned to your house, there were only two carpet men?"

"Yes, as I've already told you."

So she had. Kat thanked her and hung up with her thought processor in overdrive.

"Where is the crew that did Oliphant's work?" she asked Redhen.

"Back on the island. Woody and Tiny." The cigarette joggled in his mouth. He squinted against its eye-searing smoke tendrils. "They're installing carpet in an unfurnished spec house. Four thirty-six Paperbark Lane."

"They'll be there now?"

Redhen shrugged. "Should be. It's an all-day job."

She got out of that choking atmosphere and in the parking area took her first deep breath since she'd gone in.

The house was another piling structure. She climbed the entrance steps and opened the door without knocking. The gray-painted rough-cut wood exterior belied the sumptuous interior. Though the place was devoid of furniture, she could see the money. Across the gymnasium-sized great room, two men banged away at their knee-kickers to secure rich gold carpeting along the sliding door access to a huge deck beyond.

"Woody and Tiny?"

The sound of her voice whirled both of them around.

"Detective Curtci, Malabar Island Police."

They crouched motionless and wordless.

"Which one of you is Woody?"

"That'll be me." The man on the left stood clumsily, no doubt having been on his knees most of the day. "Ed Woodworth." He was a skinny whip of a guy. In his late thirties, she judged.

Dark hair beginning to thin. A face narrow as Fred Astaire's in late-night movies.

"And you must be Tiny." The other rug mechanic was only fifty pounds shy of Sumo requirements, she thought, as he struggled to his feet.

"Yeah, that's me," he rumbled through his dense beard. Charles Birch. What's the beef?"

Kat walked to the counter that divided the open kitchen area from the rest of the room and placed her open handbag in easy reach. Her 17-shot 9mm Glock was top item in there. She leaned against the counter with her right hand resting near the handbag.

"Well, gentlemen, maybe you can clear up something that's bugging me. On the Oliphant job, I'm told there were three of you at the start and just two at the finish. What happened to the third man?"

She caught their furtive glances at each other. Paydirt!

"He cut out around noon," Woody said. "When he broke for lunch. Asked him would he want to go back to the Beachwalk Café with us, he said no, and when we came back maybe thirty, forty minutes later, he was gone."

Through that, Woody's eyes were all over the room, and his blink rate quadrupled. Throw in his convulsing Adam's apple, she thought, and you've got yourself a liar here.

"Does that square with your version?" she asked Tiny.

"Huh. Whatever— Oh, yeah. Sure does."

"What was the man's name?"

"Ganelli," Woody offered, "or Gianelli. Something like that."

"You didn't know him?"

"He came up from one of those labor pool outfits. We picked him up in town. No, we didn't know him. He was a temp. Lotta them are drifters. They come and go."

Kat let that simmer a long moment. Then she said, "If the three of you came in the truck I saw parked outside, and this Gianelli disappeared around noon, how did he get back to the mainland?"

Another silence. Then Woody said, "Hitched a ride, maybe?"

It came out as a question. These two were simply atrocious liars. She gave them another long, silent stare. That produced a lot of shifting footwork and throat clearings on the other side of the room.

Then she offered what she hoped came off as a warm and friendly smile. "Oh, come on, you two. You just aren't very good at the cover-up game. What really happened that day in the Oliphant house?"

Woody stared at her like a man ready to bolt. Tiny hunched his hairy face down between his huge shoulders. A man ready to charge? Kat's fingers slipped toward a reassuring touch of the Glock.

"This Gianelli," she said, "was he a white man, medium build, fairly long black hair?"

"That's about right." Woody's voice sounded as if he were strangling.

"He floated into a canal yesterday. With a bash in the head that looks exactly like the working face of those knee-kickers you're using. When I take them in for testing, I wouldn't be surprised to find traces of blood on one of them."

Tiny's glittery little eyes held hers for a long moment. Then he astounded her. His huge legs gave way. With a moan, he sank to the floor with his hands thrust out palms-up in a really supplicating gesture.

"Damn, Woody. I tol'ja-"

"A nightmare," Woody blurted. "That's what it was. Still is."

Kat's heart pumped furiously. "What happened?"

"Gianelli was a goddamn thief," Woody burst out. "That's what happened. I figure the som' bitch took labor jobs to case houses, or if he could, swipe stuff while he was on a legit job. That's what he did here soon's the old lady left."

"That's the God's truth," Tiny boomed. "I caught him about to lift stuff in the bedroom. Outta a jewelry box half an hour after the missus left."

Ergo, the ring in the vic's pants pocket. "Then?" Kat prompted.

"Then," Woody said with a shudder, "he pulled a gun on us. Said to back off and let him get out of there with what he'd grabbed, or he'd plug both of us. A real bad situation. He goes, we get blamed. So there's him in the bedroom with a gun on Tiny. Me in the great room with only a knee-kicker in my hand. So I-"

Kat shot out her left arm, hand up in a stop signal. "Hold it right there. We're going to make this nice and clean. You have the right to remain silent-" she recited the entire Miranda warning.

"Hell with that!" Woody's eyes were huge in his narrow face. "I gotta get this off my chest, now I've gone this far. I never felt so bad in my whole life like I did these past coupla days."

He swallowed hard. "It was like this, see? Tiny backs outta the bedroom into the great room. Alla time, Gianelli – or whatever his name was – has a damned .45 on him. So when Tiny backs through the door, I'm flat against the wall. As soon as he's all the way in, I rap him with the knee-kicker."

"Some rap," Kat said. "You stove in his skull."

"That made us both sick, sick and scared. We panicked. Rolled him in a piece of the old carpet and stowed him in the trunk until quittin' time. Then we drove out to the east end of the island and waited 'til it got dark."

"Sure takes a long time to get dark," Tiny said.

Woody shot him an impatient look. "When it did, we carried him out on one of the docks and dropped him in. figured the tide'd carry him out to the gulf."

"And the gun?" Kat asked.

"Threw that in, too. A diver could find it."

"What you didn't know," she said, "is a body first sinks then comes back up a few days later. "You're both under arrest," she added conversationally.

Woody's voice was suddenly scratchy. "For murder?"

"For various," she said. "Sit down, both of you. I've got to cuff you. Regulations."

She fished in her handbag. She had only one pair, so she cuffed Woody's skinny wrist to Tiny's huge one. Neither of them, to her immense relief, showed the slightest sign of resistance.

She took out her cell phone. When Moby answered the phone in the squad room, she said sweetly, "Any progress?"

"Damn right!" he boomed. "Got an assist lined up from the FBI to help us figure out the wound pattern. That's a big step forward. So what have you done?"

"Oh, I found out what the murder weapon was, though I think this case could end up being a matter of self-defense-"

"Jeez! What was the weapon?"

She ignored that. "Also determined who the victim was — and he just might have been the series burglar you've been beating your brains out to find."

"Wha — Who-"

"And I know who did him in. There are two of them."

Silence. Then, "Come on, woman, give!"

"I have them shackled right here with me. Read them the Miranda. Now I'm-"

"Where!" Duckworth boomed. He sounded as if he were strangling. "How!" Another pause. Then he said, much quieter, "You're kidding me, Detective?"

"Would I ever kid you, Moby?"

His voice sounded as if he'd just been hit in the gut as he asked. "Do you need back-up?"

She gave him a silvery chuckle. "That could be helpful, Detective Duckworth. We're at Four thirty-six Paperbark, and we'll wait."

LAST THE BEST

When Alban "Sicko" Van Ness was released on a technicality, Detective Kat Curtci fought her almost overpowering compulsion to scream at the judge: You fat-faced, dull-brained idiot! The man's a menace.

That might be emotionally satisfying, but Kat knew such an outburst would be career suicide. And the legal lapse had been her own doing. So she silently cursed herself for being an over-eager cop. Van Ness's running a stop sign had brought the man to Kat's attention. She was standing beside her computer when NCIC's data on Van Ness rolled out of the printer. Some rap sheet! It even included his nickname, "Sicko." He had last been detained on suspicion of B & E in Indianapolis, got out of that on a technicality also. Currently, he wasn't wanted anywhere. Here he was vacationing – or maybe something less innocent – on her beat, Southwest Florida's laid-back Malabar Island.

Boy Wonder Brice, the arresting officer at the stop sign bust, had been distraught over a lack of outstanding warrants on Van Ness. He was hot to nail the guy for something more career-enhancing than running a damned stop sign, but in the squad room, Chief McReady put the quietus on Brice's eagerness.

"You're assigned to traffic, Brice. Detective work we leave to the detectives." Whereupon the chief gave Kat a copy of Brice's arrest report. Brice bristled at that, and McReady swung back to him. "I'm well aware of your beef: she's new, and you're yearning. But she came here with FBI crime scene training. Life is unfair. Now get back out there, Brice, and do something constructive about the winter season traffic."

"Friend Brice is leaving in a high dudgeon," Detective Duckworth murmured to Kat.

"Drives better than his customary blue funk," she riposted with a straight face.

Van Ness's local address was an isolated rental beach house on Lonely Bayou at the north end of the island. Kat made it a point to drive out there frequently, but all was serene until the night of January 18. A cinder block through Island Jewelry's display window was the smash part of the smash-and-grab that relieved the shop of $10,000 in gold baubles.

The case was Kat's, and she knew who had done it. Instinct, not evidence. She subsequently saw the evidence through the window of Van Ness's rented house: a black felt Island Jewelry bag carelessly left under a table in the living room. She knocked. No answer.

Then she made the mistake that had just set Van Ness free. She busted into the place – and no one was there. If she'd had a search warrant... But she hadn't, and now in the county courtroom, Van Ness walked past her, a free Sicko, his chilly blue eyes riveting on her as he strode by. His bloodless lips moved. *Watch your ass.* An icicle slid up her spine.

"It's nothing to worry about," Kat's sometimes partner Ellis "Moby Duck" Duckworth told her as they inched through the heavy seasonal traffic on Melaleuca Way, Malabar's main drag.

"Then why are we riding together, Mobe? You supposed to be keeping an eye on me?"

Duckworth, his impressive gut just short of impeding the steering wheel, chuckled. "Call it reorientation, Bela." He'd hung her with that handle when he'd heard her father was a Romanian exile from the Transylvanian Alps region.

"Hey," Moby said into the air-conditioned silence. "Don't take this as a reprimand. You just got a little ahead of yourself, that's all."

"I should have known better than to bust in without a warrant."

"Yeah, you shoulda."

"By the time I got one, he would have gotten rid of the evidence."

"Yeah, he woulda."

"Stop that, Moby! I'm trying to make some serious points here. If I – WATCH IT!"

Ahead, an Ohio Chevy had stopped dead. Moby rammed down the brake pedal, stood their unmarked Ford on its nose, and squealed to a halt ten inches short of disaster.

"Jeez! I'm going to have seat belt burns in five-mile-an-hour-traffic."

"Eyes on the road, Detective," she said. "Listen, how long do we play partner?"

"Want it straight?"

"No other way."

"Until I'm convinced you're not going to go flying off on your own and try something else stupid."

Kat turned to gaze at Moby's doughy face with its three chins. Her dark eyes narrowed. "What's it going to take?"

"Your word."

"You kidding?"

"I know it's a mission impossible. But that's what McReady wants. I think he sees me as your father image."

"I've got my own father, thank you. And I'm a big girl."

"Yeah, I've noticed that. Five-ten?"

"Five-eleven, stocking feet." She tossed back her mane of coal-black hair and gave him an exaggerated shrug. "So, okay, Dad, I'll be a good girl."

"And not burst into any more houses like that. And maybe even get in touch with me if you're in doubt."

"About what?"

"About anything, Bela."

His tone surprised her. The big lunk sounded as if he really cared.

"Okay."

"Okay, what?" he pressed.

"Okay, I'll get in touch when I have a problem bigger than I can cope with."

He turned to grin at her.

"Mobe, watch the damned road!"

He kept grinning. "You're a real case, Bela."

"How so?"

"You don't think you ever will have a problem you can't handle, do you?"

"Not if I stop raiding empty houses." He was right, though. She knew damned well she could handle anything that came her way.

That was before she got the valentine.

In was in her mailbox two days later, the traditional red heart-shaped box, an inch deep, sealed with Scotch tape. Her name was hand-written on a piece of paper taped to the top of the box. She walked slowly from the mailbox up her sand-and-shell drive, flipping through unwanted catalogs and a couple of bills. She studied the box again. No stamps. Somebody had personally slipped it into the box.

She grinned. Moby, you're a surprisingly sentimental old tub of lard.

In the kitchen, she slit the cellophane tape with a paring knife, set the box on the counter and slipped off the cover. Chocolate covered cherries, she hoped. She had a thing for choc–

"My God!" She jumped back in horror. Coiled inside the box was a black racer, surely a yard long, and very dead. The scales were shiny blue-black, terminating in raw scarlet where the head had been chopped off.

The chill that shot through her turned hot. She pulled out one of the dinette chairs and sat down hard. Her fingers trembled, and a fine sheen of perspiration broke across her forehead.

"Oh, damn it!" she moaned. Then, as a cop, she forced herself to look at the box and its incredible, grisly contents.

Fingerprints? Could be, if she hadn't smeared them all with hers. Anybody notice the delivery of this... this thing? She lived pretty well isolated here at the end of Strangler Fig Lane. Only two other houses in the quarter-mile stretch from Melaleuca Way. She would ask, of course.

But first, and she hated herself for the way her mind jumped right to it, she was going to call Moby.

She grabbed the phone, pressed 472... Then she set the phone back in its cradle. This was the act of a panicky woman, not a cop. So she'd gotten a snake valentine from a sick-in-the-head non-admirer. Morning was soon enough to mention it to Duckworth. There wasn't anything wrong in taking precautions, though.

She took her bath with her ugly standard issue 9mm Glock 17 on the floor beside the tub. She tried to let the sudsy sandalwood warmth dissolve her disgust at what now lurked in her refrigerator, and she wondered if she'd really been smart to move out of the rented condo into this cheaper but far more isolated bayside home.

When the fat detective arrived to pick her up at 8 a.m., he got in the first word.

"I think this procedure might be kinda dumb, Bela. Ride with you on day-shift then leave you alone out here all night. Know what I'm saying?"

She held the door open for him. "Come on in. I've got something to show you."

She took the heart-shaped box out of the refrigerator by its edges. No sense putting more prints on it than she had to. "This little gift arrived in my curbside mailbox by unseen messenger yesterday. Might be prints on it, but take a look."

Carefully fingering only the box sides, he jiggled the top off. "JEEZ!" Duckworth recoiled two steps backward. "Who in the hell– Oh, Van Ness, of course."

"It would seem so. He didn't wait long to get started, did he? Well, his prints surely are in the Indianapolis AFIS, so if he was as careless with this repulsive little token as he is obvious, we should be able to nail him fast as a fax."

Duckworth yanked off his sweat-stained golf hat and mopped his forehead with a blue bandana. "Jeez, I hate snakes. What kind of moron-"

"It's not so much the snake," she broke in as she slid her Glock into her handbag. "Why did he lop off its head?"

When they were side by side in Duckworth's unmarked unit, he reached for the key. Then he paused. "Maybe he found it that way. Y'know, saw it dead on the road somewhere and that gave him the idea. Could be that's all there is to it."

"That's one way of looking at it," she agreed. But she didn't think so.

"Anybody on this road see the delivery?"

"I checked them by phone before you got here. Negative from one. The other recalled only a police unit on patrol."

He turned the key, and they rolled into the day's first assignment, routine investigation of a break-in at the Scoop Du Jour ice cream store in the Malabar Pines Shopping Center.

On their way south, they passed Brice's unit heading north on his traffic patrol. He scowled as they rolled by.

"Now there's a guy too eager and much too arrogant for his own good," Moby said. "Instead of having his nose to the grindstone, he always seems to have his finger in the air."

Around one, they stopped at the Nations Bank branch so she could use the ATM.

"Hey!" He'd rolled down the driver's side window to call after her, "Catch you here in ten minutes. A burger okay? Then we'll hit that stolen boat complaint out on the south end."

She nodded, not thrilled by the prospect of a fat-laden offering from the Garden of Eatin', but she would offset it tonight with a green salad and nothing more. A few extra pounds might not show on her lank frame, but she could always feel them.

Kat walked up the bank's entrance steps. The ATM was to the right of the doors. She stood back and waited in the unshaded Florida heat while an outsider in white ducks and a green sports shirt alternatively muttered and kicked at the machine's base.

"Hate the goddamn thing," he grumped as he walked past without looking at Kat.

She stepped up and accomplished her $65 grocery money withdrawal without trouble. Even under the bank's portico, she could feel the sun's power.

Then she felt something else. A quick little chill, but not one of temperature. She swung around. Just the row of empty cars in the bank's parking lot. Nothing but non-threatening tourist traffic out on Melaleuca Way. Even one of Malabar's own green-and-whites waited at the corner stop sign for a break in the through traffic.

Then Duckworth pulled into the lot and stopped at the bottom of the stairs.

"You set?" he called.

"Yep." She slid into the A/C coolness. Real coolness, not the freakish little ripple she'd had up by the AATM. A cold flash? Come on, Kat.

She fastened her seat belt, and Duckworth nosed into the eastbound snail's pace.

The picture arrived in the next day's mail. There she stood, her back to the camera but her head half turned from the ATM so that it was obviously she. Nice fast work, Postal Service. Would that all first-class mail came as promptly. But it really hadn't been much of a trick. Drop it at the Malabar P.O. before five, and local delivery would handle it the next day.

Even photo processing could be had in an hour at two island locations. Take a pic and have it hot from the processing machine 60 minutes later, guaranteed.

Of course, Van Ness was too clever for that. He knew she certainly would check with every hour-photo processing set-up within a plausible driving distance.

Not a chance of that, Kat realized as she stared at the tiny but heart-chilling feature that made this picture a real stand-out. The guy had used Polaroid. An untraceable print developed right in his camera. Smart, Van Ness. And you really know how to pull my string. Across her neck in the photo, he had drawn a fine line with red ink.

"A decapitated snake. A photo with a cutthroat. Oh, I'm just having a ball, Moby," she said into her phone slippery with palm sweat.

"I'm gonna pick up that som' bitch right now!" Duckworth barked.

"That sounds fine, but we both know you can't. No proof. The Valentine box turned out to be clean except for my prints and yours. You know there won't be any prints on the Polaroid. We've got nothing solid on him. And what if we had? What's the penalty in Florida for sending a snake and a photo to a cop? He's laughing while I'm sweating."

Duckworth was silent. Then he said, much more calmly, "You want I should come over?"

She almost blurted, Yes, yes, for God's sake! Not like herself at all, that panicky impulse. Damn it, she was an experienced detective, a big girl – two inches taller than Moby Duck, come to think of it.

"No," she said. "He's getting his kicks from taunting me. It's becoming something of a pattern."

She pulled a knife from the kitchen drawer. Be an interesting moment for Van Ness to show up, wouldn't it, with her standing there armed with a 10-inch pig sticker. She grunted with a trace of humor at the thought and began chopping carrots for her atonement salad.

The phone rang at nine, just as she was about to switch to Unsolved Mysteries. Moby again.

But it wasn't.

"Detective Curtci." A harsh whisper, and so close, as if he had the phone almost to his mouth.

She said nothing. Hang up, she would have told any victim of a call like this. But she didn't.

"Did you enjoy your valentine, Detective? And your portrait?

Well, that neatly connected him with those incidents. She was surprised at how well a whisper disguised a voice. But would she have recognized Van Ness's natural voice? She'd heard him mutter only a few words to the judge. Wasn't there some way to wrap him up for delivery back to the court, this time with the hard evidence of threatening the life of a police officer? Which, she realized, he actually hadn't done.

"Cat got your tongue, Katherine?"

"Listen to me, Van Ness!" she bristled. "So far all you've done is threatened. Leave it at that. And get your ugly butt out of this part of the country. Because I swear-"

"Oh, my, such a temper!" the hideous in-her-ear whisper taunted with a sibilant little chuckle. "Ever hear this one, Katherine? 'First, the worst, second the same. Last the best of all the game.'"

The line went dead.

She stared at the handset. First, the worst, second the same... It was a kid's rhyme. First had come the headless snake. Second was the throat-slit Polaroid.

Last was the best of all the game.

My God, what would that be?

With shaking fingers, she tapped in Duckworth's number, hating herself for it.

He wasn't there. Oh, God. She had a wild impulse to "call the police," but she was the police. A 911 call would unleash seven kinds of confusion, and just because she'd had a whisper call that technically hadn't been threatening at all.

Enjoy your valentine?

Cat got your tongue?

Such a temper!

First, the worst, second the same...

That would look just great in the responding officer's report. There wasn't any love lost in the ranks for her ascendancy to detective status, but they'd just love this.

It came down to securing the house as best she could and sleeping with her gun. Locks and Glock. Why hadn't she done something about the sliding glass doors to the lanai off the kitchen? The right tools and you could probably lift them right out of their tracks. Why hadn't she done something about that? If he did work on the glass doors, at least there'd be noise. She hoped. And believe me, she told herself, I'm an instant light sleeper.

Not in her bed. She hoped extra blankets properly plumped would look enough like her sleeping. In black slacks and a dark blouse, she opted for the wicker chaise in a secluded corner of the living room. The Glock, with 17 in the clip and one in the chamber, lay in her lap.

The silence itself was scary. As her eyes adapted to the darkness, wan starlight made hazy rectangles of the two windows across the room. The tiniest of moves made the wicker crack beneath her. She waited.

Then she thought, this is useless. The chances of Van Ness showing up are… what? One in a hundred? Better than that. Much better. Was it the blood of ancestral Romany gypsies that made her so certain he would show? Last the best of all the game. He was coming.

From the kitchen, a loud creak made her heart race. Settlement groan? Her fingers trembled on the pistol's chunky plastic grip.

This had to be incredibly stupid, sitting here waiting for a looney to break and enter. She should have taken up Moby's offer to babysit. God, it was hot in here. She had killed the A/C's rattle. But suddenly it went on. No, no, that was the refrigerator, its hum exaggerated by her over-sensitized hearing.

She caught herself drowsing and shook her head to clear the gathering cobwebs. Checked the luminous dial of her watch. Twelve-thirty. Twelve-thirty! She must have slept for nearly 15 minutes. That would never do.

Was she overreacting to nothing more worrisome than a joker who got his kicks from threatening then leaving his victim enmeshed in self-regenerating fear? Maybe Van Ness was already halfway to Orlando, chortling at how cleverly he had–

What was that? Another house noise… No, it was the kind of metallic grating that would be made by somebody prying up a sliding glass panel of the lanai entrance. She'd asked for this, hadn't she? She'd known how easily those panels could be lifted out, and she'd done nothing about it.

She wanted Van Ness in here. Wanted him in here so she could blast him out of her life. Aren't you the cold-blooded bitch, she marveled at herself. But her mouth went dry at the realization.

Now the house was alive with stealthy rustles. Imagination, or nutso Van Ness creeping in? She sat statue-still, the gun held in front of her in both trembling hands.

A shadow drifted soundlessly across the dim window rectangles. Not even the merest of bumps against a chair or the coffee table. He must have checked out the house through the windows while she was on duty. Ice water broke across her shoulders. Incredible how silently he moved. Toward the bedroom. Into the bedroom, she heard a ripping sound, a burst of breath expelled.

Now she sensed rather than she saw he was in the bedroom doorway trying to pierce the darkness, trying to find her.

His voice was low and raspy. "Cute trick. But it won't help."

A new jolt of fear heightened her senses. She could see his dim form against a less dense grayness of the bedroom behind him.

He moved forward. "I see you now! See your watch."

The damned luminous dial! "Stop right there, Van Ness. Hands behind your neck." Her voice sounded a lot steadier than she felt. "Another step and you're a dead man."

"Ah, Bela, you don't have the guts." And he lunged for her.

With a two-handed grip, she aimed where his chest should be —

Bela?

Barely in time, she jerked the gun downward and fired three quick shots.

The charging figure crashed to the floor. There was a moment of absolutely dead silence. Then she heard someone banging into the kitchen through the lanai entrance, someone with heavy feet. A blinding shaft of white light shot across the room, darted about, then centered on the fallen man — a husky man, all in black, wearing a black ski mask, groaning in pain. A boning knife glittered on the carpet near his right hand.

"You okay, Bela?" said the voice behind the flashlight. Duckworth.

"You're a tad late, Moby," Kat managed.

"I got to thinking about you isolated out here with this guy on the prowl. Drove out, didn't see any car but yours, started to check out the house, saw the lanai doors had been forced. Heard the shots and damn near busted my butt charging into your kitchen."

He played the flash over the crumpled man on the floor. "Looks like you took pretty good care of Van Ness all by yourself."

"It's not Van Ness," she said.

"Say what?"

"He called me Bela. Nobody outside the department would know that. He's one of our own."

"Which is why you knee-capped him instead of following regs and shooting for the chest?"

"Something like that."

"Well, let's see who this som' bitch is." He bent down and jerked off the ski mask. "Shoulda guessed," he said into the pain-contorted face of Boy Wonder Brice. "You really did resent Bela here Leap-frogging over you. Looks like the department was right in holding you back, you miserable excuse for a cop."

"Ambulance," Brice muttered. "I need an ambulance."

"I'll call it in," Kat offered. She stood on rubbery legs and hit the room's light switch. In the glare of the ceiling floods, Brice's right leg was twisted in a way legs don't normally twist. Blood pooled beneath the shattered knee.

After everyone else had cleared out in the wake of the ambulance's howling departure, she managed to put coffee together. She and Moby sat in her kitchen wide awake at two-thirty a.m.

"Found Brice's car one street over." Moby's thick fingers turned his coffee mug around and around. "Must have walked here along the shoreline." He shook his head slowly. "I feel like a real idiot assuming it was Van Ness."

"That makes two of us. It's pretty obvious now. Brice figured he could get me out of the way and Van Ness would be blamed. I wouldn't be surprised if Brice's next move was to track down Van Ness and rig a 'suicide.' That would have tied it all up in a neat package."

Duckworth nodded. "If you hadn't been so fancy with that pistol, Kat, you could have been one dead cop."

She nodded.

"Lemme ask you something. If you hadn't tumbled to the Bela thing, would you have shot to kill?"

"Yes."

"You should have asked for more help early on, kid."

"Can't argue with that."

He set down his cup and cocked his head. "Kat, are you putting me on?"

"Would I ever do that, Moby?"

Kat. He was calling her Kat.

He'd crashed in a little after the fact, a little late, but all on his own, this fat, sloppy - wonderful man got here for her.

She felt a wild impulse to leap up, grab him and dance around the kitchen. But she settled for another cup of coffee.

CUT AND DRIED

On a slow night when Malabar Island Detective Kat Curtci and Detective Sergeant "Moby" Duckworth were on their second mugs of coffee, the call came over the radio speaker from Officer Sid Durnham, a uniform on routine patrol.

"I've responded to… ah, an apparent suicide by gunshot at Three Thirty-six Sanseviera Lane. Who's catching?"

Kat strode to the radio set-up in the corner of the near-deserted squad room and grabbed the mike. "Curtci and Duckworth on our way, Durnham. Secure the scene and stay out of it. Do you read?"

"Roger, but EMS is already here."

"Do the best you can. Curtci out."

She banged the mike back down on the desk. "Let's get out there, Moby, before Durnham and EMS make a promenade of the crime scene."

"Who said it was a crime?" Duckworth muttered as they rushed for the department's unmarked Dodge.

"Reflex, I guess. You've got a point. Durnham did say suicide."

The house was one of the remaining one-story ground-levels built before federal flood regs put later barrier island houses up on pilings. The place at this midnight hour was an island of light in a humid sea of inky black. Malabar PD required investigation of suicides, thus Kat's and Moby's arrival on the scene. They parked behind two emergency vehicles – lights still flashing - and Durnham's green-and-white. He awaited them at the front door, a worried little man in Malabar chocolate brown, bare-headed, running his billed cap through fidgety fingers.

"Jeez!" Moby peered through the open front door. "It's a three-ringer in there."

"I told them, Sarge. I told them EMS people to be careful."

On rational second thought, Kat wondered how do you secure a scene with an ambulance full of dedicated paramedics thundering inbound in search of a spark of life?

"Fill us in," she suggested.

Durnham's bony face swung her way, looked up. Almost everyone in the department had to look up at five-foot-eleven Detective Curtci, which, she knew, aggravated the majority. Except Moby. A porky five-seven or so, he was too near retirement to give a damn about comparative statures.

"You know them medics," Durnham pleaded. "The victim was still breathing when I got here, and they all barreled in. No use though. Died just before I called you. Now they're packing up to leave."

"We're sure you've done your best." Kat resisted the temptation to pat the distraught and defensive officer on his sweaty little balding head. "Now fill us in."

"Albert Brandenburg, he-"

"Brandenberg, the contractor?" Moby put in. "The guy who built most of Leisure Estates over on the mainland?"

"That's the guy."

"He killed hisself?"

"No, Sarge, the victim is-"

"Victim?" Kat said.

"Sorry. I'm a little shook up." Durnham took a deep breath, blew it out in a shaky gust. "I'm a traffic-ticket ace. Women shot in the head aren't on my usual regular agenda."

"Mrs. Brandenberg shot herself?" Kat deduced from Durnham's ramble.

"That's it. I got the mister to stay in the great room, but I couldn't do much about the paramed-"

They were already past him. Beyond the front door was a large, low ceilinged "great room," beigely carpeted wall-to-wall. The far end was mostly sliding glass doors that opened onto a blue-tiled patio and kidney-shaped pool. The outside lights were on back there. The whole place was a blaze of light as if a flood of illumination might burn away the dark hover of tragedy.

Kat's attention was first caught by the cluster of paramedics departing the bedroom to the left. Then, as she swept the room, she saw the man sunken in the wing chair near the glass doors.

"Mr. Brandenberg?" she called.

He barely looked up, a big man with a florid face, now deflated, shrunken. A grief-laden man in maroon pajamas under a royal blue robe.

"Moby," she said quietly, "I'll do him, you do the body."

"Right," he said. No problem with her taking the lead though he had the rank. She knew he no longer cared about rank. He wasn't exactly coasting to retirement, but he wasn't bucking for anything, either. Made him easy to work with... Or, she sometimes wondered, was this his way of, well, seasoning her to the job? Could he be that subtle?

She pulled a straight-backed chair closer to the listless man in pajamas and sat down. "Mr. Brandenberg, I'm Detective Curtci. We are required to investigate situations like this. That's why Sergeant Duckworth and I are here."

"I-" Brandenberg cleared his throat. "I understand."

"I know this is extremely difficult for you, but can you tell me what happened?"

She sat back. Waited.

Silence.

Then it came out in a monotone. "I was watching CNN on the set over there." He aimed a listless thumb at the big-screen TV in the opposite corner. "Heard a shot. Thought it was outside somewhere. Our bedroom door was shut. Then I wondered why Irma hadn't come out to see what it was. I went in the bedroom..." his voice drifted into a croak. "In the bedroom. The lights were on, and she... she..."

"Your wife usually retired before you, Mr. Brandenberg?"

He nodded. "I stay up for the late news."

"At what point did you call Nine One One?"

"When I saw the bullet hole. Took her pulse. Could barely feel it. I called Nine One One right away."

For a normally robust man of about 60, she judged, he looked awful. Cheeks a lifeless putty color, jowls slack, gray hair askew across his balding scalp.

"Was Mrs. Brandenberg depressed, distraught over anything serious enough to drive her to... this?"

He stared at her, apparently unseeing.

"Mr. Brandenberg?"

"This is a nightmare."

"Look, maybe we should let this go until tomorrow."

He shook his head slowly. "Like to get it over with now." As if he could. Newspapers, TV – then lawyers, the IRS, the tide of paperwork. Death was not a private affair.

"I wondered if your wife was disturbed, depressed over something serious enough to"-

"No, no, of course not. We were close. Very, very close. I really loved that woman. I don't understand this. I don't."

He sat there numbly, hands palms-up in his lap.

"Can I get you a glass of water?"

"I need something stronger than water. In the dry bar over there."

She found a fifth of Jack Daniels, poured him three fingers in a squat glass. The paramedics – three men and a woman who looked as if she could lift stretchers all by herself – watched in bemusement Kat's playing barmaid. Moby appeared behind them and summoned her with a nod.

"Cut-and-dried," he told her as she joined him in the white-carpeted, Scandinavian-furnished bedroom. A large room, with its own glass exit to the rear patio, now closed off with gold-painted Venetian blinds.

"Gunshot to the right temple at close range. The standard quick exit."

In a pink silk nightgown, Irma Brandenberg lay on her back, angled across the bed. Her naked heels dug into the carpet's rich pile.

"For a woman in her late 50s or early 60s, she looks good," Moby said, "except she's dead." The wound was just above the corner of her right eye. Looked like .25 or .32 caliber.

"No exit wound," Moby pointed out. "Little pistols can do a lot of damage. Slug bounces around inside the skull."

The bed was neatly made up. The whole room was crisply neat. Nothing apparently out of place. Except one thing, Kat realized.

"Where's the gun?"

"That's what the medics wondered. Me too. Took a while, but guess where I found it?"

"Couldn't begin to." Did they have a possible murder here?

"On your hands and knees, Kat. Take a look under the night table."

Nestled in the deep carpeting beneath the nightstand was a snub-nosed revolver.

"Know what it is, Kat?"

"From the odd front sight and unusual handgrip, I'd guess Charter Arms."

"Good guess."

"A better guess would be, what's it doing under there?"

"Recoil. Flung her arm out—see, it's stretched straight to the edge of the bed. Gun falls, bounces under the nightstand. It's only in the movies where's it's still neatly in the gun hand with the finger on the trigger."

Not moving from beside the bed, she scanned the room again, "I wonder if our friend in the great room knows about that?"

"Come on, Kat. If he staged this thing, she'd be lying there, gun neatly in hand."

"I still wonder."

"Hell, we can close this thing right now. Suicide confirmed – and go home. Or we can bring in the ME and his guys and end up drowning in paperwork over an obvious cut-and-dried, open-and-shut self-inflicted."

"You forgot 'black-and-white.'"

"That too." He frowned at her, chewed his bottom lip. "You're serious?"

"It's the way Brandenberg answered out there. A little too insistent on how much he loved dear Irma."

"Jeez, that's some wobbly peg to land a case on." Moby ran a chunky hand across his thinning brown hair. Wobbled his ear side-to-side deliberating with himself.

She waited. She had seen this reaction before.

"I really feel for that poor bastard out there." He shrugged. "Hell, okay. We'll wake up Doc Hewlett." To the medics, he called, "Thanks, guys. You can go home. We're bringing in the medical examiner."

Hewlett, a banty rooster in khakis with an Orioles baseball cap hiding most of his white hair, didn't arrive until two a.m. Kat had suggested to Albert Brandenberg that he lie down in one of the guest bedrooms on the other side of the great room, but he selected to sit frozen in his chair.

The ME's team of three swung into full press. They photographed, dusted for prints, vacuumed and bagged the yield. The body, encapsulated in black plastic, went out on their folding gurney. Not until 3:24 a.m. – Kat had just looked at her watch – did they find the pillow.

Hewlett called them into the big white and chrome master bathroom. "Megargee just unearthed this, from the bottom of the clothes hamper."

It was a small and decorative pillow, about 12" by 24", with an edging of lace. A dainty, little feather-stuffed pillow, made significant by the hole in its middle, a powder-burned ragged puncture where the bullet went through.

"Anybody care to hazard a guess?" Hewlett asked roguishly.

Moby was already charging out to the great room.

"Albert Brandenberg," they heard him announce. "You better get dressed."

"Cut-and-dried," he reminded Kat three days later, a blistering Southwest Florida afternoon with the department's A/C's flood of cold air rustling desk litter.

"So you've chortled daily," Kat shot back across their facing desks. "But..."

"Get with it, Kat. When you saw where the gun was, you thought he'd done it. Now that we have the evidence, you're thinking maybe he didn't? It's still an open-and-shut – he shoots her through the pillow. That's why none of the neighbors heard it."

"They all had their windows shut and their air conditioners going. They wouldn't have heard it even without the pillow."

Moby held up a copy of her report, slapped it with the back of his hand. "Says right here when you interviewed an Edna Trumbell-"

"Next door neighbor to the west."

" —she let it slip that 'everybody knew' old Albert had something going with his sales manager. A Silvia Hansen. You interviewed Hansen, and she as much as confirmed that."

"Agreed, Moby. Common knowledge, so common that the neighbors thought Irma Brandenberg knew it, too. Irma had turned 'tight-lipped and sour,' as the neighbors put it."

"You're proving my case." Moby moved his forefinger down the sheet. You say here that loveable old Brandy lied to you about him and Irma being a happy twosome. You'll be able to tie this up tick-tight with a looksee for Hansen gift tie-ins in his charge card records, maybe his bank statements."

"Probably could."

"So why aren't you out there digging, Kat?"

She brushed back an errant raven-black strand. "Because I'm hung up on that damned pillow. Where's the blood? A bullet impact causes blowback. The shot to her head should have left blood blowback on the pillow. But there isn't any."

"So he held the gun and pillow far enough away so the blowback wouldn't reach it."

She shook her head. "Not likely. Even if she were asleep, it's too hard to aim through a pillow except from a few inches away. Another problem. If Albert shot her through the pillow, why did Doc Hewlett find traces of what is apparently blowback blood on the gun?"

"We're working on that."

"So I don't think it is so cut-and-dried, Moby. I'm going back to Three Thirty-six Sanseviera."

She stood in the great room and pondered. They'd had an easy call until that damned feather pillow had shown up. Why, though, if Brandenberg was the doer, had he made the set-up less obvious by shoving the gun under the night table? She couldn't accept his knowing that suicides can result in guns being thrown some distance from the shooters. Something was amiss here.

She sank into a chair by the glass door expanse, stared at the crystal pool beyond. Either Albert did it, or he didn't. If he didn't, Irma did. Or a proverbial bushy-haired stranger hit-and-run? Highly improbable, given the locked bedroom door to the patio – unless Albert arranged to leave it open for a contractual shooter? Eliminate the wife, and it's clear sailing with the sales manager. But would a paid hit man plant that bloodless pillow?

Did Albert have an enemy or enemies unsavory enough to frame him? In her interviews, she hadn't turned up a single anti-Albert comment. A nice guy, aside from his being an unfaithful husband.

If not Albert, it had to be Irma.

Kat stared unseeing across the patio's china blue. The damned pillow... She let her imagination ramble, percolate.

The bedroom and bathroom had been minutely checked, but not – was it possible? Not–

The garage was accessed through the kitchen. Kat snapped on the overhead fluorescents. Two cars in there, a jumbo-sized black Mercedes, no doubt Albert's, and a smaller, Irma-sized gold-flecked Lexus. The car's interior was immaculate. After three long minutes of searching, Kat's confidence in her bizarre theory began to erode. Then she found it, wedged up under the passenger seat. A fluffy little feather.

Kat replaced her desk phone in its cradle. Gave Moby a thumbs-up. "That was Doc Hewlett. The feather's a match."

"Well, I'll be–" Moby's sunburned forehead rumpled. "Better run all that by me again. It's a little complex for one take."

"My pleasure, Sergeant. Irma finds out Albert is smitten with Hansen. Hates him for it. It's eating her up. The marriage is doomed. From her viewpoint, her life is over. She works out a unique act of revenge. Not only will Albert be filled with remorse, a common suicide motive, he will be jailed – maybe even executed, the bastard, for murdering her."

Moby hunched forward, folding his arms on his desktop and growled, "Can't imagine anybody coming up with a scenario like that."

"Because you've never been a woman scorned, Moby. She needs to hide evidence where it will be found. The decorative pillow from the bed stuffed in the clothes hamper should do it. Now she needs a bullet hole in the pillow."

"The car, Kat. How did you know to check out the car?"

"She didn't want to chance the noise of the gunshot in the house, in the neighborhood. Her gun, by the way. He bought it for her after some break-ins in that neighborhood last year. So she drives out somewhere deserted, opens the passenger door or window and shoots through the pillow."

"Uh… huh. Stays in the car because she wants to be able to get out of there fast just in case."

"Problem is, the shot blows out a bunch of feathers. She cleans them up but misses the one I found under the passenger seat."

Kat stood, picked up her empty mug. "So that's why there's no blowback on the pillow, Moby. And that's why you're going to drop the charge against Albert."

Moby brought his chair back down with a thud. "Dammit, Kat," he said as she headed for the coffee machine. "At least I was right about why the gun was under the nightstand."

She turned and grinned down at him. "True, Sarge. At least you were right about that."

RED ON YELLOW, DEADLY FELLOW

"**M**alabar Four, are you on the east end of the island?"

"Ten-four, Dispatch."

"We have a report of a man down in the backyard at 936 Kudzu Lane. Check it out, Collins."

"Will do."

All of that, Malabar Island Detective Kat Curtci picked up on her radio as she drove toward the east end's Sporty Sand Dollar shop. A little morning-off browsing was not likely now.

"Curtci also responding," she said into the two-way radio she always carried with her – and always had on. Couldn't break the habit, even on a day off. Thus two side streets later, she swung her five-year-old Pontiac into Kudzu. First on the scene, she noted with satisfaction. Corporal Carleton Collins – "Three Cees" to everyone on the force – was nowhere in sight.

Kat trotted to the rear lawn and crouched to take a prelim scan of the prone figure that was indeed back here. And alone. Not another soul in sight.

Male Caucasian, probably in his sixties, stocky build, balding. And flat on his back. Khaki slacks, white golf shirt, thong sandals, no socks. No pulse, either.

She heard a car pull into the gravel drive out front. A long moment later, Three Cees pounded around the end of the one-story, ground-level stucco house and stood behind her, not even breathing hard.

"Yo, Kat." Beneath his tailored uniform shirt, his abs rippled. "What've we got?"

"What you see is what we got. Not another soul around. Who called this in?"

"Dispatch says the call came from the medevac 'copter on its way to a problem on the beach. Happened to spot this guy as they flew over the river."

"Heard you chiming at the front door. Nobody home?"

"Nobody answered." Three Cees bent over the body. "Heart attack?"

"Seems likely. He got a wallet?"

"Yep." The cop lifted the body enough to extract a slim fake alligator hide billfold. "Harold Wharton." He read from the driver's license. "This address."

"Any medical emergency card?"

"Nope. Couple credit cards, and forty bucks cash."

Kat surveyed the stand of ferns between the lawn and the scarlet blaze of bougainvillea hedge along the back lot line and halfway down the sides. No wonder no one at ground level saw him back here.

"Weeder." Three Cees pointed at a pronged hand tool just inside the ferns. "So here he was, out in the Southwest Florida sun, no kind of hat on that bald head, and down he went."

Three Cees stood beside her, impressive chest thrust out, shoulders in a near-military brace. As tall as he could manage, Kat noticed. But he still came up shorter than her five-eleven.

"All that shrubbery." She peered at the body again. "What's that?" She hunkered back down to study the splayed feet. "Check this, Three Cees."

The twin punctures were just below the left ankle joint, about a quarter-inch apart.

"Fire ants?" Three Cees suggested.

"More like a snakebite."

"I don't want to hear that." Three Cees scanned the ferns like a man besieged. "I hate – Yiii!"

Kat sprang to her feet. "What in the world-"

"Snake! Snake!" Three Cees leaped backward from the ferns, thrusting out a shaky finger. "In there!"

Kat peered into the fronds. Sure enough, a snake, a pretty one. Banded in red, yellow and black.

Red on yellow, deadly fellow. And the thing had a black nose.

"Coral snake, Three Cees. But it's dead. Looks like its head's been stepped on."

"So it's not a heart attack. Poor bastard is doing some weeding, the snake nails his bare ankle and down he goes."

"A possibility."

"A possibility? The evidence is staring right at you, Detective."

She glanced at Three Cees, who wore a little grin. So, okay, he'd said that tongue-in-cheek. She was touchy about challenges to her status and had verbally flattened a couple of the department's macho-mouths.

"Since it could be an accidental death instead of from natural causes, at this point the medical examiner gets in on it. Put in a call to Doc Hewlett, Three Cees, while I do a neighborhood check. Then stay with the body."

A glance along the street told Kat that almost all of the neighbors were winter residents, and this was summer. The piling house directly across the street had its hurricane shutters in place, as did the ground levels on either side of 936. Diagonally across to the right, though, the windows were naked – and the garage door was up, with the rear of a car visible inside. Slipping her badge and ID card out of her handbag, she strode across the hot macadam.

As she crunched into the gravel drive, she heard the clang of a hood slamming down. Seconds later, a middle-aged Charleton Heston-type emerged in grimy T-shirt and khakis, wiping his hands on a yellow polka-dot rag. He was wonderfully tall…

"Good morning, sir." Kat held up her badge. "Detective Curtci."

"You're here about the swimming pool truck-" He peered at cars in the driveway at 936; her red Pontiac and Three Cees' patrol unit. "What's the problem over there?"

"I'm afraid Mr. Wharton's had an accident. No one answers the door. I wondered if I might-"

"Harry? What happened to Harry? Can I help?"

"I'm afraid not, Mr…?"

"Palmer. Ed Palmer."

"Mr. Wharton is dead, sir. In his backyard."

"Dead?" Palmer was visibly stunned. "What the hell happened?"

"It may have been his heart, Mr. Palmer. He lived with his wife?"

"Yes. Thelma. She and Essie – that's my wife – are out shopping. Left a couple hours ago. They should be—Lord, now what?"

Siren screeching, an orange and white EMS ambulance rocked into Kudzu Lane and scruffed to a stop at 936.

"I'd better get over there, Mr. Palmer. Here's my card. Please have Mrs. Wharton call me as soon as she and your wife get back." Halfway down the drive, she stopped, turned back.

"What was that about a swimming pool truck?"

"Oh, a pool maintenance truck was parked for a while at the Kirshners', right across the street. Around seven. I thought it was rather odd, so I called the police."

"Well, I do see a pool enclosure behind the house."

"Oh, there is a pool there, but last year Sy Kirshner filled it in - after their daughter nearly drowned in it. Now it's a jumbo-sized planter. Anyway, the guy left just after I called you people."

"Apparently that call got lost in the excitement. I'd better get back over there. Thanks for your help, and make sure Mrs. Wharton calls me."

She loped over to 936, thumbed back a stray lock of raven hair and tore into Three Cees.

"You were supposed to call the M.E., not the paramedics. They've got more to do than check out bodies. That's a job for-"

"He didn't call us, ma'am," said a youthful voice behind her. "The medevac pilot did. Might as well take a look while we're here."

"Don't you disturb anything," Kat warned.

The young paramedic - were they taking them right out of high school now? - eyed her badge.

"Wouldn't think of it, ma'am."

"Detective Curtci."

"Oh, sure. Heard you solved that so-called suicide a couple months ago. Good show."

Well, maybe he wasn't such a green kid.

"You on the case here?" he asked.

"I'm not sure it is a case-" She peered at his nametag. "Richard. You'll have to excuse me. I've still got some checking to do."

The other nearby neighbors still in residence – the Syzmanskis two doors down from the Palmers, and the Markesons, two houses up on the Wharton's side – had heard or seen nothing at all.

"Oh, except," said iron-haired and pillowy Anna Markeson, "I heard a car or truck go by just after I woke up. Around seven. On this dead-end street this time of year, there's never any traffic that early."

That by itself was no lead at all, but there was the matter of the truck at number 938. Dispatch may have forgotten it, but she hadn't, and she strode back across the street.

"Sorry to bother you again, Mr. Palmer, but could you describe that pool maintenance truck?"

Ed Palmer, having emerged again from his garage mopping his greasy hands on his polka dot rag, squinted down his Heston-like nose at her. He had to be six-four, at least. Some women have all the luck.

"Consider this the response to your truck call, Mr. Palmer. Can you describe it?" She realized she was here maybe 60% because of the truck, and 40% because... because Charlton Palmer here had really blue eyes? God, how unprofessional!

"It was white, more like an SUV than a truck, now that I think about it. Had the name of a pool maintenance company on the door."

"License number?"

"Sorry. Probably Florida, or I might have noticed."

"And it stayed there in the driveway for how long?"

"I don't know. Essie and I were having breakfast. I just happened to look out when I heard the door slam."

"Did you see anybody walking around over there?"

Palmer flicked his rag at a curious yellow jacket. "Not when I was watching. It just pulled out and left."

"Did you see the driver?"

"A man."

"That's it?"

"I'm afraid so, Detective. Now that I've been questioned, I realize how dumb it was to report it. Or try to. A new pool man lost and just using the drive to turn around. Or one given the wrong address."

No reasonable way to linger with the compelling Mr. Palmer-Heston. "If you think of anything more, please give me a call," she said in resignation. And she left, chiding herself for conduct unbecoming a detective. A really tall one who was dateless a lot more than dated. Oh, get a grip, Curtci. The man was married... Probably loved his damned car more than Essie.

"Don't you have something better to do?" Sgt. Ellis "Moby" Duckworth twitted her when she walked into the squad room. He hunched forward in his squeaky swivel, plunked his elbows on his desk and rested his chin on tented fingers. "This was supposed to be your day off."

"Tell me about coral snakes, Moby."

"You taking up nature study?"

Closing in on retirement, Moby had given up on his waistline. He had slowed down to mostly deskwork – which he detested. Rode as a partner with Kat when he could get away from paper-pushing, but let her take the wheel and the initiative. She could never quite decide whether he had lost his edge, or was slyly helping her develop hers. What he did constantly hone was an encyclopedic knowledge of Malabar Island.

"I'm taking up coral snakes, short term. Found one near this morning's body, which had what looked like a fang wound on the left ankle."

"Well, now," Moby sank back in his chair. "Prettiest snake there is, with those red, black and yellow bands. Confused a lot with the scarlet king snake and the Florida scarlet. But your coral has a black nose and 'red on yellow—'"

"-'deadly fellow.'"

"Yep. He's in the cobra family. Same kind of venom. Not much of it, though. Your coral's usually not more'n two feet, two-and-a-half long. Odd thing is, they don't seem to know the punch they got. Usually come out at night and without much of a temper. I watched a guy over at the Snaketorium pick one up and play with it for ten minutes, no gloves, no problem. Your guy must have really agitated the one that got him."

"Could have. He was working with a weeder."

"Maybe dug the coral out of a sound sleep."

"How long does it take for the venom to act?"

"It's not right away. Can take up to an hour."

She pondered. "Something's wrong. Why didn't he go for help?"

"Maybe he didn't know he was snakebit. Fangs aren't more'n pin pricks. Could've thought it was a fire ant and shrugged it off."

"But the snake was dead. Its head was crushed."

Moby shrugged. "Stepped on it after it got him?"

"Then he stayed there, knowing he'd been bitten? Come on, Moby."

The chunky detective sergeant shrugged. "Maybe he stepped on it by mistake."

"Huh!"

"You're trying too hard, lady."

"Don't call me that. I hate it!"

Moby grinned. "You're trying to make a case against a dead snake, Kat. Let it lie."

Kat's response was cut off by her phone. Thelma Wharton. "Ed Palmer told me to call you. Oh, God, this is just awful! Terrible! I can't believe it!" She choked back a sob. "To get home to find poor Harry gone. Ed told me it was a heart attack. Nobody called 911? Why didn't somebody call-"

"Mrs. Wharton-"

"Why didn't anybody-"

"Mrs. Wharton, listen to me. No one could have seen him back there—not until the medevac helicopter flew over. They did what they could. Notified us, called the EMS people. We all got there as soon as we could. But I'm afraid he was already gone."

A long sigh on the other end. "Well, I guess it was going to happen sooner or later."

"Is there someone there to, uh, be with you, Mrs. Wharton?"

"There's Essie Palmer and Ed, of course. They're here now. The medical examiner took him. Does that mean an... autopsy?"

"What may have been an accidental death requires an autopsy, Mrs. Wharton. We found a coral snake nearby, a dead one. And what looked like fang marks on your husband's ankle."

"Oh, my stars! I knew there were snakes in our ferns, but I never dreamed there might be poisonous snakes back there. How dreadful!"

"It could have been a heart attack, Mrs. Wharton."

As if that would make the poor woman feel better about it. "We're just being thorough."

"Well, I hate to think of poor Harry all... I just hate to think of it. Harry wanted to be cremated. When might I be able to-"

"That's up to the medical examiner. If you don't hear from him shortly, I'll be glad to follow up for you."

"That's very considerate of you, Detective. Thank you."

Kat hung up and turned to Moby. "In three minutes, Thelma Wharton went from near hysteria to calm courtesy, Mobe."

"Quit looking for an answer when we already have one. Four little words."

"Four little words?"

"The snake did it."

The next morning before she had a chance to stir her squad room coffee, Doc Hewlett called. "Toss up," he told her. "Could have been venom, but it's kind of unusual for a coral snake to drop an adult on the spot."

"If he knew he was bitten."

"A coral snake attack isn't like a rattlesnake job, Kat. Your coral hangs on and chomps for a while."

"Well, he certainly would have felt that."

"Yeah, except he'd had a pretty stiff dose of barbiturate. Enough, I estimate, to discourage weeding in the hot sun."

"Barbiturate?" Her brain shifted into high. "Enough to knock him down?"

"I'd say so."

"How long was he dead before we found him?"

Hewlett snorted. "Body temp is no help in 90-degree sunlight. But the pooling of his blood—the lividity—makes four, five hours a fair guess."

That would put Harry Wharton down around seven or so.

"The lividity was consistent with the position we found him in?" she asked.

"Flat on his back, yes, and that wraps up my preliminary. I'll be in touch if anything else - oh, almost forgot. Quite a coincidence yesterday. A coral snake nailed your guy, and the same morning, another guy shows up at Health Center with a coral snake bite. They're pretty rare, but there came two of them the same day."

She heard a clatter in the background.

"Oops, there's an incoming," Hewlett said. "Gotta go. See you soon."

Oh, I hope not, she muttered to herself. Two coral snake bites yesterday morning?

"Moby, I'm off across the causeway to Health Center."

"You sick?"

"I think I've got fang fever."

"Take an aspirin," he muttered without looking up. "I'm telling you, the snake did it."

"Ronald Gilroy was kept overnight for observation then discharged this morning." The vastly overweight ER receptionist looked up from her computer. "It was a snake bite on his wrist, but apparently he didn't get much venom."

"Did Gilroy say how he happened to be bitten?" Kat asked.

"No record in the computer."

"Address?"

"Four forty-one East Ibis. That's here in Fort Bristol."

It was indeed; in a little residential development a block west of U.S. 41, wedged between a used car dealer's vast, balloon-festooned lot and a cramped industrial park. The houses were identical one-story stucco ranches with single-car garages. Today was Saturday, but number 441 looked closed up tight. Kat pulled into the short concrete driveway, radioed Malabar dispatch where she was, and crunched along the gravel walk to the door.

The plastic doorbell button had yellowed with age. It chimed the standard ding-dong.

Footsteps. Then the door creaked open on an irritated man in his fifties, built heavy with short-cropped dark hair. He wore rumpled olive slacks and a sweat-stained green tank top.

"Ronald Gilroy?"

"Yeah." His little eyes squinted against the sun's glare. "Who are you?"

"Detective Curtci, Malabar Island Police." She offered her badge.

If that shook him, she couldn't see anything change behind his leathery tan.

"Kind of out of your jurisdiction, aren't you?"

"I'm investigating an incident that took place on the island."

"An incident?"

"You live alone here?"

"Just me and my problems."

"What happened to your wrist, Mr. Gilroy?" She nodded at the Band-Aid.

"Little gardening accident."

"A snakebite."

His mouth tightened in disapproval. "You been checking up on me?"

"A coral snake, I'm told. How did that happen?"

"I don't have to talk to you, Detective."

"That's correct, Mr. Gilroy, especially if you have some reason not to."

He stood eye-to-eye with her, unblinking. Then he muttered, "In the garden out back. I was doing some weeding, and zap! He got me. I drove straight to Health Center.

"Did you save the snake?"

"Save it?"

"To help the doctors determine the proper antivenom."

"Hell, lady, I know it was a coral snake. Anyway, it got away. Look, I got things to do. Saturday's my day to keep this place glued together."

"What kind of work do you do, Mr. Gilroy?"

Solidly entrenched in the doorway, he thrust a hefty arm against the doorjamb. A reflex, she thought, signaling how much he resented the intrusion.

"I work for a fencing company. County Fencers up in North Fort Bristol."

"Yet you were weeding your garden yesterday. On Friday?"

"Before I went to work, but I didn't get to work. Had to call in from the hospital. You can check on that."

"What I'd like to check on is your garage, if you don't mind."

"Jeez, lady, you got a real bug up your-" He shrugged. "Well, okay. Wait here. I'll open it from inside."

She walked over to the garage and waited for long seconds. Had a vision of him loping away across the back lot. Then the door creaked slowly upward.

Her eyes adjusted to the gloom in there. An SUV.

Gilroy appeared through the connecting door. "Look, lady, I need to get into town. You got any more questions?"

"Not at the moment."

"Then I'll see ya." He stepped into the SUV and it blapped into life.

Dark blue. Damn.

Behind her, a man's voice said, "Sounds smooth enough to-" His words were lost in the snorting of the truck as Gilroy gunned it, then backed out.

The man behind her, smiling, trim, in his brush-cut blond forties, jerked his thumb over his shoulder.

"Live across the street. Name's Arnold. Arnie, to everybody but the tax man. Who might you be?"

A man on the make. She could tell from the toothy smile.

"Detective Curtci, Malabar Police, Arnie." She watched him wither.

"Uh huh. Well, I just came over to say hello to Ron. Nice meeting you."

She drove back to 41 in gnawing frustration. She could hear Moby now: "Told you, Kat. You're letting yourself get snakebit over a freak accident."

But two coral snake bites in the same morning when there normally wasn't even one a year in all of Southwest Florida?

She and Officer Three Cees had found Harry Wharton not four feet from the dead snake. Doc Hewlett told her coral snake venom had a delayed reaction. But barbiturate didn't. No other record of a coral snake bite on Malabar. Ever. She checked.

Instead of turning south on 41 toward the island, Kat turned north.

The blindingly white limestone Snaketorium hulked behind its macadam parking area among the as-yet-undeveloped farm fields six miles north of Fort Bristol.

The front door with its brass cobra handle opened into the chilly air-conditioned gift shop and ticket counter – the tickets to admit gawkers into the open-air snake pits and wire cages out back. Kat had been here several times, entertaining her mother from Baltimore, then her brother and his wife from Scranton.

"Hi," Kat said to the gum-smacking teenaged clerk behind the counter, wondering how the girl managed that with a silver ball-thing piercing her tongue. "Is Cal around?"

"You wanna see Cal, he's upstairs."

Kat climbed the metal staircase in the corner and emerged in a short hallway. She knocked at the door with a hand-lettered file card taped at eye-level: C. Talbot, Fangmaster.

"Yo! Come on in!"

Behind a work table littered with papers, Priority Mail cartons and a rack of test tubes, a scrawny old man in a stained lab coat peered over his half glasses.

"Well, if it isn't Malabar's finest. How are you, Kat? And your delightful mother and her, well, not so effusive brother?"

"I'm fine, Mom's fine, and I apologize for my Uncle Fritz. He just plain hates snakes, but Aunt Karen couldn't wait to get here."

"Sorry for the mess." He waved an arm at the table. "Today is venom shipping day to the medical lab in Miami. So... what can I do for you?"

"I'm here on a case, Cal. Well, maybe a case."

"Ah, the coral snakebite on Malabar. Heard about that."

"Did you also hear about the one in Fort Bristol?"

"When was that?"

"Yesterday. Same morning. That victim was a fence worker. Told me he was bitten in his backyard, drove himself to the ER."

"Corals can be tricky. Deliver a lethal dose, or maybe not. A lot of factors involved."

"Can anybody buy one?"

Cal placed both hands flat on the table and leaned toward her. "What, dear girl, are you thinking? Yes, you can buy one. You just have to know where. Certain hobbyists love the idea of owning something that can kill them."

"You can buy one locally?"

"About ten miles east on Route 80. Little place called SerPenthouse. Tell Mort Mortenson I sent you." He grimaced. That sounded like a used snake dealer's pitch."

"Sweet," Kat said. She tore her eyes from the bright yellow sign above the tiered cages behind him: If you don't love me, then kiss my asp. "You are Mr. Mortenson?"

The frog-like man behind the counter nodded, agitating several chins. "Morton Mortenson. Call me Mort. What can I do for you?"

"I'm told you sell coral snakes."

"Coral snakes? I don't deal in venomous-"

"Cal Talbot said you might. And I've got this." She smiled and showed her badge. "I'm after information only, Mort."

"Oh, sh...lithering serpents." All 300 pounds of him undulated in what she interpreted as distress. Then he leaned on the counter and peeked up at her like a schoolboy trying to turn on the charm.

"Why coral snakes, dear lady?"

"Oh, come on, Mort. You read the paper this morning, or saw it on TV." The stringer who haunted police HQ had salivated over this one.

"Jeez, Detective, all I did was sell a snake. What happened after that isn't my problem. And how do you know it was my snake that was involved."

"I don't think we've got a sudden invasion, Mort. I'd like you to describe your customer."

"Am I in trouble?"

"Only if you want to be."

"Gotcha. Heavyset. Dark hair cut short. Squinty eyes."

"Name?"

"Paid cash. I didn't need a name."

"Well, that would have tied it up neatly, but I know who he is."

"'He'? She was a woman."

Kat left Mort's SerPenthouse in a state of fuddle – until just a mile westward she realized she had never actually met Thelma Wharton. So it was possible that heavy, short-haired Ron Gilroy's coral snake encounter was a coincidence.

Back on the island 45 minutes later, she chimed the Whartons' – well, now the Wharton, singular – doorbell.

"Thelma Wharton?" she asked the blonde, wavy-haired, noticeably slight woman who answered. Hope not, hope not. Maybe the cleaning woman?

"Yes. And you are?"

"I'm Detective Curtci," Kat managed. Talk about chagrin! "Just passing by to see how you're doing."

"Why, how considerate." Thelma's blue eyes sparkled. "I'm doing just fine, thank you."

"By the way, what medications was your husband taking?"

"Medications? Only Hytrin for his blood pressure, and he had headaches. He took phenobarb for those."

"Every day?"

"Whenever he had a headache. Like yesterday morning."

Innocent, or a cover-up?

"If there's anything else you can think of, Mrs. Wharton, please give me a call."

Thelma frowned. "What do you mean?"

"It's just that a coral snakebite isn't an everyday occurrence."

"Certainly not for me, either." That with a bit of a snap.

"I'm convinced I have most of the pieces," she told Moby back at HQ, "but some don't fit and some are still missing."

Moby shook his head. "Tried to tell you, Kat, you can't make a case. There has to be a case."

"There is a case here, Mobe. I feel it."

"Uh oh, that's the worst case."

"Listen to me, Mobe. We've got a bite from one of the world's most placid snakes."

"A placid venomous snake."

"The victim giddy or prone with Phenobarbital. Another coral bite, but that vic had the wrong SUV. And whoever bought the coral snake was neither the second bitee nor the wife of the first. Maybe too many pieces, Mobe."

Duckworth heaved his bulk back from his desk and stood up surprisingly fast for such an overweight sergeant.

But he said, "Know what I think? I think it's time to visit Corporal McCase."

In his own little cubicle, Willard McCase the computer ace looked not like a cyberspace nerd but like Hulk Hogan without hair. McCase had two interests in life: pumping iron in weekly tonnages and periodically clicking computer keys with a near-magic touch.

In a remarkably few minutes, he had unearthed two pertinent financial facts. "One, Harry Wharton had only an unexciting $25,000 life insurance policy with Great American."

"Damn," Kat muttered.

"And two, Thelma Wharton had no policies on Harry, but she does have her own trust fund set up by her father, Jonas Gilroy of Athens, Ohio."

"Nothing there, Kat," Moby grumped. "Kat?"

She was already out the door. Maiden name Gilroy!

On East Ibis, she turned not into Ronald Gilroy's drive but into the driveway across the street. On Sunday, chances were good that he was home. And he was. The door chime was answered by the same man she had so blithely neglected to consider yesterday. Full treatment today. Badge, smile, extended hand.

"Detective Katherine Curtci again, Mr.-?"

"Majeski. Jim Majeski." Ah, that toothy grin. Majeski was back in form today. "What can I do for you, sweetheart?"

Cripes. Worse than "lady."

"You said something yesterday about Mr. Gilroy's SUV sounding fine. What was that about?"

"Oh, he'd had some engine trouble Friday. Had something to deliver and asked to borrow mine."

"He used your SUV Friday? May I look in your garage?"

"I don't see the point, but sure."

Majeski's SUV was white. She walked in, checked the dusty front doors.

"Thank you very much, Mr. Majeski."

"What's going on?"

"Routine investigation." Lull, don't intimidate.

Back at her desk, she went to work on Yellow Pages listings for makers of magnetic signs. Scored a pool service sign hit on the third call.

One last loose end. And a hunch, Moby, no matter what you think of hunches.

Essie Palmer answered the door, a big woman – with cropped blue-black hair, squinty little eyes. Time, Detective Curtci, for some serious grilling.

"It didn't take that long," Kat told Moby after the warrants had been served. "The two women hated Harry. Thelma, because he had become a brutal husband, adept at whacking her where it didn't show. Essie, because he had attempted to rape her. Both of them were terrorized, afraid to tell anyone all about Harry."

"Nice retired old geezer. But you lost me back there in all the snake coils."

"Okay, one more time. Essie bought the snake, gave it to Ronald Gilroy."

"Thelma's brother."

"Right. His motive, in addition to relieving his sister of an onerous husband, was the twenty-five thou from Harry's life insurance. Afraid his SUV might be noticed, Gilroy borrowed Majeski's – the white SUV indeed spotted by Ed Palmer, who had nothing to do with any of this."

"Except for giving you that hot lead."

"Well, true. So Gilroy arrives early Friday with the snake, in the borrowed SUV with magnetic pool service signs on its doors. Harry's already down, from the phenobarb Thelma put in his coffee. Gilroy puts on gloves, takes the snake from its box and applies it to Harry's ankle. When he finally pulls it loose, it's in a foul humor and gives him a shot just above the glove."

"So now Essie Palmer comes over as planned, and the two lethal ladies go on a shopping trip while stupefied Harry dies out of sight in his backyard," Moby chimes in. "Woulda worked if it wasn't for that autopsy they didn't figure on – and that second snakebite."

"I don't think it would have, Mobe. Too complicated, too many people involved."

"And one other thing," Duckworth said impishly, "A tall, persistent lady named Curtci."

"Cripes, Mobe. You know I hate that."

"Tall?"

"No, I mean that 'lady' business."

"Right. You're no lady. You're a cop."

"That's more like it."

"Absolutely." He grinned. "…Sweetheart."

"Moby, for Pete's sake."

TOTOO

Malabar Island Detective Katherine Curtci spread her beach blanket, slipped off her robe and exposed her bikini-clad 5'-11" sun-screened elegance to the Southwest Florida glare.

Her beeper turned her sigh of contentment into a groan of exasperation. She plunged into her beach tote and yanked out her cell phone.

"That you, Kat?" Sergeant Duckworth rasped.

"Moby, it's Monday, my day off."

"Wouldn't have called you, except I figured you'd be on your favorite south end beach, and we just got a call from over there. Lost dog."

"Lost – did you say dog?" she pictured Duckworth, girth spilling over his belt, chuckling to himself.

"Yeah, lost dog. But it's wearing an owner's tag same name as the missing person's call that came in earlier this morning. A Beverly Bridger, white female, age 20, from Clarks Summit, Pennsylvania. Dark hair, wearing navy shorts and a white top when last seen. She's down there on vacation with a friend name of Lister. Sandra Lister. She's the one called in the missing report."

"Okay, Mobe. I'll check out the dog, then I'll interview Lister. Where's she staying?"

"The Gulf Sands, just north of where you're at. The dog's on the beach the other way, toward the lighthouse. A snowbird has him."

My punishment for finally getting a break, Kat fumed to herself. She yanked on her hibiscus-patterned robe, stuffed the blanket back in the tote and plodded southward, barefoot on the hard sand at the water's edge.

The dog, on a leash looped to the arm of a beach chair, was small, black and sprawled flat in the chair's shadow. The chair's occupant was large, pasty white – and visibly delighted at the approach of a tall, raven-haired woman in a loosely-sashed beach robe. He was still grinning after she officially introduced herself, complete with badge folder.

"M'god, cops are sure pretty in these parts." His eyes roved. "In all parts."

"To business, Mr.-?"

"Davidson. Sam Davidson. From Norwalk, Connecticut. Down here to soak up the sun for a week."

"Better take it in short increments, Mr. Davidson. You're already medium-rare around the shoulders. Tell me about the dog."

"The missus went shopping and I came out here about half an hour back and found him groggy on the sand. Took him in for some water and cooling off, and called nine-one-one."

"Maybe a vet would have been more-"

"No phone book in the unit."

"Did you put the leash on him?"

"Nope. He came equipped."

She crouched, let the dog sniff her hand, patted his head and inspected the tags on his plaid collar. Rabies up to date. A Lackawanna County license. And a name tag: My name is Totoo. My owner is Beverly Bridger. Plus a phone number with a 570 area code.

The collar and the leash were encrusted with salt.

"You didn't take him into the surf, Mr. Davidson?"

"Hell, no. He was nearly too weak to walk at all. I kept him inside for a while, then brought him back out to wait for you." Davidson craned around in his chair. "Seems a lot better now. Not a bad looking mutt."

"He's a Cairn terrier."

"A what?"

"A Cairn. Scottish breed. Smart and determined."

"You're a dog lover?"

"Had a friend who owned one. I'll take him now, sir. Thanks for-"

"Jeez, you had to call me 'sir'? I'm not gray yet."

"Thanks for your help, Sam. And either get yourself some major sunblock, or you'd better go inside and watch TV."

She carried the Cairn back to her car in a public access lot a quarter-mile north. Drove a few blocks to the Gulf Sands and led the dog to the motel office.

"Sandra Lister?" the short-cropped, henna-rinsed manager repeated as she squinted at Kat's badge then riffled through a box of file cards. "Okay, she's in Unit Seven. She do something reprehensible?"

"Lost dog."

"That little guy there? Thought that belonged to the roommate."

"Have you seen the roommate today?"

"Nope. They usually don't show their faces this early."

Kat and swiftly recovering Totoo made it halfway to Unit 7 when its door burst open and a pony-tailed blonde in orange halter and shorts flew out and rushed up to her.

"Ohmigod, you've found Totoo! But where's Bev? It's been hours since I called."

"I'm sorry. We're stretched pretty thin in-season. Why don't we go back inside where we can talk?"

She and Bev were co-workers and close friends at a Scranton-based computer service company, Sandra said as, with hands trembling, she handed Kat a mug of instant coffee. They sat side-by-side on the unit's small sofa. The two girls, both in their adventurous early 20s, had come to the island for a brief, carefree vacation, though Sandra felt Bev's dog had been something of a downsider.

"I'm not a dog person, but Bev loves the thing. Even has permission to take him to work."

"He's not a great vacationer?"

"He's okay, I guess, but he's a dog. Has to be taken out, walked, fed. Screws up a lot of potential, but she's devoted to him."

"How did she come up with a name like that?" Kat hoped their chatter would calm Sandra to a degree of reliability.

"'Totoo'? He's just like that dog, Toto, in 'The Wizard of Oz.' First she called him Toto Two, then that turned into Totoo."

"You reported Bev missing early this morning. When did you last see her?"

"She took Totoo out for a walk around eleven last night. I was worn out and I went to bed. When I woke up at seven, she wasn't here." Sandra struggled to keep her voice steady. "Her bed hadn't been slept in, and the dog wasn't there either. This isn't like her at all. I called the cops and, surprise, I didn't get that forty-eight hour waiting thing. A couple of hours, though. But here you are. I really appreciate it."

"Has she been out all night before?"

"Not in the five days we've been here. Hasn't even met anybody to be all night with, if that's what you're asking.

I can't imagine where she could be. What makes it worse is him." She nodded at the dog. "She would never... just would never..."

"Did you two have an argument? Might she have gone back home in some sort of-"

"No! We're like sisters. We've never even had a cross word." Abruptly Sandra Lister broke into tears. "Oh God," she gasped, "I just know something... something awful has happened."

Kat slipped an arm around Sandra's shoulders. "Why don't you tell me whatever you can that might help. Do you know where she went for her walks?"

"At night, she liked to walk down that street across the road, the one with the boats at the bay end. She enjoyed the view across the bay, the lights over there."

"Do you think that's where she went last night?"

"She always took Totoo there for his last time out. Is that where you found him?"

"Not exactly, but in the general vicinity." She set her mug on the coffee table, stood and smiled at the tear-stained roommate. "There's surely a logical reason for this, Sandra. Let's give it a full twenty-four hours. Then, if she doesn't turn up, we'd better apprise her family."

"She has no family. Her mother died when Bev was born. Her father was killed in an industrial accident last year. Totoo - and I, sort of – are her family." She sobbed, gulped. "I'm sorry. I'm a mess. What about the dog?"

"Looks like he's in your care for the moment."

"No, I can't. I just can't. I don't know the first thing about dogs. Don't the police have cages for lost dogs until their owners pick them up?"

"Yes, we do."

"Well?"

Kat glanced down at Totoo, who stared up at her. A lousy cage after whatever he'd been through? The dog would be better off with... Hell, with her until Bev Bridger was found.

"I'll see that Totoo is in good hands."

Sandra Lister nodded. "I really appreciate that."

At the door, she touched Kat's arm. "I've got a perfectly awful feeling. Please find her."

Kat patted her hand. "I'm sure there's a logical reason for all this. I'll be in touch." Empty words, she was afraid. If only Totoo could talk.

Not good. A naïve young woman on a late night walk wrapped in tropical vacation euphoria. Half the department's work was responding to calls from stunned visitors: "I left my purse in the car and it's gone." "My beach bag was out of my sight for not more than four minutes." But a woman disappearing on an evening walk? Had Beverly Bridger suddenly decided to go home for some reason Sandra was covering up? Not likely without her dog. Or had she met some irresistible hunk out there in the dark and spent the night at his pad? And let Totoo wander off by himself?

Kat had just one potential lead, if she could even call it a lead. She left Totoo at Island Vets for a check-up. Then she drove to her little mid-island beach house to change into more businesslike gray slacks and white blouse. At 11:15, she drove back to the island's south end.

Opposite the Gulf Sands, she turned off the main road into Baylook Drive. The street was a short one, flanked by towering Australian pines. Three homes nestled along each side. At the bayside dead-end was a community dock. Beyond the dock and its four tethered boats, the bay glittered in the unrelenting sun.

Halfway down the shaded blacktop, Kat parked. "Door to door," she muttered. And with nothing to sell. Well, maybe a degree of information-eliciting charm.

Forty plodding minutes and five nothing-seen-or-heard houses later, she was running out of hope. The last residence loomed imposingly on pilings, with its ground level neatly boxed in to provide a two-car garage. The Clymers, the stylized alligator mailbox announced. Clymers, indeed, with towering steps to the main floor.

A white-haired gnome answered the door chime, an ancient fellow in rumpled khakis. He stood barely up to Kat's breast line, which he savored at his piercing eye-level.

"Mr. Clymer?"

"Alban Clymer, at your service, unless you're selling goods or goodness."

She showed him her badge folder. "Detective Curtci, Mr. Clymer. Hoping for a little help."

"Sweetie, I'll be overwhelmed to help you any way an old man can. Bring yourself in and set yourself down. Coffee? Tea? A pinch of pinch bottle?"

"Nothing, thank you. Do you live here alone, Mr. Clymer."

"Alban, for gosh sakes. And no, my wife is on the mainland getting her hair youthenized. I'm eighty-six, though, so you don't have a heck of a lot to fear."

She perched on the edge of an overstuffed chair near the brick fireplace. Why did people move down here to escape snow country then insist on a fireplace?

"So what can I do for you, darling? Oh my, that's a beautiful head of hair you have. Shines like licorice."

Oh, great. She had skewered come-on artists for less than that. But he was eighty-six, and he was teasing, not demeaning. "Thank you, sir."

"Come on, girl. Between us, it's Alban."

"Were you awake around eleven last night, Alban?" Fat chance. She wasn't sure he was completely awake now. Possibly a bit aglow from a pinch of the pinch bottle?

"I'm awake every night at eleven, honeybun. That's when the wife's asleep and HBO starts its skin shows."

Good lord.

"Might you have noticed anything unusual out in the street? Or anything at all?"

"Anything at all on this street at that time of night would be unusual."

"So you didn't-"

"Don't jump ahead of an old man, dear. I heard a boat."

"Out in the bay?"

"Right out there at the dock. Then it went out in the bay."

"Is that unusual?"

"Yep. Those boat owners are sixty, seventy. Not given much to moonlight cruising."

Worth pursuing? What else did she have? "Any idea who it might have been?"

Alban shrugged. "Heck, I know exactly whose boat it was. Recognized the sound."

She waited.

"Don't you want to know whose boat it was?" he asked.

"Sure, Alban. Whose?"

"John Spencer Kingman's. That's whose."

Was the old coot playing with her? "Alban, John Spencer Kingman is a U.S. Senator."

"You're a very smart babe. That's who owns the boat that makes a peculiar burbly sound. It's an inboard. I'd guess a six-figure inboard. The others are rackety outboards. Last night that boat went out just as 'The Bottom's Line' was ending. Those skin flicks are short."

"What time was that?"

"Eleven-thirty, thereabouts. The senator has a place up around the corner. Second one northward. Uses it for a couple weeks when Senate's out of session. Like now."

"Did you hear the boat come back in?"

"Nope. Past my bedtime by then, honey."

"Well, Alban, you've been a real help," Kat said as she stood.

"I'll bet you say that to all the snitches."

She couldn't help grinning. "I do, but so far, none of them have made a U.S. Senator my next stop."

"The senator says he will see you." The Hispanic maid, in uniform no less, had left Kat on the front deck of the imposing three-story house. Now she led Kat down a pine-paneled entrance hall, through a two-story-high "great room," then out on the vast screened-in rear deck.

The view of the bay was magnificent. The view of the senator, in voluminous white slacks and surely a triple-X ivory golf shirt, was forbidding. Not because of his imposing size, but because of his scowl.

"Better be a damned fine reason for the local police to interrupt my siesta time. I'm down here to get away from interruptions, not to welcome them." He hadn't budged from his wicker chair, and he didn't invite her to sit down. From the third-story deck overhead, she heard recorded country nasal enough to compete with Willy Nelson.

"Detective Curtci, Senator, Malabar-"

He waved an impatient hand. "So Esmeralda informed me. What business can you possibly have here?"

"I'm investigating the disappearance of an island visitor, Senator. A woman named Beverly Bridger."

"Never heard of her."

"She went for a walk last night around eleven, probably down Baylook Drive. A resident at the bay end of the drive states your boat left the dock around eleven-thirty."

"I know absolutely nothing about any boat leaving the Baylook dock last night, Detective. And I do not understand why you think a departing boat concerns me."

"It was your boat, Senator."

"You say you have a witness?"

"Yes." If not an eye-witness, at least an ear-witness.

Senator Kingman glared at her. Then he looked at the ceiling and bellowed, "Gary, get your butt down here!"

The music overhead cut off in mid-twang. She heard footsteps thumping downstairs, more than one person. An athletically trim youth in khaki shorts and a blue T-shirt thudded onto the deck from the great room. He was followed by a less trim boy in jeans and a rumpled tan gold shirt.

"My son, Gary, Detective, and his buddy Edward Herkiser. Penn State seniors celebrating spring break. Gentlemen, this local detective lady claims our cabin cruiser went out late last night. Might you know anything about that?"

Silence. Herkiser glanced at Gary. And Gary shrugged. "Yeah, Dad. We took it out for a short spin around the bay. Came back maybe an hour later."

"There you are, Detective...Kersey, is it?"

"Curtci, Senator."

"Whatever. Mystery solved."

"No, the mystery is what happened to Beverly Bridger." She turned to the two collegians. "Did either of you see a young woman out there on Baylook Drive last night?"

"No," Gary Kingman said. "Not a soul, did we, Herk?"

"Not a soul," echoed young Herkiser.

"Not when you left in the boat, not when you came back?"

"Nobody," Gary said.

Herkiser echoed him again.

"Satisfied?" Senator Kingman rumbled.

Gary and his sociopathic friend stood there blank-faced. No, not quite. What was that twitch playing at the corners of Gary's mouth? A feeling of superiority as he watched his powerhouse father handle an upstart woman cop? Or was something more going on here?

"Senator," she said, "may I have your permission to check out your boat?"

"No, you may not, Detective. I'm tired of this ridiculous fishing expedition of yours. If you have no further questions, I believe I hear Esmeralda sounding the luncheon chime."

"Gentlemen," she said to Gary and his pal, "you will not leave this island until you are cleared by me, you understand?"

"GOOD DAY, DETECTIVE!" Senator Kingman thundered, finally hoisting himself out of his chair. "Leave!"

Thus bounced from the senator's vacation retreat and fuming at his high-handed attitude, Kat drove to Island Vets to pick up Totoo.

"He's still a touch shaky," young but balding Doc Harter told her, "but with a little TLC, he'll be fine."

"The man who found him told me the dog was completely exhausted, dehydrated. Could a night on the beach have done that to him?"

"If he was in the surf. He'd been completely immersed in seawater. Salt residue all over him. Gave him a bath. Now he's a pretty little Cairn. Smart one, too. Found the biscuit bin a second after I put him on the floor."

"He's cleared to go?"

"Oh, sure. Just give him that TLC I mentioned, and he'll be fine."

Totoo wasn't going to get much tender loving care in a police retention cage. "Looks like you and I are going to spend the night together," she told him.

At the Island Mart, she picked up a bag of dog food and a box of biscuits. Totoo zeroed in on the biscuits while they were still in the bag. No appetite problem with this guy.

Tuesday morning, she couldn't bring herself to leave the little Cairn alone all day. She took him with her when she reported in. She was relieved when Moby welcomed the company.

Totoo curled up in a corner of the squad room. "Take him out a couple times, will you, Mobe? I'll leave you a biscuit supply."

"You going back for another sensational filibuster? Know what I think? I think the girl fell off that dock at the end of the street, drowned and the tide took her out."

"Possible, I guess, but why would her dog walk across the island and end up exhausted on the gulf shore crusted with sea salt?"

"Huh. Keep digging."

"While I'm doing that, how about having our resident computer ace check out those two midnight boatmen for possible rap sheets."

She called the Coast Guard. No bodies found anywhere in the area for the past month. If Bridger had sunk, she wouldn't come back up for a couple more days.

Kat drove across the three-mile causeway to its pair of tollbooths on the mainland end. The two attendants now on duty hadn't been there Sunday night, but they told her neither of the Sunday night shift had mentioned seeing anything at all suspicious in any departing vehicle.

She returned to Malabar Island. Interviewed the occupants of several houses in the vicinity where the dog had been found. Nobody had seen anything.

"Not much of a ratchet forward, Mobe." She lamented as the descending sun splashed the squad room with hot orange. "I'm dead certain those two college hotshots knew more than a shrug's worth. I'd like to take a look at that boat, but with what I've got so far, the chances of a search warrant are nil. Especially with the senator backing up Gary's and his buddy's story."

"What did you expect a father to do, Kat? He's not about to—Hey, Totoo, supper time's coming up. Hang in there, will you?" Moby swiveled back to Kat. "Never saw such a dog. Sits and just stares at you all day until you give him the biscuit."

He shuffled through the papers on his desk. "Computer came up with this much. Herkiser's clean, but young Kingman's had his jollies. A slew of speeding and reckless driving raps, fines paid but no convictions. High spirited kid stuff, except for a charge of assault in an Altoona, Pennsylvania tavern. No conviction on that either."

"A pattern, though. An unruly son protected by a prominent father."

"Seems so, Kat. Looks like you're up against the proverbial stonewall. Or maybe these two didn't have anything to do with the girl's disappearance, after all. Maybe she just bugged out."

"Sure, Mobe. And left her dog? Get real."

"Get real yourself, Detective. In two days you've got nothing at all."

"I've got a boat leaving."

"Boats leave all the time, Kat."

"And, as a long shot, I've got Edward Herkiser. He might be the key, but not while he's with Gary."

"So get him in here. Hasn't the senator told you to stay away from his house?"

"Good point, Mobe. Very good point."

Day three, and she was still nowhere. Now, though, she had a plan. Came to her last night as she played stare-a-biscuit with Totoo.

"Kingman residence," said Esmeralda in a monotone phone voice.

"I would like to speak with Gary, please. This is Katherine."

Apparently, that was the kind of call Gary was used to getting. He came to the line in seconds.

"Hey, Katherine? Do I know you?"

"We've met, Gary. This is Detective Curtci. There are just a few points I need clarified." She ignored his snort of derision and pressed on. "It would be a help if you and your friend would come by to the station today. Say, in an hour or so."

"I don't think-"

"I really don't want to bring you in on material witness warrants, Gary."

"We're not under arrest or anything like that?"

Interesting question. "No, no. Just an informal chat." Said the spider to this formidably-backed fly.

"I'll see." Off-balance for sure. Would he run to Papa, a worried son with something to hide? Or swagger in here like the arrogant clod his rap sheet appeared to spell out?

Or perhaps the senator had deduced she wasn't going to let this drop until she interviewed them without him present.

A few minutes before noon, the two of them pulled into PD parking, an arrival timed, perhaps, for lunch hour to cut her short. Wouldn't work. She never ate lunch. The car was a lustrous forest green Jag, no doubt the senator's vacation buggy.

She took Gary first, leaving Herkiser in the drab little waiting area. The interrogation room was also barren of décor, just a center table, and two hard chairs.

"No two-way mirrors? Gary quipped.

"You've been in these before?"

"I've seen them in movies."

"We're not that fancy here."

Gary plunked into one of the chairs. Kat sat across from him. For a long moment, she said nothing. The calculated silence seemed not to bother him at all.

"Let's go over what you told me Monday, Gary."

"Sure. We took the boat out around eleven-thirty or so. Cruised the bay nowhere in particular. Came back an hour later. We saw nobody when we left or when we came back. That's all there was to it."

"You're sure?"

"Sure, I'm sure."

That went on for a few more minutes, but she hadn't expected to hear anything else. Her target wasn't Gary Kingman. It was Edward Herkiser.

"All right," she finally sighed. "You can go back to the waiting area while I talk to your friend."

He grinned. "Okay, Katherine. Want me to send him in?"

"I'll come for him in a few minutes. She needed those minutes. Then she stepped out to Moby's desk. "I'll take Totoo now, Mobe." With the Cairn on his leash, Kat beckoned to Herkiser. He followed her into the interrogation room.

"You going to interview this dog, too?" he asked as he sat where she told him. "What's he doing here?"

"Visiting. Relax," she advised Herkiser as she took her chair, the leash still on her hand.

"Is this going to take long?"

"Up to you, Herk. Is that what they call you?"

"That's what Gary calls me."

"I'll call you Edward. Time to tell me the truth, Edward. What really happened out there on Baylook Drive?"

"How many times do you want to hear this? Around eleven-thirty, we took the boat out. Came back an hour later. We didn't see anybody when we left or when we came back in. That's it."

Almost word-for-word identical to Gary's statement. Rehearsed? Or was she at a dead end here? Maybe they truly hadn't seen Beverly Bridger and her dog. Even if they had, were they to stick to their story, there was no hint of another lead. It all came down to this moment with this close-mouthed boy.

She let the leash drop.

Then she leaned forward, her eyes hard on his. "Did you perhaps hear anything unusual that night, Edward?"

He seemed not to hear her. Totoo had wandered from

under the table and stopped beside Herkiser's chair. Edward's attention had swung to the dog. Motionless on his haunches, the Carin stared upward, unblinking.

"I'll ask you again, Edward. Did you hear or see anything unusual out there that night?"

"Uh, anything what?"

"Unusual."

"Huh-uh." He was trying to ignore the dog's unrelenting gaze. Totoo's attention riveted on Herkiser. Who twitched uncomfortably. On his forehead sweat glistened.

"She was a twenty-year-old girl, Edward. About your age. Just out for a walk with her dog. With that dog, Edward."

He swallowed. Blinked. Wiped his eyes with the back of his hand.

"Dammit," he whispered. To the dog. "It was an accident."

"It was what, Edward?"

"An accident," he wailed. And like a pent-up flood behind a ruptured levee, the story poured forth.

"In a way, it was an accident," she told Moby after the arrests, the Senator's predictable explosion, the hastily summoned lawyers. "They ran into Beverly out there and talked her into a moonlight boat ride. Just a chance encounter. God knows why lonely women fall for invitations from strangers, but she and Totoo went aboard. Kingman and Herkiser had two six-packs with them. When they left the bay and cruised into the gulf, the six-packs were in them. That, plus his cocky arrogance, prompted Kingman to make a pass at Beverly in the cabin. It escalated into serious grappling. According to both of them, her head smacked the cabin wall hard enough to kill her."

"Manslaughter and attempted rape."

"That's what they realized, too, Mobe. It got uglier, if that's possible. They tied her body to one of the boat's two anchors and into the gulf she went. About five miles offshore,

Herkiser estimates."

"But the dog-"

"Herkiser said Gary made him throw Totoo overboard, expecting him to drown. But that's a tough little canine. He obviously swam toward lights on shore – five miles of doggy-paddling with those stumpy little legs. Some dog, that one."

"Damn near human, too. You say he's the one who cracked the case – with his hard, beady stare?"

"It was more than Herkiser could take, an accusing stare from a little dog he'd tried to kill. Totoo's a great interrogator. Come on, Totoo, let's go home."

"He's yours now?"

"Beverly had no family, Mobe. Her friend doesn't want him. So it looks like I've got a partner."

Moby chuckled. "In your case report, you gonna give your partner a mention for the assist?"

"Not a bad idea." What she wouldn't mention, though, was the dog biscuit she had taped under the arm of Herkiser's chair just before his interrogation.

CZECH FOR A SHORT BIER

After I left the interstate, the first thing I found out was that Dooganville was one truly isolated Appalachian Mountain town. After I'd wound along State Route 53 for a half-hour of autumn-crisped trees and sharp turns around rocky outcrops, the second thing I found out was the guy I'd come to see was dead.

But I'd had to push hard for that news.

"Who?" asked the lean and mean-looking Sheriff Mac Lindquist in his storefront office at the near end of his single-street town. He hadn't bothered to take his combat-booted feet off his desk when I'd come in, and they were still there. "You say his name was Komensy?"

"Rad Komensky, from Radnor, Pennsylvania," I told him. "Rad short for Konrad."

"Oh, you mean Radnor Rad. Fella just over three feet tall." Fingers laced behind his balding head, Lindquist nodded. "Guess Rad was the fella you're looking for."

"'Was'? He wasn't more than forty, forty-five. What happened to him? Heart?"

"Head." Lindquist wormed his rump deeper in his creaky swivel. "Bashed it against some rocks when he fell down a drop-off in the woods over by Wold Lake. Broke his neck."

"When?"

"A month back. Why you so interested in a dead dwarf, Mr... What'd you say your name was?"

"Montgomery. Elrod Montgomery. Mr. Komensky was an employee of mine – a friend. I'm a PI, Philadelphia area. Rad worked for me for a time."

"Radnor Rad was a PI? Don't seem appropriate. Too easy to spot."

"Who'd expect a little person to be a PI?"

Lindquist nodded. "See what you mean. Back in Pee Eh. Thought you said he was a foreigner."

"His parents were immigrants from Czechoslovakia." I leaned against the filing cabinet in Lindquist's dinky office. "How'd he come to take a fall like that?"

Lindquist had put a little twist on the name I'd never really liked, but I didn't appreciate other people sneering at it. I usually tell folks just call me Rod, but I was beginning not to appreciate Sheriff Mac Lindquist.

"First vacation I've had in years," I told him. "Man edges up on fifty, wife long gone, decided he'd better see the country while he's still able. I thought I'd drop by for a couple hours and chew the fat with Rad. Now you tell me he's dead."

"It's a fact. So you might as well move on, Elrod. There's

nothing here for you."

That struck me as an odd thing to say. I got the feeling the sheriff wasn't telling me everything. Rad had come here two years ago to take care of his normal-sized but asthmatic sister. He'd written me he'd found himself a job; then a couple months back, he'd written that she'd died. But he was still working, doing okay, and he hoped I remembered him. That was when I'd decided to drop by to see him on this vacation swing.

"Nothing here for you," Lindquist repeated.

"Well, it's a tad late in the day. This burg got a hotel?"

Lindquist sighed, and his boots finally hit the floor. He pushed out his chair to stand a good half-head over me, but he wasn't nearly as heavy.

"Look, Elrod, it was an accident. He was heading for the lake in the dark, fell down the bank."

"What was he doing wandering around in the woods at night?"

"Checking something at Grady's Docks, I assumed. That's where he worked. Caulking, painting boats, repairing the slips. And he wasn't wandering in the dark. He had a flashlight. Got it right here."

He reached into a drawer and pulled out a three-celled flash with a sliding switch. "It was in working order. I turned it on to check."

"You're the one who found him?"

"After old man Grady reported he hadn't showed up for work for two days."

"A motel?" I pressed.

The sheriff shrugged surprisingly narrow shoulders. "Dooganville Lodge, other end of town."

The other end of town was visible from this end. I slid back into my dusty Ford and drove the three blocks. Calling the four clapboard cabins huddled under a stand of maples a "lodge" was a high compliment. In the office shack out front was a woman who could have been a stand-in for Ma Kettle in the black-and-white movie days – when Dooganville must have been built.

Her voice was as dry and crackly as the old farm auction poster on the wall behind her. "You'd be the friend of Radnor Rad."

Shook me for a couple seconds. Then I nodded at the dial phone on the counter. "Didn't take the sheriff long to give me an intro."

The thin lips grinned around tobacco-stained teeth. "You're right quick, mister. Never did cotton to Mac Lindquist's prying into everybody else's business. Sure don't appreciate his telling me to keep my mouth shut 'bout that poor little fella Rad."

I came to full alert. "He told you that?"

"Word's out all over town to keep shut of that particular subject. Burns my buns."

I signed the fly-specked registration pad. "Rad was an associate of mine. A friend." I looked up at her. "You got something to tell me about him?"

"That's the problem. I don't."

Then she looked through the window behind me, checked the empty street and leaned close. "But I do know somebody who does – if she would talk, you being a stranger and all."

"Maybe me being a friend of Rad might make a difference. She got a name?"

"Sarah Brauer. She worked at the After Hours 'til about a month ago when she quit. Now she just putters around her house. Husband's went off with somebody else, son's gone off to the navy. She's all alone."

"How can I get in touch with her?"

"There's the phone. Here's the book."

Sarah Brauer didn't want to meet me at her house. She suggested a fast-food place all the way back to the interstate interchange. One scared woman, I gathered.

Driving there, I got the feeling I was being followed. Who wouldn't, the way this was shaping up? But the road was so twisty through these hills, I couldn't check more than a tenth of a mile behind me. Didn't see anyone at all.

The countryside was fading to evening purple when I reached the cluster of gas stations and food shops along I-81 and pulled into the Queenburger. Fair crowd in there, but I spotted Sarah right off because she wore the mustard-colored scarf she'd mentioned on the phone.

At the counter, I bought a combo of Chicken Digits, slaw and coffee, then swivel-hipped through crowded tables to hers in a remote corner.

"Mr. Montgomery?" Her voice was squeaky. Not a bad looker in a washed-out sort of way. Mid-forties. A little make-up would have helped, along with replacements for her shapeless blue dress and baggy white cardigan.

"Sarah Brauer? Really appreciate your meeting me on short notice." I eased onto the hard plastic seat opposite her. "Don't you want more than coffee? I'd be glad to-"

"Not hungry, thanks. You go ahead." She glanced around like a cornered rabbit. The way the place was filling up, I figured we were lost in the crowd.

She took a nervous sip of her coffee. "I shouldn't be doing this."

"Nobody'll ever know."

"I didn't see it happen. I was back in the kitchen."

"At the After Hours?"

She nodded. "It's a tap room, but they have a little kitchen behind the bar. I was back there-"

Her eyes had riveted on something or somebody across the restaurant. I looked over there. Just crowd.

I turned back to Sarah. "What is it?"

She already had her purse in her hand. "Gotta go. Sorry." And she was gone, slipping through the jammed restaurant like a spooked eel.

By the time I got outside, she was in her car, heading outbound. I jumped into mine, but after I dodged an overeager Buick trying to zip into my space, she had whipped her Toyota out of there. I watched her taillights wink out around the first bend in the road back to Dooganville.

Couldn't catch her. Almost did, halfway back, but a black pickup bounced out of a side road, slewed sideways and stopped dead in front of me. I damn near broadsided him.

A cloud of blue smoke from maybe three months'-worth of burned-up tire wear drifted past my headlights. As it cleared, I sneezed then looked up into the meanest pair of squinted eyes I'd seen this side of Clint Eastwood.

My door flew open. A blue-shirted arm snaked in. I was yanked into the night by a two-legged mountain. He bunched my shirt into one hand and began to slap me with the other. Thank God he didn't make that dinner plate of a hand into a fist. As it was, my face felt like a piece of beef under attack by a tenderizing mallet.

"Don't even think about going back to town," Platter Hands rumbled. "You hear me?"

Then they were gone, just like that. I slithered down the side of my car and through swelling lids watched the pickup's taillights disappear Dooganvilleward.

I was 200 miles inland, but I thought I could hear the ocean. Then I realized that was my ears singing. I felt my jaw. Nothing broken there. Maybe a couple of eardrums.

Above the rise, I heard a car. Coming from the Dooganville direction. It stopped with its headlights on me.

"Ohmigod!" Sarah Bauer wailed. "When I saw the pickup pull out just after I went by, I stopped in a driveway. A couple minutes later, it roared past. When your car didn't show up, I figured... Omigod, look at you!"

"Superficial." I managed, trying hard to stand on legs made of pudding. "Who were they?"

"I'm not naming names. They might... You might-"

"For Pete's thake, Tharah —" my tongue was swelling up. "Tell me thomething."

"Can you drive?"

"Think tho." I groaned back into the Ford. "Yeth."

I shut my door and rolled down the window. She leaned in. "Ask them at the After Hours about the broken light."

"The what? Tharah, come back here!"

She had run back to her car. At full alert for menacing pickups, I followed her back into Dooganville until she pulled into a narrow side street in the middle of town, then into a driveway. Anything more to be gained by pushing into her house? I thought not, and there was that one little piece of info she'd given me. A broken light?

I hadn't passed the After Hours on the east side of town, so I deduced it had to be somewhere out on the west end. Found it soon enough, not by the halo of neon I'd expected, but by the gaggle of cars around the dark building. The single-story structure was a frame ramble, tastefully facaded in gritty tarpaper. Nightlife in Dooganville.

I parked heading outward for an efficient departure, should that become a necessary option. Head still ringing but tongue subsiding, I made for the door.

I heard music in there. Well, maybe by some standards. Kind of a gut-curling thump with a wailing fiddle override. Boondocks Beguine. When I opened the solid plank door, the noise rolled all over me. But when I made it through the crowd and bellied up to the splintery bar, it stopped. Or my ears had finally given out.

A voice like a 50-gallon drum rolling downhill rumbled, "Man ain't got the sense of a cockeyed tick hound."

My God, it was Platter Hands, sucking up beer no doubt to celebrate the expunging of an unwanted visitor. But here I was, as dumb as corncobs, ready for another facial treatment. Except I hoped there was some safety in numbers.

I looked around the room, not at the sour faces flanking me at the bar, no doubt waiting for rumble-gut to make a decision, but at the lights along the walls. Dim little pairs of plastic candles with fake flame bulbs. What had Sarah Brauer been talking about?

Then I looked up. Three chandeliers hung up there, wagon wheels with bulbs at the ends of their spokes. Four bulbs in the middle one, all on one side, were a lot brighter and not as fly-specked as the rest.

When I looked back down, I was ringed by a cluster of redneck types, one small and worried-looking, the half-dozen others as reassuring as pit bulls aquiver. All were towered over by Platter Hands, apparently top dog.

"You in a barrel of trouble, boy," he rumbled. "PI outta his jurisdiction. Mac Lindquist told me," he said into my surprised expression. "Sheriff and me is close as spit on a sidewalk."

I squinted at the worried fellow among them. Since life itself is a bad-odds gamble, I was going to take another.

"The Philadelphia Spiel was a cover. I'm from the state police."

Worry Wart's face twisted in anguish. "The state?"

"Yep." I flashed my private eye badge. "And my people know I'm here."

His eyes bugged. "Wasn't my toss!" he squawked. "Not me. It was Thursday."

"Shut up, Ernie! Platter Hands roared. "Lissen, you clowns, this ain't no state cop. That was a PI Badge he flashed. Now you," he yelled at me, "you get your butt outta here! Hit the road whilst you're still able. Let him through, boys. He's going on his way like a good fella."

I got out while the getting was good. Heading back into Dooganville's tatty metro center, I wondered if I'd learned anything at all. Look for a broken light, Sarah Brauer had said. I'd found it. "Wasn't my toss," Worry Wart had yipped. What in hell did that mean? And his crack about Thursday? None of this made sense.

Except for the curious state of Rad's flashlight.

I parked close to my drab little cabin. Figured maybe I could hear any fiddling with my car going on out there during the night. Then I discovered there weren't any towels in the phone booth-sized bathroom. I walked over to the office. The light was on, and the place was still open at 10:00 p.m. I went in and rang the counter bell.

Ma Kettle shuffled through a door behind the counter. In a raggedy terrycloth robe. She lived back there.

"Mr. Montgomery?"

"Sorry to be so late, but you forgot to put towels—"

"What happened to your face?"

"Big man, little brain, wants me out of here."

"That'd be Thursday."

"No, that'd be tonight."

"I mean Ben Thursday," she said. "Hands like coal stove lids, voice like a bull. Ben Thursday. He... He... I'll get your towels."

When she came back, I took the threadbare things. Then I looked straight into her watery blue eyes. "What is it I should know about our friend, Ben Thursday?"

She dropped her gaze to stare at her dusty countertop. "Everybody's afraid of him, except... You know about women who are kind of, uh, drawn to that sort of man? His power, maybe."

"You afraid or drawn?"

"Afraid, I guess, like 'most everybody else." Then her washed out eyes hardened. "But I'm mad, too, damn it!"

"About what?"

"About... You gotta swear you never heard this from me."

I nodded. "So sworn."

"I'm mad at him and Jenny."

"Who's Jenny?"

"Jenny Lindquist." She said, meeting my eyes again. "The sheriff's wife—and my kid sister."

"Your sister and Ben Thursday are a 'thing'?"

She nodded sourly. "Jenny told me. It's like an addiction. She can't get herself to break it off, but she's scared to death Mac will find out."

"Who else knows?"

"Nobody, I reckon. 'Cept you now. She and Ben meet at the lake at night when nobody's there."

Platter Hands Thursday and the sheriff's wife! This was a stunner. I hadn't seen her, of course, but I'd seen juiceless Mac Lindquist. It was possible his neglected wife could be drawn to a virile mountain like Thursday, despite his crudeness. Maybe because of it.

A light dawned. "You're hoping I can break it up, somehow, aren't you?"

Her thin, bluish lips tightened into something close to a smile.

I walked back to the cabin with my arms full of towels and my head full of confusion. Took a shower, turned on the battered A/C unit. The thing made a noise like a kid running a stick along pickets. Turned it off. Opened the paint-starved window a crack.

I lay in the sticky dark to toss and turn. Toss? Wasn't that what Worry Wart had blurted back in the After Hours? "Wasn't my toss. It was Thursday," the guy had whined. Thursday's toss?

An ugly thought hit me. Then the whole thing hit me, and I don't think I slept more than an hour. Radnor Rad was becoming a forgotten man because certain people here for sure didn't want to remember him.

Sheriff Mac Lindquist eyed my misused face. "You here to press charges? Word on the street is you got slapped around some last night."

"Not much of a street out there, not much of a word you got, either, if that's all you got."

Lindquist poured liquid tar from a Mr. Coffee machine into a mug inscribed with What People Say Behind Your Back Is Your Standing In The Community. "You look like you could use some yourself," he offered.

"No, thanks." I gestured at the mug. "Appropriate sentiment."

"Specially in this town."

"That's the truth."

"So what brings you here this morning?"

"I'll bet you had an autopsy done on Rad, right?"

"It's the law in a death like that."

"You got a copy?" I asked him.

He rooted in a drawer of a filing cabinet and handed me the stapled form.

I skimmed it and found what I'd expected. "Didn't it bother you that glass particles were found in the facial abrasions?"

"Figured he'd hit pieces of a busted bottle somebody left out there."

"Sheriff, it says here the particles looked like they came from a 'thin-walled glass object.' My money's on light bulbs. The busted ones at the After Hours joint."

Lindquist didn't change expression, but his eyes took on a hard glitter.

"Covered it up, right, Sheriff? Better than even money you were there yourself."

"It was an accident."

"No doubt illegal in this state, isn't it? A sick fad a couple years back. But dwarf tossing is illegal most anywhere now. How low can this town go?"

He glowered at me. Then he slumped. "Ah, hell. It was only a game, tossing for distance into mattresses the boys brought in their pickups after the place closed for regular business. Rad didn't mind. He was getting paid five bucks a toss."

"And Thursday's toss crashed him head-on into the chandelier."

"It was-" Lindquist licked dry lips. Cleared his throat. "It was an accident," he repeated.

"Maybe. So after Ben Thursday threw him hard enough to break his neck, Rad was carried into the woods by you sportsmen and put at the bottom of a drop-off. But you made a mistake with the flashlight."

"What mistake?"

"You told me you turned it on when it was found next to Rad's body. If he'd been picking his way through the woods at night where he had to know there was a dangerous drop-off, he surely would have had his flashlight on."

Lindquist sank into his chair and took a deep drag of coffee. And wheezed a deep sigh. "We took up a collection and buried him in the town cemetery. The undertaker in Frampton put him in a kid's coffin. A kid's coffin..."

He looked up at me. "What did you mean, 'maybe' it was an accident? I was there."

"You know what kind of a woman chaser Ben Thursday is?"

"Everybody knows that. I'm not even surprised you know."

"I'll give you odds Rad went out to Wolf Lake to check

something he was working on, saw Ben out there with somebody's wife, somebody Thursday sure didn't want to find out about their torrid tangle out there on the dock. My thought is he spotted Rad watching them, and when the chance came, it was lights out for Rad. No pun intended."

"You've flipped your wig, Montgomery, coming in here with a wild story like that." But now there was no steam behind his words. Then he said, "Whose wife?"

"Rumor, Lindquist. Big man about town."

I kept my eyes on him. Watched the color drain from his face.

"Hit the road, Montgomery. Now. Get on with your vacation. Go on, get out of here." Not friendly. Not unfriendly, either.

I got. But as I went out the door, I shot a look back at him. He was strapping on the biggest Colt .44 I'd ever seen outside the silver screen.

On the way back to I-81, I passed the entrance to the Dooganville Cemetery. Stopped, backed up. Drove in. I found what had to be the grave. Just a small, unmarked mound. I couldn't help Radnor Rad now, the little person who'd wanted to be remembered.

I set out again for the interstate. Then I stopped and turned back toward Dooganville. At least I could do something about a headstone.

TEE FOR TWO

On the 11th tee, Merv Atherton sucked in his gut and addressed the ball. When he was younger, he'd had a stance as good as the Golden Bear's. "The second Nicklaus," they'd begun to call him on tour. That was before his putting went to hell, and he couldn't make the cut anymore.

"Merv!" Ed Mittleman said behind him, "that twosome is only a hundred yards or so ahead."

Atherton straightened in irritation. "Dammit, Ed, they've dragged their butts on every hole. Now they're not even on the fairway, bumbling around in the brush under those palms looking for a ball they'll never find anyway. They won't even know we've played through."

He set his feet again, well back from the ball in his awkward, belly-offsetting stance, and eyed the green 310 yards distant. He brought the driver through his trademark-slow backswing, paused, then whipped the club downward.

A good enough drive, but not quite on the sweet spot. Atherton could tell by the sound. The ball arrowed straight out for 50 yards. Then it began to hook.

"Tsk, tsk," Mittleman burlesqued. "Only bad drive of the day, and it's gonna cost you."

The ball arched high, soared further leftward, then streaked down into the wide hedgerow of booted cabbage palms and underbrush that separated the 11th hole from the parallel 8th.

"Cripes, Merv, that's just about where-"

They heard a distant shout, then one of the duffers burst out of the bushes waving his arms and yelling.

"My God!" Atherton's voice sounded as if he were strangling. "You don't suppose my ball-"

All this, I got later from Ed Mittleman, about the same moment Merv Atherton's ball clunked into the hedgerow bordering the 11th fairway. I clinked my iced coffee glass to Ike Lebber's iced tea.

"Damn, it's good to see you again after all these years, Ike," I said. "Too easy to lose touch."

"Ain't that the truth?" He gave me a long look. "How's business for Elrod Montgomery, private eye?"

Ike rolled that around as if he didn't really believe it. Usually, I told people I was in the shoe business, not the gumshoe business. Saved a lot of dumb comments, but Ike had already heard somewhere what I really did for a living.

"I'm looking a tad hefty, my friend. And the thatch is thinning. The PI business? No car chases. No fireworks. Just observation and imagination." I filled him in on how rich I wasn't getting. "Time came for a vacation tour of the country and a chance to look up some of my old buddies. You were on the list, manager of the tap room here, so-"

The wail of a siren racing up the clubhouse drive put the rest of that on hold. I swung around to the window behind me. An orange and white county ambulance bumped over the driveway curb and barreled straight down the 10th fairway.

Then a guy stuck his brick-red face through the Tap Room's quaint swinging doors. "It's Russ Patterson, the lawyer. Hit by a wild drive on the 11th!"

"He okay?" Someone asked - inanely, I thought, with the ambulance's siren howling down the course toward the 11th hole.

"Hell, no. He's out like a light."

Reflex shoved back my chair. I found myself on my feet. Then I wondered what I was doing. Not my case. Not a case at all. An accident.

Ike grabbed my arm. "The golf carts are just outside." Which is how I came to be chasing an ambulance down the 10th fairway like a starving shyster, with Ike Lebber hunched over the wheel.

We hummed past the 10th green and skirted the 11th tee, flushing a trio of squawking crows. I spotted the ambulance, 200 yards down the fairway, close to the palms. When we got there, the two paramedics had unshipped their emergency gear and were being urged into the brush by a distraught guy in pink slacks and a white and gold shirt.

I was out of the cart before it stopped. With Ike wheezing behind me, I followed them into the hedgerow.

A stretch of Florida brush isn't like the northern kind. It's dense right down to the ground with prickly stuff among the ferns. I was glad the pink and white golfer and the paramedics were breaking the trail.

The victim of the errant drive lay about 20 feet in, face down in a stand of ferns. I could see a perfectly round, golf-ball-sized dent in his left temple, about a half-inch deep. Some blood. A yard this side of him lay the golf ball.

"You with him?" I asked the guy in pink and white.

"Yeah." He watched the paramedics check vital signs. Then he scowled at me. "You a member? Haven't seen you around before."

"Visitor. Name's Rod Montgomery. Friend of Ike's here." I stuck out my hand.

"Harry Kimmel." His grip was icy limp.

"Hell of a thing," I said.

"Yeah." Kimmel stared at his golfing partner on the ground. "Ball zipped in here, smacked Russ on the head and down he went."

I heard one of the paramedics mutter, "We're losing him."

They rolled Russ Patterson onto his back. His face was pasty white, and his bulging eyes weren't blinking. One of the medics began mouth-to-mouth. The other locked his hands together and pumped Patterson's chest. The rest of us stood around in the ferns, all eyes riveted on the three men on the ground.

The tension got to Harry Kimmel. Had to be some kind of shock to have a ball zip out of the blue and flatten your partner right in front of you. Head down, he began to pace. He held an iron, and he swished the club back and forth through the ferns.

On the fairway behind me, I heard a car pull up. I looked through the palms to see a big-boned, sunburned guy in khakis pick his way into the hedgerow toward us. When he reached our little fern patch, I saw he carried a dark green campaign hat in his hand. He wore a badge over his left shirt pocket – and a nameplate over his right. B. BARRETT BRUNDAGE, COUNTY SHERIFF.

"Awright, what've we got here? Somebody called in an accident-" He spotted the prone golfer. "Oh, yeah. Say, ain't that Russ Patterson??"

"Yep," somebody said. Harry Kimmel glanced up from his nervous swishing.

"Fella with the lawsuit to stop the condo development over in the east end of town?" the sheriff said to no one in particular. "Guess this could put a crimp in his court appearance."

"Sure will." The medic straightened up. "He's gone."

Now I became aware of how many people were in the ragged circle around the late Russ Patterson. Apparently so did Sheriff Brundage.

"Okay, I gotta make out a report, so everybody tell me who you are." He whipped out a little notebook from a hip pocket, fished a pencil out of his shirt, licked its point and nodded at me. "You first."

"Elrod Montgomery," Ike said for me. "He's a visitor with me. A gumshoe."

"A who?"

"A private detective," Ike said.

"I'm in charge here," Brundage announced, and he made a note. "Who're you?"

"Ike Lebber, manager of the club's Tap Room. Heard the ambulance, came down with Montgomery to-"

"I'm in charge," Brundage repeated. He turned to the pink and white golfer.

"Harry Kimmel," the guy said, glancing up from his fern inspection. "I was with Russ there, looking for the ball I'd two-stroked in here. He was helping me look; then Merv's ball zipped in, smacked him on the head and down he went."

Brundage licked his pencil again and nodded at the big-bellied golfer across from us. "You?"

"Merv Atherton. I'm afraid I drove the ball that hit him. Bad hook." He stared down at Russ Patterson, who stared straight up through the overhanging palm fronds. "I can't tell you how rotten I feel about this."

At that point, I noticed how little mourning was going on here for a dead attorney.

"Atherton," Brundage repeated. "As in Mervin Roger Atherton, the developer? Wait a minute. Ain't you and Kimmel here partners?"

"That's right."

"Working on that east-end condo deal?"

"That's right too."

"Well, ain't this one hell of a coincidence? Your partner's out here on the fairground-"

"Fairway."

"Whatever. He's out there with the lawyer who's trying to put the blocks to your business deal, and you clonk that particular guy dead with a wild drive. Some coincidence."

Atherton shifted his bulk. "Not at all. The golf course is neutral territory, so to speak. We thought Harry could talk some sense into Russ during a friendly round. Ed Mittleman-"

"You Mittleman?" the sheriff asked the tall, jug-eared guy next to Atherton.

He nodded, and the sheriff made another note.

"Ed and I," Atherton went on with an impatient scowl, "we just happened to be behind them. They were slow as turtles, so on the 11th, we decided to play through."

"'Just happened,' huh?" Sheriff Brundage turned to Mittleman. Atherton's stringbean partner had a greenish tinge to his cheeks. He wasn't having a nice day.

"You in this real estate lash-up, too?" Brundage asked him.

Mittleman licked his lips. "N-no. Merv was looking for a partner, and I was handy. I was flattered, too. Merv's the best golfer at the club. Used to be a pro on the circuit."

He looked down at Patterson's body. "Do we have to… stand around here?"

Brundage shoved his notebook back in his hip pocket and hitched up his slacks. "Good point. All of you, wait over by the ambulance. Nobody leaves 'til I tell you to. That means you, too, private eye."

As we trailed out of the scrubland, Ike murmured to me, "Don't mind the sheriff. He's running for reelection this year. Makes him a little hyper."

I looked back to see Brundage pull a glassine envelope out of his shirt pocket, crouch down and nudge the ball into it with his pencil. The paramedics had lifted Russ Patterson's body onto their stretcher and were covering it with a yellow plastic tarp. The others trailed behind us toward the golf carts on the fairway, with Harry Kimmel lagging for a final swish then picking up his golf bag.

"Where you from, Montgomery?" Brundage had his broad-brimmed hat on now, and he looked properly official.

"Pennsylvania. Just outside of Philadelphia."

"What kind of work you handle?"

"Scut, mostly. Divorce, straying spouses, missing people the cops have run out of leads on. It's a living."

"Uh huh."

In his green and white Dodge with big gold stars on its front doors, I sat next to him on the passenger side of the front seat. Ike hunched on the back seat, no doubt thinking of the lousy publicity all this was going to bring the club. In the mirror on my side, I watched the ambulance's flashing lights bounce up the fairway toward the exit drive. Brundage had sent the others back to the clubhouse, and I wondered why he'd kept us here.

"You believe in coincidence, Montgomery?"

"Now and then, but not often."

"Yeah, me too. Fact, it's kind of a coincidence you being here."

I shrugged. "That's one you can believe in. Ike and I went to high school together. I'm on a vacation trip, he works at the club, so I dropped in to say hello."

Brundage swung around to Ike. "That right?"

"God's truth, Sheriff."

"Tell me something 'bout Atherton."

Ike said, "Golfwise or otherwise?"

"Whateverwise."

"Used to be a pro on tour. Then his putt went to pot. Couldn't sink them for sour apples. But his long games always held up. He can still drive like Babe Ruth used to call his homers. It's got to be a real jolt to him hooking that drive so bad on the 11th."

We sat silent in the sheriff's Dodge, hot even with all the windows open. A pair of crows glided past, heading for the hedgerow with a hoarse caw.

"Crows down here sound different," I said.

The sheriff squinted out his window, watching the crows land in one of the cabbage palms. "They are different. Fish crows. Yours up north are carrion crows." He turned back to me.

"Don't forget I'm in charge here, but what do you think, PI? We got a guy at the tee who your buddy says can call his shots like the Babe. And we got his partner two hundred yards out in the bushes with the guy who's filed a lawsuit that's maybe going to cost them both a bundle. Catchy scenario, but damned if I believe Atherton – or, hell, even Arnie Palmer – could be good enough off the tee to snipe some guy he can't even see six hundred feet away."

My sentiments exactly.

"Suppose you're Atherton," Brundage went on, "and you want to knock off Russ Patterson and make it look like an accident. How'd you go about it?"

I knew this interrogation technique, but surely the sheriff couldn't think I was somehow going to hang myself.

"Remember," I reminded him, "I was in the clubhouse and Ike here-"

Brundage waved an impatient hand. "Come on, Montgomery. You don't see my cuffs out."

"Okay. In the first place, I'd do just what Atherton did. Partner my buddy with him, then have his buddy – Harry Kimmel, in this case – drag around the course until he saw a likely-looking spot and flub into it. Kimmel said he two-shotted in there, not hard for even a duffer. Then I'd ask Patterson to help me look for the ball."

"But how in the hell could Atherton hit him on purpose from that tee way back there?"

"The hook Merv could work out easily," Ike offered behind us. "But hit a target he couldn't see?" Ike shrugged.

"So he gets the ball about where he wants it," I said, "but a million to one it's going to smack Patterson on the head. You know what I think? I think we should assume the ball didn't hit him."

Brundage held up his evidence envelope. "Take a look at it. It's Atherton's, all right. Got an MRA monogram on it. Marvin Roger Atherton. To my eyes, it fit that dent in Patterson's skull exactly. You tell me what else is going to make a dent like that. And look here, you see specks of blood."

"Okay," I agreed. "Then let's assume it did hit him. But not out of the blue."

From the back seat, Ike said, "What are you getting at, Rod?"

Brundage looked interested. "So the ball slams in there but doesn't hit Patterson. You saying Kimmel picked it up and whacked him with it hard enough to kill him? It'd take some doing to batter a guy to death with a golf ball."

"How about making something like a... a slingshot."

Brundage stared at me. "A kid's toy?"

"I tried one of those 'kid's toys' at a flea market a couple years ago. The kind powered by heavy-duty rubber tubing. I sank a ball bearing half an inch into a pine board. And the thing was small enough to hide in a golf bag – which I noticed Kimmel had with him in the ferns, not back in his golf cart. Why would he lug his whole bag in there to look for a lost ball?"

"A point, a point," Brundage allowed. "He never did find his ball. Just kept swishing through the weeds with his iron."

"Now why," I wondered, "with his partner dying in front of him, was Kimmel so intent on finding a damned golf b-"

Then I got it. "Oh," I said. "Very neat."

Brundage thumbed back his campaign hat, leaving a red mark low on his forehead. "You're doing all the talking, Montgomery. What's so 'neat'?"

"A theory, Sheriff. When the timing and location are right, Kimmel flubs a couple of shots to get Patterson in the hedgerow. That's not hard for a halfway competent golfer. Then he waits for Atherton's ball to zip in. He's got a pilfered monogrammed MRA ball in his pocket. He hears Atherton's drive sock in. He whaps Patterson with the extra MRA ball."

"Using a slingshot."

"Give you odds. Then the idea is to quickly find and pocket the ball Atherton drove so there won't be two MRA monograms lying around when the crowd gathers. Obviously, he's got to leave the killer ball where it is. He has a couple of minutes before Atherton and his partner get down here on their cart. But he can't find the ball Atherton drove. When we all crowd in, he's panicked that one of us will stumble on it. He can't stop himself from looking. That's what all that fern swishing was."

"But," Ike put in, "if he'd found it, we would have seen him pick it up."

"Uh huh," Brundage rumbled, "but all he'd have to say is, 'Oh, I just found my ball,' and stick it in his pocket. We'd have figured he was in shock and didn't realize what goofed-up behavior that was."

Had I sold Brundage? "If I'm right," I pressed, "it means Atherton's ball is still in the hedgerow."

"And that could clinch it?" Brundage pondered. "I might go along with that."

"How about the three of us spread out and walk the length of that stand of brush?" I suggested. "One pass ought to cover it."

One pass did. We found three golf balls, all of them obviously long residents of that particular stretch of brush. But that was all we found. Our main accomplishment was to roust a gaggle of crows out of the cabbage palm in there.

Brundage whipped off his hat and wiped his forehead with a blue bandana. "Kind of shoots the theory, Montgomery, don't it?"

Behind him, the crows glided back into the nearby tree. They sure loved–

Observation. Imagination.

"Ike, you're not a very heavy guy," I said. "Let me give you a boost up there."

Brundage scowled. "Now what? I gotta get back to the office, file an accident report."

The crows weren't happy about Ike standing on my shoulders in there. It was a long shot, and I began to feel like a middle-aged grandstander with nothing to show for–

"Hey, lookee here!" Ike cried above me. He reached among the foot-long "boots" left by the broken-off fronds of years past. And he held up a golf ball.

"Monogrammed 'MRA'!" he called down to us. "Looks like you're right on the money, Rod."

"Well, I'll be damned," Brundage relented. "No wonder Kimmel couldn't find the ball Atherton drove in here."

He swung around and rushed to his car radio. By the time I helped Ike down and we pushed out of the scrub, Brundage was all smiles.

"Just raised one of my deputies out on the main road. He stopped Harry Kimmel as he was driving out of the club. Searched his bag. One Super Duty Power Sling is being held as evidence. Arrested Kimmel, all points out on Atherton. Gotta give you credit, Montgomery."

"No, you don't," I told him. "I'm just passing through. You take the credit. Get yourself reelected. This country needs reasonable lawmen." I gave him a grin. "In charge."

DOTTY BLUE

Bizzibee turned out to be a nice looking little town. It straddled both sides of a state road that angled off US 25, the highway that parallels the east side of the Rockies from New Mexico to Wyoming.

The town was two blocks of mostly ma-and-pa commercial enterprise, a rustic lodge named The Mountaineer, then a string of decent enough houses. In front of one of them hung a shingle: F.X. GOSLING, MD, COUNTY CORONER. That was what I was looking for.

I was here not because F.X. Gosling was the local county coroner or because he was an MD. I was here because Dr. Gosling had been a high school classmate of mine back in Philadelphia. He went on to Johns Hopkins Medical School. I joined the U.S. Marines. By the time I'd served my hitch and joined the Philly PD, Gosling had a general practice going, and I signed on as a patient. As time wore on, no big problems other than too much weight.

Eventually I quit the force, set up shop as a PI. Put on more weight, though when you're just shy of six feet, it doesn't show all that much. Then came the Gosling case, after which Doc Gosling and I parted company.

All this flashed through my sun-dazzled brain as I pulled my travel-worn Bronco into his graveled semicircle driveway. An adobe wall screened the entrance from the highway. I supposed it was there to protect the sensibilities of neighbors and passing motorists when bodies were delivered here for Gosling's autopsical findings.

I pushed the doorbell button, heard a muffled chime and waited. The house was wide and low, rough tan stucco, the oak door extra wide – for gurneys, I supposed.

I ran a quick gamut of mixed feelings. He had been a high school buddy, my doctor for decades, then he'd turned cold and mean when I found his wife was making appointments of her own. Notably house calls on quiet afternoons with a suave Dr. Finley. Gosling had hired me to check her out, then cut me dead when I turned in my report. Still, he once had been my friend – and we were a long way from Pennsylvania out here at the foot of the looming Rockies.

The latch rattled and the big door swung open. Dr. Francis Xavier Gosling, once known as "Goose," later as "Doc," stood there, a rotund balding double for a Guy Kibbee of old movie fame.

"Yes?" Doc Gosling said. "Can I be of-" He squinted, peered up at me. "Well, I'll be a monkey's grandfather! Rod Montgomery!"

I couldn't read his reaction. "I was in the neighborhood," I said. Somewhat true, except that neighborhood had been a vacation stop in Albuquerque, and this was a multi-hundred-mile side trip.

"I can't believe this." Doc's sandy brows were at high surprise. "You. Out here."

"Same thought I have about you," I told him.

"Simple enough. After Melba and I... split, I came out here to visit my daughter. She manages The Mountaineer Lodge. I liked it here. Stayed here. Bought this place, sent for my furniture. Got myself elected coroner."

"Didn't know you were a forensics man."

"I read a lot." Doc suddenly slapped his forehead. "Why are we standing out here in the heat? Come on in, Rod."

"I gather I'm forgiven?"

"For what?" he said over his shoulder as I followed him into the air-conditioned coolness.

"The case."

"The case? Oh. The Melba business. I acted like an ass, Rod. Hired you to get the goods on her, then hated you when you did your job. Shameful example of killing the messenger. Sit." He curled his thumb toward a pretty darned ugly overstuffed chair. "Have a ginger beer or something stronger?"

"Ginger beer is fine."

While Doc clanked around in the adjacent kitchen, I took in the strange décor of the big main room. Tan stucco walls here, too. Philadelphia 1950s furniture in a Mexican hacienda. Across the entrance hall were a pair of metal swinging doors.

"That's my little morgue," Doc said behind me. He held out a frosty glass of pale ginger beer. I sank back into the chunky chair.

"I've made a discovery, Rod," Doc said from the mushy-looking sofa. "There's a lot less anxiety when your patients arrive already dead."

"You get much, uh, action?"

"Accidents and heatstrokes." He grinned. "Cut and dried,

you might say. Now and then something more interesting turns up. Got one in there now."

"Other than cut or dried?"

"This one's broken. Care to take a look?"

Well, that was a novel offer, but I wasn't so sure I wanted to take him up on it this peaceful western afternoon.

"Broken?" I said.

"Neck. Purportedly a fall. Too bad. Can't be more than thirty-five or so. Something about it bugs me. Come on, I'll show you."

How could I refuse?

Doc's morgue was a stark white room, its own A/C seemingly set on freeze-dry. At the far end was a cluttered lab set-up. Two steel tables graced the middle of this unappealing chamber. On one of them lay a sheet-adorned body.

Without preamble, Doc Gosling folded back the sheet at the head end. "Meet the late Dorothy Blumentripp, local artist, found dead yesterday afternoon in her own studio. Broken neck, apparently from an accidental fall."

"Fell how?"

"She seemed to have tangled her feet in an extension cord and took a header down the steps into her sunken studio."

"Sunken studio?"

"Originally a sunken living room. Quite the architectural fad when her house was built. She'd converted the room into an at-home art studio."

"So Blumentripp tripped."

"So Chief Dixon deduced. And so he has officially reported."

I peered down at the mortal remains of Ms. Blumentripp. Quite pretty. Gracefully arched eyebrows, stubby little nose, full mouth. No make-up. Gray complexion, but she was dead. Shoulder-length blond hair, lots of it.

"So what bugs you, Doc?"

He fingered the hair aside at the nape of her neck. "See those bruises? What kind of a fall gives you bruises like that?"

"You think she was strangled."

"No, Rod. Her neck has been snapped."

Doc nodded thoughtfully.

"But?" I prompted.

"No motive, no suspects. Dixon likes a lot of evidence to go on, not just a few suspicious bruises."

I looked down at Doc Gosling's current patient. I had no particular place I had to be next. Had as much time as God was willing to give me.

"I'm kind of partial to suspicious bruises, myself," I told him.

Doc gave me a big smile. "I was hoping you would be."

"But I'm two thousand miles out of my area of license."

"You want to play, I'll call you my special consultant."

"Fair enough." I gestured toward the supine Ms. Blumentripp. "Now that I'm on the case, what else can you tell me?"

Doc leaned against the empty autopsy table. "Federal Parcel Service driver found her around 4:00 p.m. yesterday when he made a delivery to her place. Chief Dixon called me, and I got there around 5:00 p.m. Figured the time of death was around noon, give or take an hour or so. It's an inexact calculation, you know. Too many variables."

"Anybody else seen around her place yesterday?"

"The gardener. He was working in the back lawn most of the day. Said he didn't see anybody at all. Woman across the street did, though. Maude Ruddy. She's got an older house with a front porch. Spends her day on it, sitting and knitting. She told Dixon that the deceased had a visitor around lunchtime. Maude knew who he was, too."

"You going to tantalize me or tell me?"

"Fellow by the name of Trimbull. The deceased's ex-husband. They broke up about a year back."

"Two callers, then. Ex-hubby and the parcel man. That's it?"

"So Maude called the chief."

I nodded at the body. "How'd you find her?"

"On the studio floor, flat on her face. Feet were up on the little step I mentioned, and an extension cord from a lamp was looped around the left one." Doc shrugged. "Looked like an obvious accident – until I spotted the neck bruises."

"Forensically speaking, Doc, you got anything else?"

"I have this." He walked over to the lab set-up and handed me a glassine envelope.

I held it up toward the ceiling fluorescents. The plastic envelope had a collection of what seemed to be snippets of colored paper. And a scatter of little blue dots.

"You know what this stuff is?" I asked him.

"Paper and plastic bits. Art residue, you might call it. The police report calls this an accidental death." He tapped an envelope with a forefinger. "I call it 'The Case of Dotty Blue.'"

Dotty Blue? Oh, the blue dots. "Not an accident?" I said.

"There are those neck bruises. Should be a big one on her head where she hit. There isn't one. Should not be bruised under her jawline. But there they are."

"Where'd that stuff in the envelope come from, Doc?"

"Her hair. When I combed it out. Standard procedure."

"You think it might be some kind of an oddball beauty fad?"

"Nope. You're staying around for a while?"

"Thought I'd get a room back at The Mountaineer for tonight."

"I've got a spare room, Rod. You can bunk here. First thing after breakfast, I'll show you the crime scene. Well, what I think is a crime scene."

"You can do that?"

Doc Gosling gave me a crinkly Guy Kibbee grin, "We're not very formal around these parts. And I'm the coroner. I have a key."

Dotty Blue's house crouched at the top of the road's gentle rise north of town. White adobe and redwood, a jarring combo of two architectural worlds. Precisely pruned shrubbery set off a beautifully manicured lawn. I swung the Bronco into the short black-top drive and nosed up to the garage door.

In the rearview mirror, I spotted an elderly woman on her porch across the street. Her weathered two-story farmhouse was way out of place among its pseudo-hacienda neighbors. I realized I was duly noting Maude Ruddy duly noting us.

I followed Doc to the multi-paneled front door. No crime scene tape. But in the eyes of the local cops, this wasn't a crime scene. Doc fitted a key into the ornate brass lock, and we were in.

I'd judged the house and grounds to be in the mid-six-figures category, pretty upscale for a town like this, but inside, the place looked like a pig-sty. Well, the flagstone foyer was neat enough, but the big room it led into was a housekeeper's nightmare.

"Told you she'd converted this into a studio," Doc said as we plowed in there. No question about that. Big room with lots of windows, a domed plastic skylight with three large drafting tables clustered beneath it, a crowd of filing cabinets, several drafting stools and a scatter of white resin chairs. Some nice landscapes and portraits on the off-white walls.

But none of that was instantly grabbing my attention in that room. What widened my eyes in disbelief was the floor. Over in one corner, I was able to observe that it was expensive parquet. But everywhere else, it was littered – snowed under – by a blizzard of chopped paper and plastic bits. The room looked like the aftermath of the world's wildest New Year's Eve party. Except this stuff wasn't confetti. It was snippings, the same sort that was in Doc's evidence envelope.

"What in hell kind of artist was she?" I wondered, toeing the underfoot mess.

"Called herself a 'collagist.' All her work was made up of bits of paper and plastic glued to Masonite 'canvasses.' Doesn't sound like much, but take a close look around you. That's her work on the walls."

I took a closer look. What I'd taken for landscape and portrait oils were not oils at all. They were made up of tiny bits of paper and plastic, not a dab of paint anywhere. Yet when I stepped back a few feet, each work blended into what looked to my untutored eye to be damned fine "paintings."

Doc pointed. "That one over by the door, 'The Last Hunt.' She got old Ben Crowfeather to pose for it. Liked to use local people as models. Looks just like him. He wanted to buy it, but he couldn't afford it. One of her works hangs in the lodge. Collage of pioneers heading west. The lodge owner bought it for five figures. That's what she's getting now – or was, before somebody put an end to it yesterday."

"You're convinced that's the case?"

"Follow me through on this," Doc said. He walked to an area at the rear of the room. "Here's where the body was lying. Face down, just about here. See that single step there, coming down from the rear hall? That's what her feet were up on."

He stepped up to crouch behind a table on the landing. Held up an electric cord. "And this extension cord was looped around her ankle. Come on up here and take a look at this set-up. Anything strike you as odd?"

I checked the lamp on the table and its copious cordage. Seemed okay to me… No, it didn't.

"The lamp's cord is long enough to reach the outlet under the table. Why did she need the extension?"

He clapped me on the back. "Exactly! I think the killer rigged that up after the fact to fake the accident scene. The cord probably came from one of the drawing table lamps. Problem is, this isn't quite enough to pin anybody with murder."

I made a slow round of the walls, peering at length at each of Dotty Blue's remarkable works. Then I scanned her drawing tables and the floor beneath.

Doc watched all this in silence, but ultimately he had to ask, "What in the hell are you looking for?"

"Blue dots."

"Should be blue dots in with all the other bits and pieces. She had them in her hair."

"Can't find a one. Not in any of her collages, not on the work tables or under them." I pondered. Then I said, "Aha!"

"Aha, what?"

"Precisely where was her head when you got here, Doc?"

He took two paces from the step and waved his pointing finger in a small circle. "Right here."

And right there, I found blue dots. Just a few, but they looked exactly like those in the envelope back in Doc's morgue. Then, on my knees in this same small area, I found several more of the dots.

"Interesting." I stood up.

"Got something?"

"Stiff muscles, Doc. I'm not as young as-"

"Come on, Rod!"

I grinned at him. "I've got half a theory. What I need to do now is talk with the two people who dropped by here yesterday."

"So you have got something," he chortled.

"I might. You told me the Federal Parcel driver discovered the body. Any chance I can interview him?"

Doc Gosling cogitated. "Makes his Bizzibee deliveries, if he has any, late afternoon. We'll keep an eye out."

"And the ex-husband?"

"Manages the Gold Pan restaurant in the lodge. How about lunch there?"

"Sounds good to me, Doc. Mind if I take a look through the rest of the house?"

"Take your time. I'll be in here admiring the artwork."

The kitchen was most notably green marble Corian and hanging copper bottom pots, a combination of low and high maintenance. Through the window over the steel sink, I saw the gardener hard at work with manual clippers on the yew hedge along the back lot line. Must have been paid in advance. Conscientious man.

I opened the kitchen door and stepped out onto the lawn. The hedge clipping stopped. The grass was dense and spongy as I walked out to the tall, sun-leathered gardener who sported a nose that would be an eagle's envy.

I stuck out my hand. "Name's Rod Montgomery. Doc Gosling's asked me to give him a hand with the, ah, unfortunate situation here. Like to talk with you about it."

"Bingham. Ned Bingham. Terrible thing." He set the hedge shears on the grass, stripped off his grubby work gloves and stuffed them in a hip pocket. His grip was firm, calloused, what you'd expect from a man who made his living with his hands. There was a tang of yew sap in the still air.

"I'm kind of surprised to find you out here, now that Ms. Blumentripp is no longer with us."

Bingham stroked his great blade of a nose with thumb and forefinger. "Already paid me for the month."

Diogenes would have been fulfilled.

"You see anything out of the ordinary yesterday, Mr. Bingham?"

"Folks call me Ned."

"Ned, then."

"You mean around the time she fell?"

"I mean anytime yesterday, Ned."

He swept a denim-sleeved arm toward the back of the property. "Plenty of hedge to trim. I spent yesterday on it, finishing it up today. When I clip the hedge, that's what I see. Got no time to lollygag around, poking into what ain't my business."

"I take it that's a no."

"No what?'

"No, you didn't see anything unusual yesterday."

"You got it right." Bingham picked up his hedge clippers. "You got any more questions?"

Not at the moment, but I certainly reserved the right. I walked back to the kitchen door and went on with my tour.

Dotty Blue's bedroom, like the kitchen, was a model of neatness, in wild contrast to the mess on the studio floor. I wasn't learning a thing back here, so I rejoined Doc in the studio.

"If there's anything more to see here," I told him, "I've missed it. Care to join me in a neighborly visit across the road?"

"I'd better introduce you," Doc cautioned. I soon discovered why.

"Who?" Maude Ruddy yelped in a razor-edged voice loud enough to slow traffic.

"Rod Montgomery," Doc repeated patiently. "He's helping me on the Blumentripp, uh, case."

Maude Ruddy was eighty-seven, Doc had told me, Bizzibee's longest-in-residence widow. Beneath her abundance of snowy hair, she was built of sharp angles. Her blue sundress draped loosely from a frame of wire and had a barbed wire outlook.

"Case!" she snapped. "Thought she fell and broke her neck."

"That may well be, Mrs. Ruddy," I ventured, "but I-"

"A lot you know about it!"

"I've filled Rod in," Doc said.

"What I'd appreciate your telling me," I said with utmost

civility – funny how blatant peckishness produces that reaction – "is what you observed across the road yesterday while-"

"You mean who went in and out and when they did it? Already told that to Chief Dixon."

" – And how they seemed to be reacting when they left, Mrs. Ruddy."

"Oh. Didn't tell him that. He didn't ask." She stopped her flank speed knitting and squinted up at me. "Tad Trimbull, ex-husband. In just before noon, out in ten minutes. Looked fit to be tied. Screeched his tires when he drove off. Federal Parcel driver walked straight in at three-fifty-five, out in three minutes. Looked like he'd seen a dead body. Which he had. He waited out front for the police to arrive."

"And that's all? Could you possibly have missed someone? Maybe when you went in for lunch?"

"Don't have lunch. That's how I keep this girlish figure."

I smiled.

"You're sure, Maude?" Doc put in.

"'Course I'm sure, Dr. Frankenstein."

We thanked her and ambled thoughtfully back across the blacktop to my Bronco.

"What was that Frankenstein bit?" I asked him.

"Oh, she found out somehow that I'd been a GP. Wanted me to take her as a patient. But I'm out of that now, so she has to go to the clinic up in Cloudman. Hates me for it, hates what I do." He slid into the passenger seat. "You want to talk to Trimbull? It's just about lunchtime."

The Mountaineer lodge was rough-hewn pine outside and in, lots of it, and lots of Navajo ruggery, floor, and walls. Over the fireplace hung a giant painting – no, it was the collage Doc had told me about. Wagons West, with a pioneer's prominent profile in the foreground. Looked familiar.

Doc made a courtesy intro to his daughter, a pleasant, plump and preoccupied blond in her mid-thirties. Then we strolled into the Gold Pan restaurant, its rough-cut pans presumably used by prospectors long gone, and other gold-mining artifacts. The menu was compatible with the décor: "Nuggets of Chicken," of course, along with "Mine-estrone Soup," "Candied Carats," and "Ore-eo Pudding." Our lanky waitress wore a gold lame mini-skirt.

"Waddle ya have, gents?" Her hair was gold washed and piled high.

"We would like to have a word with Mr. Trimbull," Doc said. "Is he available?"

"Tad's always available," she said saucily. "Lemme gettim."

A few minutes later, Trimbull swivel-hipped among the tables and pulled up at our booth. Terrific tan, nifty contrast with his blow-dried, prematurely platinum hair. Dark trousers out of Brooks Brothers, plaid jacket out of Pimlico.

"Hi, yuh! Oh, Doc, it's you and-?"

"Friend of mine. Rod Montgomery from Back East. He's helping me on the Blumentripp matter."

"You need help for a simple accident case? What help?"

I thrust out my hand. "Good to meet you, Mr. Trimbull. Why don't you join us for a couple minutes."

Puzzled, Trimbull slid his lithe length into the booth, opting to sit next to Doc. "What 'Blumentripp matter'?"

"Some minor points we're trying to clear up," I assured him. I didn't need him any more defensive than he already was.

"Like what?"

"I'm told you visited yesterday. Around noon."

"By old Maude Ruddy, no doubt."

"Seems to be a reliable witness."

Trimbull's steely blue eyes narrowed. "You a lawyer?"

"No, I'm what Doc told you — an old friend of his."

Trimbull's unblinking stare didn't waver. Then he smirked. "Retired cop."

I met his smirk with one of my own. "Call this a hobby. What was that yesterday, a social call?"

"I don't have to answer questions from you, Red."

"Rod. Of course, you don't. But that would make both of us wonder what you might be hiding, wouldn't it?"

He mulled that over. Then he said, "When Dorothy and I split a year ago she got the Mercedes, I got the Chevy. But they were in both of our names. Couple days back, I bought a new Buick. When I went to trade in the old Chevy, there was her name on the title. I went out to her place to get her signature."

I took a swallow of ice water our gold-plated waitress had just plunked down. "What shape was she in when you got there?"

"Same shape as when I left, Rod. Just as nasty as ever."

"She sign the title?"

"After giving me a bunch of lip."

"Don't you need a title signature notarized?"

Trimbull smiled icily. "Once a cop. Happens I know a notary who'll fudge a bit. She put her seal on it yesterday. Buick dealer has it now." He looked smug enough to slap. "Anything else?"

"Maude Ruddy said you looked a bit out of sorts when you left. 'Fit to be tied,' she put it."

He shrugged. "She's right. But that's how I feel every time I have business with my former beloved. A real bitch on wheels she is – was."

He stood. "Gentlemen. Would you like to order now?"

The Fed Parcel truck came through Bizzibee right on schedule. There wasn't any real urgency in talking to the driver because he'd arrived at Dotty Blue's place after she'd been dead for three to five hours. But I've always been task-oriented, and the Fed Parcel man was part of this task.

It was a simple matter of flagging down the red and blue truck as it reached Doc's place.

The driver was a size XXL raw-boned guy in a dark blue FPS jumpsuit. Shoulders like a grizzly. Thick black hair combed straight back.

I threw him a quick smile and reached up to shake his hand. "Rod Montgomery, friend of Doc Gosling's. Helping him out on the Blumentripp death."

He shut off the truck's clattering Diesel, swung out of the open-sided cab and swallowed my hand in a huge paw.

"Sid Mankel," he said. Like a lot of big men, he had a surprisingly gentle voice. "Glad to help, if I can. She was a steady customer of mine. Art supplies near every week."

"A witness tells us you walked straight into the Blumentripp place."

He smiled. "Mrs. Ruddy keeps close tabs on things. Dorothy hated to be interrupted to answer the door, so I had a standing order to walk right in. Door was never locked. Like I told the police, I got there just about four yesterday. God, I was real sorry at what I found. Her on the floor. Dead."

"How'd you know she was dead?"

"Checked her pulse. Nothing. And she was real cold. She was dead all right, way past CPR. We're trained in that. I called 911."

Parcel man Sid hadn't told me much of anything, but I hadn't expected him to. I had my man.

The phone call came just as Doc and I finished packing in tender roast chicken and home-fried red-skinned potatoes. He could have shamed the chef at the Gold Pan.

Doc's side of the conversation was, "You don't say!... Well, I'll be a monkey's grandfather... How about that!" and similar interjections. When he hung up, he came back to the kitchen table, plunked down and stared at me.

"Well?" Doc said.

"Well, what?"

"How'd you do it? Chief Dixon sweated him like you suggested, and he cracked. How'd you know he'd asked for a piece of the dough she got for the collage in the lodge he'd posed for? How'd you figure out he was so mad at her go-to-hell attitude that he slipped in through the kitchen door, threw a fatal neck-snapping hold on her and rigged the 'accident' scene? How could you know all that? Nobody else did."

"I'm a good PI," I said smugly.

"Oh, sure." Doc shoved in a forkful of chicken, chomped, swallowed, chased it down with a long pull of ginger beer and banged the bottle down on the table. "Come on, Rod, how'd you do it?"

I wondered if I should tell him that since nobody else was seen going into Dotty Blue's house yesterday, it almost had to be Trimbull or the gardener – unless somebody else slipped by Maude when she might have been dozing, or sneaked through the kitchen door when Ned Bingham was preoccupied with yew hedgery. Unlikely in both hypotheticals, but possible. But all that was beside the point.

What clinched Bingham as the murderer were the blue dots. I'd seen dots like those before: rows of non-slip plastic dots lining the palm of a pair of work gloves I'd once owned. When they got old – like the gloves Bingham had stripped off when we shook hands – the dots began to shed.

"Rod, Doc pleaded. "For God's sake, tell me!"

I relented. "It was a matter of eyeing all the dots."

"Huh?" Doc said.

BLOWBACK

Cold rain sliced through my headlight beams. I knew the night was going to be miserable, but in the half-light of early dusk, I had no inkling of how miserable it would shortly become. At the moment, I was preoccupied with my memories of Homer Pitt.

Homer had been a reporter for the *Philadelphia Inquirer* at the time I'd taken early retirement from the City of Brotherly Love's police department and set myself up as a PI. He was the only reporter who believed I'd had no part in what became nationally infamous as the "Schuylkill Scandal." I was clean and he knew it, but the cover-up needed a patsy. Me. I resigned in disgust. He resigned in protest and exiled himself clear across the country to these foothills of the Cascades where autumn rain now pelted the roof of my travel-weary Bronco.

The slick macadam wound through a pine-forested valley. The town of Horsewhip was no more than a mile or two ahead. I hoped that the burg had a passable motel – or that Homer might have a spare room for a night or two. This was the westernmost point of my vacation swing, and I needed a breather before I turned back east.

The black hill on my right gave way to open country. The road made a tight swing to the left. I drove past the first scattered houses in Horsewhip. On the phone yesterday, Homer had told me to watch for his place on the right. A hundred yards further, there it was. The office of *Tri-County Watchword* – a blaze of light even at this dark hour. But Homer had told me he'd be working late on a breaking story. "Not much of a hardship," he'd said. "I live upstairs."

I pulled up out front, stepped bareheaded into the downpour and dashed across the sidewalk. Then I froze, but not because of the frigid mountain air.

The first-floor office was a single big room behind a gray-tinted plate glass storefront window with TRI-COUNTY WATCHWORD in a gold-lettered arc at eye level. In there was a desk, filing cabinets, a cluttered work table, an electronic type-setting machine and some other items I barely noticed. I barely noticed any of it after a first glance because my attention was nailed to the most significant factor in that one-man newspaper office. Homer Pitt, himself. Sprawled on the floor beside the typesetting machine.

Dead. That was obvious even from out here in the dismal rain. A portion of his skull was missing. And now I spotted the bullet hole in the window, just below the first W in WATCHWORD. A hole big enough to accommodate a .45 caliber slug.

Though nothing could be done for Homer now, I tried the adjacent door. Ex-cop's reflex. It was locked. I stood there a moment. What now?

A light had flashed on in an upstairs window across the road. As I glanced up there, I heard a car start a couple hundred feet down the macadam. I squinted through the darkness. The car's dim shape leaped away from the shoulder. No lights. Then, just before it disappeared around a bend toward town, the taillights flicked on and the brake lights flared. Well, one brake light. The left one.

Talk about suspicious behavior! I swung around the rear of the Bronco, yanked open the door and scrambled in. I got the thing fired up, howled off in hot pursuit, whipped around the bend and found myself in downtown Horsewhip.

I raced along the main drag, three blocks of assorted businesses, a couple of side streets that climbed the mountain to my left and dived into the valley on the right. A scatter of dim streetlights. Nobody on the sidewalks. No sign of the other car.

But a big indication that this little whistle-stop had a police department. Or at least a police officer. He straddled the middle of my lane with both hands wrapped around a revolver of significant size. It was pointed straight at me.

I stood on my brakes. The Bronco screeched to a halt with the front bumper just ten feet from the crouching cop.

"Out of the car!" he yelled. "Hands where I can see 'em!"

I shut off the ignition, climbed out with my arms crooked upward, mindful that it doesn't take much these days to activate a trigger finger.

"Face the car. Hands on the roof." The metal was as cold as his voice. Frigid rain stung the back of my neck as I felt his hand pat me down. All he discovered was my wallet. I'd left the Glock 17 back in my office in Radnor.

"Put your hands down. Turn around."

Now I had a close look at him. Young, maybe twenty-five. What I could see of his blond hair was cropped short below his black Stetson. Ex-military, I deduced from his terse manner.

"You got any ID?" he demanded.

"In my wallet."

"Take it out of the wallet and hand it to me." This kid was all procedure.

He scanned my Pennsylvania driver's license.

"Mr. Montgomery, we're going to the station house right there behind me. Turn around, walk ahead of me and keep your hands where I can see them."

He stepped aside. I walked past him with my arms down but dangled outward.

"What about my car?"

"I'll come back for it and pull it over next to the department's unit in front of the station house."

What he called the "station house" was a converted store, its former display windows now bricked in, its door steel with a little wire-glass window. The station was wedged between a liquor store on the left and a secondhand bookstore on the right, both dark by now, as were almost all downtown businesses. The only light here came through the reinforced window in the metal door, and it was partially blocked by a head peering out at us.

The door was swung open from the inside by a chunky cop in uniform, his thinning hair showing gray. Medium height, chilly blue eyes. Clean-shaven except for a hint of gray stubble. He looked like a man who'd been around.

"This is him, Chief," the cop behind me announced. "White vehicle, Pennsylvania plates. Just like she said."

"Good job, Pincus."

Pincus? I'd hate to be a cop named Pincus.

He handed my driver's license to the chief, who studied it then said, "You. In the holding cell back there."

"Now wait a minute! What-"

"Leaving the scene of a crime," the chief said. "That'll do for starters."

"Now wait just a minute, Chief. You've got no reason to hold me on-"

"We've got a witness."

Ah, the light in the window.

"Witness told me she saw you leaving the newspaper office," the chief went on. "And she saw a body lying on the floor in there. Caught your yellow and blue rear plate. Then you come hightailing through town. I'd say that's enough to hold you on."

"Is this an arrest?"

"Call it protective custody."

"You can't-" I began to squawk, but of course he could. This was his town and I was a stranger who had just been seen racing away from a killing. The cell door slammed shut.

"Coffee's over there. You can reach it through the bars." The chief grabbed his own black Stetson from a wall rack near the door, clapped it on. "Come on, Pincus." He pulled on a navy blue jacket and said over his shoulder, "I'll be back after we check out the scene."

Out into the dismal night, they went. I heard the front door being locked from the outside. A swell vacation stop this had turned out to be. I felt a manic impulse to wail "Mother!"

The coffee wasn't bad, but the sugar substitute was. No creamer. Looked like the chief was fighting a weight problem. I sat on the cell's creaky cot, sipped Mr. Coffee's brew and surveyed my surroundings. Two battered wooden desks, the inevitable metal filing cabinets, a computer terminal, fax machine, a radio set-up.

I pondered my position. In jail more than 3,000 odometer miles from home base. The only person I'd known here was lying dead in his office, which was the reason I was in jail. My fingerprints were on the victim's doorknob, and from what Pincus had said, some vocal citizen had seen me roaring away from the crime scene. I'd been in worse spots, but I was having a hard time remembering when. The only bright part of all this was that I'd refrained from shouting, "I know my rights!" That was considered by a lot of cops to be the tagline of a criminal.

A little after nine, I heard a siren's wail, probably whatever passed for a medical examiner in this northwestern outback. A while after that, the chief returned minus Officer Pincus.

He hung up his now sodden hat and strode back to my cell. "First time I've had a suspect in custody before the crime scene was checked out. You ready to talk?"

"I've been ready since I got here, Chief. An open book."

"Uh huh. You did leave the scene in one hell of a hurry, according to our witness." The chief fished out a pack of Camels, offering it.

"No thanks." I'd given up smoking long ago.

He lit up, took a long drag that must have smoked his innards all the way to his toes, blew a cloud toward the fly-specked ceiling fluorescents.

"Go on," he said. "Tell me your story."

I told him I'd seen Homer lying there, tried the door, which was locked, then about the other car. "Didn't your man Pincus see it go past?"

"That car – if there was another car – must've gone by here before I rushed him out to stop you." The chief gave me a long silent look. "Something about you, the way you're handling this… You a cop?"

"I was. Philadelphia PD. Now I'm a Philadelphia PI. Office in Radnor." I pulled out my private investigator's card and held it between the bars.

"Oscar Fogarty," the chief said, but he didn't stick out his hand. "What are you doing in Horsewhip?"

So I gave him the background. Vacation trip, chance to drop in on Homer to offer sinfully belated thanks for sticking by me those long years ago. "Found him like you just found him, Chief. Side of his head blown off, bullet hole in the window. Somebody stood out there and shot him." I told the chief about the car with the burned out brake light. He was a good listener, so I pressed my luck. "Can I ask you a couple of questions, Oscar?"

"Go ahead, Elrod."

"Please. Rod." I hate the name, Elrod. "Question number one. Did your witness hear the shot?" Because if she did, she surely told Fogarty and Pincus that it was a while before she saw me out there. Time enough for the shooter to have run most of the way back to his car.

"She said she was in the can when she heard it, in the back of her place. She's seventy-seven years old. Took her a couple minutes to get up front. By the time she got there, she says she saw you coming out of the newspaper office."

"By the time she got there, Chief, your man was gone, and I'd pulled up. Simple as that. Your man got away."

"Unless you're my man, Rod." Fogarty's uneven teeth gave me a big smile, but his eyes didn't kick in.

"That brings me to my second question. Who in these parts would want Homer Pitt dead?"

"Interesting thought, Rod." With the toe of his snakeskin cowboy boot, Fogarty hooked over a nearby chair, straddled it backwards, rested his arms on the chair's back. "He was a pretty hard-hitting newspaperman. Owned his one-man weekly, so he didn't have to worry about what the boss thought. Wrote everything himself, had it printed over in Ferndale."

"What were his main beefs?"

"The logging business, of course. Show me an easterner who doesn't think we're wrecking the countryside out here. And there was Cascade Parksite. Homer was dead set against that."

"A housing development?"

"Worse. An industrial park. The out-of-state developers want to put it in the valley just east of town, bring in all kinds of light manufacturing."

"Sounds like it would be good for business here."

Fogarty grimaced. "It'd be a damned disaster. There aren't enough people in Horsewhip to fill a tenth of the jobs the developers say they'd have there. It'd bring in a whole bunch of new people, more than live here already. Cardboard housing, trailer parks. Boomtown, USA. Homer was against it. We all are."

"Except for somebody here who might have invested in it."

"Yeah, could be." His china-blue eyes narrowed. "By some chance, you couldn't have any money in it, could you?"

"I don't have any money to invest, period. If I did, it wouldn't go into real estate speculation. Man in his fifties needs something more like mutual funds."

"You married, Rod?"

"Not now."

"You had supper?"

"Come to think of it, no."

"The Horsewhip Café down the street is still open. What can I bring you?"

That meant I was still stuck in here. But at least the chief wasn't going to try starving a confession out of me. "What's passable?" I asked him.

"Hot beef sandwich, maybe?"

"That'll be fine. You want money?"

"Technically you're a guest of the town. It'll go on the taxpayer's expense account."

So this wasn't costing me anything but my freedom.

He was back in a half-hour with my sandwich and a side of baked beans seriously blended together in a Styrofoam container. And with a dapper fellow of perhaps forty — tall, dark, Errol Flynnish with Flynn's natty mustache. He was dressed in the very best of knife-creased trousers and a dark jacket of some nifty fabric. Raindrops glittered on its sheen. We were being visited by the local fop.

"This is Leslie Lamont," Fogarty announced by way of introduction. "Friend of mine. Ran into him at the diner. We got to talking, and he thinks you're getting a bum rap. Les is a lawyer."

Lamont thrust his hand through the bars. "Pleasure to meet you. Rod Montgomery, I believe the chief told me your name is." He had a hearty, dry grip. "Chief Fogarty is only doing his duty, of course, but I believe he has arrested an innocent man. I'd like to be of help."

I'd been in town not even two hours, and here was a Bronco chaser offering his services.

"I'm not sure I need a lawyer."

"I'm distressed at your treatment," Lamont said. "I'm offering my services pro bono."

Well, that was interesting. I chewed the plastic forkful of gravied beef. Maybe I had a living friend here after all. "What did you have in mind?" I asked him.

Lamont turned to the chief. "Might Mr. Montgomery come out of there or do I go in? I detest speaking through bars."

"You go in." Fogarty pushed the chair toward him. "Take this with you if you want."

"And, of course, you will relocate to the front of the office, Chief. My client and I wish to consult in private."

"Okay with me." Fogarty unlocked the cell door. In came Lamont with a chair. Fogarty left the cell door open and retreated up front. Apparently, he didn't expect me to flatten Lamont and make a break for it.

I'd never heard of a free lawyer in a case like this. Well, a public defender, sure. But not a sleek Leslie type with his glistening jacket – which he now removed and carefully hung over the back of the chair. Beneath it, he wore a western-style shirt of soft butterscotch suede.

"First, Elrod – may I call you Elrod?"

"You may call me Rod." I dug deep into the baked beans. Heavy on the molasses, but I like them that way.

"First, Rod. I need some background."

I sighed and put down the container and went over the whole thing again. He listened with his eyes shut and his fingers tented.

Then he said, "Do you know how much time elapsed between the point when the witness – Mrs. Wenzel, I believe the chief told me her name is – between the time she heard the shot and you saw the light go on in her apartment?"

"I have no way of knowing that. You'd have to ask her."

"The chief did, and she claims it was no more than a minute or two. Yet you just told me you saw a car start up and leave without lights several minutes after you got there. Something doesn't add up, does it?"

"Looks like her word against mine."

"And you're the outsider here. Tell me, assuming for the moment you are the killer, what could you have done with the gun? Thrown it into the woods just before you hit the curve into town?"

I bristled. "What kind of question is that, counselor?"

Lamont smiled. "Hypothetical, Rod. Hypothetical. Homer told me down at the café that you had some difficulties in Philadelphia which became public. Now, still pursuing that hypothetical line of thought, might you have come here to Horsewhip to settle an old score with former Philadelphia reporter Homer Pitt?"

I glared at him. What was this? Then I realized he had been talking loudly enough for Chief Fogarty to hear him. Either this was a put-up job between them, or–

Abruptly, Attorney Lamont stood, picked up his jacket and walked to the cell door. "I'll do what I can." A promise if kept, I figured, made this only the first of many cells to come.

Then, as he pulled on that magnificent jacket, it hit me.

"Chief!" I called as the front door shut behind "my" lethal-lipped lawyer. "Where did he leave his car?"

Startled, the chief said, "Gave me a ride back in it from the diner. It's out front."

"Check his brake lights when he backs out."

"You gotta be kidding me, Montgomery." But he peered through the little window in the door. I waited, almost quivering.

"Only one brake light," Fogarty called out.

"The left one."

"Damned if it isn't. Could be a coincidence, and it doesn't really put him at the scene of the crime."

"But there is something that does, Oscar." And I told him what it was.

Thirty-seven minutes later, Leslie Lamont returned, this time accompanied by Officer Pincus.

"What in hell," Lamont spluttered, "is the meaning of this? I know my rights, Fogarty!"

Uh oh, Leslie, the cops' rule of thumb.

"No gun in his car," Pincus reported.

"Thanks, Pincus. You can go back on patrol. Leslie, sit down," Fogarty ordered.

"This is lunacy!" Lamont protested.

"If it is, then you've got nothing to worry about."

"Well, you have," Lamont growled. "False arrest for openers."

The chief was unruffled, which made me feel immensely better. "I'd appreciate a look at that impressive jacket of yours," he said.

"Are you serious?"

"Sure am. Hand it over – and, damn it, sit down."

"I don't see what this has to do with anything at all."

"The jacket." Fogarty's voice was brittle.

Lamont eased out of his jacket. "Be damned careful of this. It's mink-dyed virgin vicuna." He handed it to the chief, who handed it to me.

With a magnifying glass Fogarty had dredged from his desk drawer, I peered into the jacket's fine fibers. No doubt about it. What I'd thought was the persistent glisten of raindrops was something else entirely. The jacket had been peppered with tiny glass particles.

I nodded at the sheriff.

"You tell him, Rod." I'll be darned, I thought, the chief is going to let me have my moment. Maybe it was to make up for his high-handed treatment of a couple of hours ago.

"Glass is elastic," I said.

"And cornbread is square. What is this?" Lamont challenged. "A physics lesson?"

"As a matter of fact, it is. You might think – I guess you did think that a bullet going through glass leaves all its debris on the exit side. But when a slug hits glass, especially a big sheet of it, the glass bends particles with the impact. Then it snaps back – hard enough to throw particles almost twenty feet toward the shooter. It's called 'blowback,' Leslie. You were a lot closer than twenty feet from that window. Your jacket tells us that. A forensics expert should be able to match these particles with the gray-tinted glass in Homer's storefront."

"This is just plain nuts," Lamont protested.

I ignored that. "My guess is that when I showed up outside the newspaper office, you were on your way back to your car. You'd parked it down the road to avoid a problem like I had with my car in front of Homer's place. You drove into town and ducked into the side street nearest the restaurant. Your leisurely appearance here could be a pretty good alibi if nobody checked the timing right to the second."

I paused, waited for his reaction, got none and plowed on.

"I figure that on your way into the restaurant, you saw Officer Pincus take me in. When Chief Fogarty showed up for dinner a few minutes later, you pumped him for details and saw the chance to come back here with him and help pin the killing on me."

Now Lamont threw me a black look. "Aside from all that fancy fiction, what possible motive could I have for shooting Homer Pitt?"

"How about the Cascade Parksites project?" Chief Fogarty suggested. "I've picked up two rumors on that. One, the out-of-state developers have a mysterious local rep. Two, Homer Pitt was working on an exposé of the whole project."

"By the way, Chief," I couldn't resist putting in, "I'm willing to bet that you'll find the gun in that little stretch of woods just before the curve into downtown. My attorney as much as told us that."

Leslie Lamont said nothing. The fire in his eyes had gone out.

Fogarty broke the silence. "You are under arrest for the murder of Homer Pitt. You have the right to remain silent..."

When he finished, Lamont stared at the floor.

"Haven't you anything to say, Leslie? The chief asked.

Lamont's head came up. He glanced at Fogarty then glared at me.

"I want to call my lawyer," he said.

We hope you have enjoyed William Hallstead's short stories. Some of these stories came from his previously published novels. You may want to peruse his list of fine reading appearing in the front of this book at www. bluewaterpress.com.